HERE ON EARTH

HERE ON EARTH

A NOVEL

BRIAN HOLERS

GIRL FRIDAY BOOKS

This is a work of fiction. Names, characters, organizations, places, events, and incidents are either products of the author's imagination or are used fictitiously.

Published by Girl Friday Books™, Seattle
www.girlfridaybooks.com

Produced by Girl Friday Productions

Cover Design: Megan Katsanevakis
Production editorial: Abi Pollokoff
Project management: Sara Spees Addicott

Image credits: cover © iStock/Nithid

ISBN (paperback): 978-1-954854-90-1
ISBN (ebook): 978-1-954854-91-8

Library of Congress Control Number: 2022946699

First edition

For Ben

CHAPTER 1

Daddy didn't break one tackle in the Miracle Run. I can see it to this day, his two pinkie fingers outstretched at a comical angle as he waits for the ball deep in the Tigers' own end zone; that first little stumble as he cuts right, then left, then right again; the clouds of breath that billow from his helmet as he darts and jukes his way through eleven Ole Miss Rebels on that cold November Saturday night in Tiger Stadium, 1968. I've seen the film a thousand times, memorized it; every little stutter step, every head fake, each imperceptible turn of his hips that vaulted him away from a tackler. I've flat-out studied it, looking and looking for something, some clue, to my father. But one thing about Daddy—you could study him all day long, and you'd never know which way he was going. People still ask me: "How did the Miracle Man run 107 yards, with no time left on the clock, without breaking one single tackle?" I just tell them, he didn't have to. When Charlie Turner put his mind to running, nobody even got a hand on him.

Daddy said he knew my name the instant they made me. I picture them there, two lost kids taking what little they had to give each other, sweating through the sheets, hearts hammering out of their chests. They rest in the afterglow of what they thought was love, on his metal frame bed at Aunt Lurleen's house with the window open as the buzzing streetlight casts a cool, gray shadow of the slow-moving ceiling fan onto one wall. Daddy had just found out, that afternoon, that all his hard work and discipline had paid off in a football scholarship to LSU. I picture them there, spread out on that same bed he'd been sent to sleep in when he was five years old, after his father had put a .45 to his mother's head, and then to his own, back in Texas. I can hear Daddy's voice as he tells my mother that all his nights dreaming and hoping for something to hold had just come true. He tells her he knew they had made a baby, and he wants to call me Tommy.

Charlie Turner played all four years at LSU, then later we lived in the country outside New Orleans when he played two seasons for the Saints. When he wasn't playing football, Daddy was just like all the other fathers, coming home to read or wrestle or shoot marbles with me. But what Daddy was really like, the last part of that tape tells me all I need to know—though I only remember the night itself in a three-year-old's flashes of purple and gold—the part when Daddy finishes his run, finds me with my mother in the first row of seats, grabs me up with his massive arms, and parades me around the field, my own arms raised in victory, as eighty thousand adoring fans scream us on.

They say he started on the pills then. I'm sure they weren't hard to get; something was always hurting, and besides that, he was Charlie Turner. The Miracle Man. I guess they masked the hurt, took him away, let him push himself further than he should have pushed. I figure they brought him a measure of relief that, at least for a time, he had always looked for. In all those afternoons of weights and drills and cramps and sweat and pain and the effort it must have taken to push those terrible things out of his mind. This was all in the days before the injury that meant the end of his football career and the only chance to get away from Branden, Louisiana, that he and my mother really had. Before the doctors finally got wise and took away the pills that filled in for the hope he had pinned on football. And way before he ended up working for a long-lost uncle back in Texas, who got him all the pills he wanted and ultimately found him laid out in an oil-stained patch of dirt in downtown Dallas with a gunshot wound in his chest.

Still, I try to focus on the positives, even if my humble beginning did help ruin both my parents' lives. As for Mama, she never did think I was anything but a mistake. But I've been in the alcoholics' program long enough I can say it out loud now, and I'm no longer glad that she's gone. If she was here right now I would tell her how much I loved her, what rare joy I once felt being buried in her cottony smell, and how I forgive her for being such a shitty mom. If she was here right now I would put my hands on either side of her pretty face and tell her she was a miracle too, that she didn't have to sell herself in their bedroom at night when she thought I was asleep, and that no one could blame her for throwing herself at a boy who looked like he might amount to something.

And I'd tell her one more thing: whatever happened between the two of them, in the few short years I really had him, Daddy meant the world to me. When the bad dreams woke me up, he was the one who came in and sang to me—"Amazing Grace," "Gather at the River," "In the Sweet By and By"—the one who lifted me from my bed and carried me outside to settle me down under the twinkling stars.

"Miracle?" he loved to say. "The real miracle is waiting for us up there. One day we'll jump on those stars and ride across the sky. And never have to run again." What finally tore him apart, it's not for me to say. The mess he left behind, it's not my place to judge; that's all between him and God. I just pray he has it all worked out by now. Because as long as I will live, the smell of Bengay ointment, the sound of Daddy's voice, and the feel of a pigskin worn smooth by the Miracle Man are what I hope to find on that glorious day when I walk with him, hand in hand once more, on that beautiful shore that goes by the throne of God, no longer lost but, finally, found.

CHAPTER 2

"Matt, please. Sit down." Tommy stood by his guest in the small living room of his rental house. The television played at low volume. He began to sit himself, then stood back up when Matt didn't move.

"It's green."

"What?"

"Your couch. It's green." Matt gestured at the secondhand sofa Tommy had bought at the Goodwill in Monroe. The sofa provided the only color in an otherwise generically white rental house, a verdant puddle of frigid ocean floating in a cumulus sky.

"It's comfortable. Please. Be a gentleman. Sit down."

This time Tommy sat. Both men looked at the television. Matt stood slack-jawed, his navy-blue windbreaker zipped all the way to the top on the warm night; droplets of sweat quivered on his swarthy face and glistened in the evening whiskers growing there. After an earlier rain, the smell of boiled earth floated in through the open window.

"Cowboys," Matt grunted. An old *Bonanza* played on the screen.

"You're welcome to take off your coat and stay awhile."

Matt laughed goofily. "Those are big hats." On the screen, Adam, Little Joe, and Hoss pushed through the swinging doors of a saloon named Cowboys' Rest.

"Suit yourself." Tommy turned his attention back to the

show. Matt stood, shoulders hunched, mouth hanging open. His pupils were pinpricks.

"I'm so thirsty, I could drink a beer the size of a washtub," Hoss said on the television.

"There's that fella we met back by the Ponderosa," Little Joe noted. *"I've got a question for him."* The man joined the three, and soon they all griped about the heat. The stranger offered to buy the brothers a drink. Before long they were having a grand old time, happy as pigs in a cool bed of mud, singing along with a fifth man in a bowler, who banged out tinny notes on a piano.

"One more, Joe. One more, Adam. Come on, fellows. Just one more beer."

Tommy had just finished his dinner when Matt had called earlier, interrupting his reading. Matt Bianchi, he wanted out of his life. No faster way to get that done than to always take the man's calls. The bowl he had used for his Top Ramen dinner still sat on the coffee table. Next to it, his AA Big Book was open and flipped facedown with Tommy's reading glasses on top of it. He picked up the tube of balm he had been about to use, rubbed some of the salve into the cracked places in his hands. Brenda had been so kind to give him that lotion, after all he had put her through. Maybe, just maybe . . . she still cared.

As his guest stood, unmoving, Tommy closed his book, put his glasses back on, and picked up the yellow pad and pen underneath it. He read once again through his two lists, thought about them for a moment. To the list marked "AMENDS" he added his son's name at the bottom. Under the column on the other, "GRATITUDES," he wrote, "Brenda—lotion."

"Ain't you gonna offer me a drink?" Matt still stood, hunched forward.

"What would you like? Water, orange juice, or a Dr Pepper?"

Matt shook his head perfunctorily, as if expecting such a response, his dark curls of hair reflecting the room's dim light. The deafening roar of evening cicadas played over the television's low volume.

"Vodka? Gin?"

"I don't drink anymore, Matt. Those are your only choices."

Matt grunted. "Just some water, then. No ice."

Tommy took his bowl to the sink and drew a short glass of water. Matt took it and popped two pills into his mouth, then drank the glass of water in one gulp.

"Dude. I don't want that here."

"*Dude?* Do you know who you're dealing with?"

"I know who you are, Matt. Let's get on with it."

Matt snorted at the screen. "Look at those fucking marbles."

"What?"

"Look." In Tommy's absence, Matt had switched the channel. At the bottom of the screen, a digital clock ticked off time, warning viewers how little was left to buy the colorful marbles offered for sale. The pitchman wore khaki slacks and a white oxford shirt, black wing-tip shoes. Not exactly an outfit for a game of shoot-out.

"A real collector's item," the pitchman said, his eyes averted to read from something off-camera. "They come in a box of three, perfect for the man in your life who has everything. Just look at that beautiful blend of colors."

"A real collector's item," Matt said aloud, and laughed. His pupils were still pinpricks. "Better not stake those in a card game, Tommy. You'd lose all your marbles." He guffawed at his own joke.

"Matt, what can I do for you?"

But Matt just stared at the television this time, as Tommy switched it back to *Bonanza*. Matt's eyes darted back and forth in his head.

Tommy took the glass Matt had used to the sink. He patted his stomach, full from his simple dinner. He almost had to laugh. As vain as he had always been about his looks, even when his life was a certified mess in those last couple of years before he did his time, he had never grown a gut before. *Too many instant noodles,* he thought. *Oh well. I guess I'll just have to look my age. There are worse things in life.*

He stared at a picture of his father above the sink, circa 1952. Aunt Lurleen leaned over him there, a tall, stooped woman with both hands on the little boy's shoulders. The two of them glared at the camera wide-eyed, as if neither knew what to make of the situation, or of each other. Even in that grainy photograph, even at five years old, the muscles in Charlie Turner's legs were bulging.

Marbles was the first game Tommy's father taught him, holding his clammy little hand as he learned to squeeze the shooter between thumb and forefinger, to put a jolt behind it and knock the other swirling beads out of the circle. Marbles was the first form of gambling Tommy learned. A handful of marbles was the closest thing Tommy had to money when he was a kid; and even at five and six and seven years old, he always came home with more than he had when he left.

As he aged, marbles changed to dice and then to cards, and if neither of those was working out for a time, his currency became whatever was the riskiest task on the jobsite. For years, as long as he had a little something to smoke or to blow he could live like he had nothing to lose; as long as he woke up breathing, it would be a day as good as the one before it, or maybe better. And, as crazy as it may have sounded to anyone else, making a living gambling, in those days anyway, made him just about as happy as he could be. So there, so be it. It is what it is, and he couldn't change it now.

He took a bottle of Dr Pepper from the fridge and returned once again to his chair. Tommy held the cold bottle to his face, let the beads of condensation on the glass cool him on the warm spring night. Lately he'd had a harder and harder time finding those glass bottles of Dr Pepper. Daddy used to say he enjoyed a bottle as an adult even more than he did when he was a kid. That in fact he so seldom had money for the sugary treat when he was a child, he intended to make up for every bottle missed in his youth. Tommy and Charlie drank them together when Tommy was a boy, sometimes as they shot marbles after football practice, out in the yard. After he finished his drink, Daddy always liked to hold his empty bottle up like a spyglass and look through, as if sizing up his next shot.

"Tommy?"

Tommy turned to his guest.

"Yes, Matt."

"Where's my fucking money?"

"Excuse me?"

Now, Matt seemed to come awake. "You heard me."

"That's why you're here? I'm making my payments. What's your problem?"

"No, Tommy. You're making your *points*. You owe us twenty-five thousand."

"So I'm making my payments. Like I said, what's your problem?"

"You're not coming in to play anymore. You need to pay up."

"Maybe you should give me a statement, like the bank does. I don't owe you twenty-five anymore. It was ten before I went in. When I came out, you told me twenty-five. I'm making payments. You're still telling me twenty-five."

"You don't make the rules, Tommy."

Tommy grabbed the top of his head with both hands, sat down heavily on the sofa. He muted the television.

"Look at me, man. I've sold everything I have. I sold my Cadillac. I sold my Mustang. I've sold all my guns." *Well, all except the two.*

"Come back to New Orleans. You have some skills. You can win your money back."

"I don't do that anymore, Matt. I'm done with it. I just want to get you your money and be done with you. I'm doing all I can."

Matt looked down at Tommy on the sofa, seemed to think about something.

"So you ain't coming back to New Orleans."

Tommy looked up, his face plaintive. "I can't, Matt. I've got my son to think about. I can't do it. I'm doing everything I can to make things right."

"That ain't my fucking problem," Matt answered. He hunched his shoulders again, and turned back toward the television.

Tommy hadn't been nervous at first about Matt's visit. After Matt had called, he reminded himself, as he did many times a day, that he had done all that could be done. *Have I lived my life today for the Lord? Have I put him first in all my actions, words, and deeds?* True, Matt was the big boss's son, and Tommy didn't want anything to do with him. But he wasn't scared. *Matt has nothing that can hurt me.* For over a year Tommy had made all his payments on time, just like the big guy with the shank and the breath that smelled of tuna fish had told him in the rec yard the day before he got out. Soon the whole thing would be behind him. It was hard saving up twenty-five thousand dollars on his wages, but he was getting it done, squeezing every dime, eating dried noodles, and most importantly, staying away from the lion's den. No. Matt couldn't hurt him. He was frankly more nervous about the end of his supervised visitation with his son, which would come to pass in only two more weeks.

Only one more day until the weekend . . . That's what Tommy had been thinking when Matt had called. As he often did when he had such thoughts, Tommy reminded himself how blessed he was to have this job, any job. Sure, running a chain saw all day until your hands buzzed was not exactly his lifelong ambition, but nevertheless he was grateful to have something steady and stable that gave him a paycheck he could count on. Good work was always hard to find in a small town, especially when you've spent two years away for dealing meth and rock, not to mention all the other things. Tommy had been awfully lucky, and he knew it. Even on the inside his fortune was good. Only God knew how many bad things could have happened. Quite a few of the guys in there didn't even remember whatever they did that got them put away for so long, little momentary lapses of judgment or just one too many drinks or snorts and then they're locked up until they rot. Without even a memory to enjoy.

But Tommy had known his boss, James Lewis, all his life, and even worked for him here and there over the years back when James just did residential tree service, when Tommy wasn't having much luck with the cards or when he just needed to mellow out for a bit, get his head out of the game and his hands back onto the earth. He understood he and James were related somewhere down the line on his mother's side. But, family or not, he knew he was lucky James had taken him on for forty hours back when he got out, and since that time Tommy had just kept his head down, done his work, and stayed off drink and drugs and everything else that ever did him harm.

Truth is, going to prison had made his drug problem even worse. Tommy stayed loaded most of the time he was inside, on shit he had never even heard of before he went in. And now, for the first time in his life, he was dealing with things. He had simply decided never, not even for a minute—and he had put his faith in God's hands—to let himself sink into pity. He'd been working the steps of the program, had a sponsor who pushed him way beyond his comfort zone, and, as hard as it sometimes was, he had simply decided to start each day being grateful.

"So you're a baseball player?" Matt walked to the shelf next to Tommy's television, picked up one of Tommy's old trophies. "Fourteen home runs, Branden High School, 1983. Fourteen home runs in one season! Tommy! I wasn't even born then!"

"I used to be a baseball player, Matt. I don't play anymore. I don't drink, I don't gamble. I don't play baseball anymore."

Matt put the trophy down. "Well, you don't have to be rude about it."

Tommy breathed out. "I don't mean to be rude, Matt. It's been a long day and I'm tired. I don't have your twenty-five thousand dollars. I'm saving it up, and paying the points until I get it all. I don't know what else I can do for you."

Matt turned back to the shelf, picked up a picture. "This your kid?"

Now, Tommy stood. "Don't say anything about my son, Matt. Put the picture down, please. I'd like you to go now."

Matt held on to the picture. "So is it true?"

"Is what true?"

"That you tried to burn your house down when your kid was with you?"

"I did my time, Matt. I'll never forgive myself for that."

Matt walked slowly into the kitchen, drew himself another

glass of water, then dropped two more pills into his hand, swallowed them, and followed with a drink. He rejoined Tommy in the living room.

"So you think you can get away from this? From the only life you've ever known?"

For an instant, Tommy felt an odd glimmer of hope. "Not by myself I can't, Matt. Only with God's help. He can help you too."

Matt ignored the comment. "And what about your kid? You don't think he'll be rolling dice soon enough?"

"I plan to give him a better life."

Matt considered. "A better life." He focused again on the television, the muted words rolling across the bottom of the screen. Once again he hunched his shoulders forward and seemed to go into another place. When he spoke again, this time it was a whisper.

"A better life."

Tommy had faced the facts, and there was only one way to say it. As much as he wished things were different, he was totally worthless as a parent. Sure, for the first few years of Jamey's life he was there, physically at least, some of the time anyway, when he wasn't away gambling or high or doing whatever else he was doing. But that was then. Since he'd been out, Tommy hadn't missed one of his visits, in fact had seen his son nearly every day, since Brenda had been so generous and hadn't tried to squeeze him into his allotted visitation.

To be fair, he wasn't that bad of a parent for Jamey's first year. He had no idea how to go about it, that was true, but he could have done a lot worse. The biggest surprise was the magnetic affection he felt for the squirming little baby. He was making good money then, his luck was pretty good, Brenda was feeding him well, and if the cards didn't fall his way for a week or two, he could always make a thousand bucks or more in a week dropping big trees for James Lewis, trees so close to power lines and houses most guys just shook at the thought of climbing up into them.

Since he'd been out, Tommy had been so good. After all that mess with the fire, he'd only been allowed supervised visits. But he hadn't missed one, and he did everything in his power not to argue with Brenda in front of their son. As angry as Brenda was at him—and he deserved every single bad feeling she had toward him—she wouldn't argue out loud if he had paid her to. Lately, to make things easier on all of them, he had been visiting his son at their house every day, playing ball in the yard with Jamey. Tommy was most grateful Brenda didn't stand out there and watch them every minute, but he wouldn't have blamed her if she had.

Still, he was grateful the supervised visitation was nearly over. He had told himself daily, sometimes five times a day, how he wasn't going to screw it up this time; he'd even dropped down to his knees, at times, to remind himself. He knew his life was a fog in those days, that he was worth just about nothing as a parent, or even as a person, for that matter. Not to mention the stupid shit he did, driving the boy around when he was loaded out of his mind, leaving him in the car when he made his deliveries. And then there was the fire, started one evening in their kitchen cooking meth. Stupid, stupid. There was another thing he was grateful for: the fact that he had never used that crap. He was so lucky Brenda had come home early from work. In his mind he could still see the burn marks on the wall, hear the little one's voice telling him there was a fire, could smell the acrid odor that wouldn't go away. He deserved whatever they gave him, and he knew it. If only for what *could* have happened.

Yet he knew not to judge himself too harshly. It didn't help anything. Because otherwise, what he did, his entire life, would just be unforgiveable.

Lately, he'd been saving his money for something nice. Something to celebrate the first time he could take his son away from home, just the two of them. And really, since it would be the first time in Jamey's life Tommy had been sober, in a way it would be the first time he spent an afternoon with his son, period. Just the two of them. Tommy'd been thinking, maybe he'd take Jamey to the zoo, or maybe to that alligator farm he'd heard about down the other side of Natchitoches. Rob, his sponsor, told him about it, this crazy place that opened up when Tommy was on the inside, where all they have is alligators. Rob told him what fun it was for kids, how they get those gators to turn circles in the water, get them to jump and snatch whole chickens right out of the trainer's hands. They even had a couple the kids could pet. Maybe that's where they'd go to celebrate. If they did, he'd let Jamey get some souvenirs, eat whatever he wanted to. Maybe he'd even convince Jamey to eat one of those alligator dogs they cook on an open fire. Rob told him about that too. He could have a giant Coke, ice cream, anything he wanted. They'd do just the kind of thing Tommy always wanted to do with his dad. Maybe he'd even spend the extra fifty bucks and wrestle the gator—its mouth was tied shut and they'd had it declawed, but the little man didn't have to know that. Tommy would just get in there and flip that son of a gun upside down, turn that permanent smile on its face into a frown.

Matt went back to the shelf and picked up the picture again. Tommy stood, moved to take it away.

"A better life?" Matt slammed the picture down on the shelf, breaking the glass. "You saying something's wrong with my life?"

"I didn't say that, Matt."

"You saying I'm some kind of an asshole?"

"I didn't say that, Matt. Take it easy. That's not for me to say. I'm only saying I want a better life for myself and my son."

"So who gave you the right to get out?"

"Nobody, Matt. I have no rights. Nobody owes me or my son anything. I'm just trying to make something better for my family, with a lot of help. That's all. Matt, listen. I know that look in your eyes. I've seen it looking back at me in the mirror a million times."

"Fuck you, Tommy."

"I mean it. You don't have to do this to yourself, Matt. I know that look. Listen, I wasn't going to go tonight, but there's an eight o'clock meeting at the hospital. You've been decent enough to me. I'll take you there. I'll go with you. You can have a different life, Matt."

Matt walked into the kitchen again, this time opened the refrigerator and took out a bottle of Dr Pepper and opened it. He picked two cookies from a package on the counter, ate them both in one bite, and followed with a large drink of the soda.

"I'm gonna tell you something, Tommy. I like you." Matt pointed the bottle at Tommy like a giant glass finger.

"Well, Matt, I can't do anything for you. If there's any way I can help you, it's a power greater than I am, working through me. It's not me. But I can take you to a meeting. I can take you tonight."

"I want my money, Tommy. I want it now."

"I need more time. Just like we agreed."

Matt stopped, hung his head. When he looked back up his face was bright red, as if he had simply willed it to color.

"Time? Time? I can always make more money, Tommy." As if to demonstrate, he reached into his jacket pocket, pulled out a wad of bills easily an inch thick and dropped it on the counter.

"But one thing I can't make more of is time. And time is running out for you."

Matt stared at the television, and neither of them said a word. He unmuted the sound and moved toward the set. Hoss and Joe were in a bar again, different from the one before, but Adam was nowhere to be found. Several men were playing cards as Hoss and Joe watched. One by one the players folded, threw their cards across the table, walked away in apparent disgust. All but one, a white-faced man who grinned like a baby and kept raking in the chips.

"You think he's cheatin', Joe?"

"Wouldn't surprise me, Hoss. Keep your eye on the lady over there. I think she's tipping him off somehow."

From the looks on the chipless men's faces, the place was about to erupt.

"You think you're a tough guy, Tommy? You think you're tougher than me?"

"I'm not tough at all, Matt. I never claimed to be. I just want to live my life, do what I need to do for my son and my family."

"You like that knot of bills, Tommy?" Matt gestured toward the stack he had left on Tommy's table. "That's just about enough to take care of what you owe me, isn't it?"

"I don't know, Matt. That's your money. Please take it with you when you leave."

At that, a black, wild look washed across Matt's face.

"So Tommy."

"Yes, Matt."

"So you know Jesus, then." Matt reached out and fingered the gold cross on a chain around Tommy's neck.

Tommy breathed out. "I do, Matt. I owe my life to Him."

"He made a great sacrifice."

"He gave His life for all of us."

"I'll make you a deal. You want out? Here's your way out. Like Jesus Christ, I'll make a great sacrifice. We'll play one hand. You win, that money's yours. You take it and give it back and your debt is forgiven. I win, nothing changes. You still owe me the twenty-five K. You have nothing to lose."

"I don't gamble anymore, Matt. I mean it. Please, take your money and go. I'll keep paying the vig and I'll pay it off as soon as I can."

On the television, the place came apart. Everyone shouted. Chairs were broken over heads. Pitchers of beer flew. A man with a wooden leg fired his pistol into the wall, scattering plaster. *"Look out, Joe!"* Hoss shouted. Little Joe ducked, swung, hit a man with granite features in the jaw.

"Break it up! Break it up! You Ponderosa boys come with me!"

"Please, Matt. Take the money and go."

"I've got a better idea, Tommy." Matt reached behind his back, pulled a flat black pistol from the waistband of his pants, and shoved it into Tommy's chest.

"Take it from me, and the money's yours."

"One thing I learned from Daddy, Hoss. Jail never did a man any good."

Tommy had never been one to think first. He reached for the gun in his chest and shoved it away as Matt fired it once into the ceiling. Tommy slapped the gun to the floor, then kneed his unwelcome guest in the stomach. Matt grunted once, then swung one hand in an uppercut to Tommy's groin but only grazed his target.

Tommy grabbed Matt's hand and bent a finger back. Matt screamed. All of a sudden the television went quiet. For several seconds the only sounds in the place were from the two men fighting. Then Tommy's phone began to ring.

Matt's hands went straight for Tommy's neck—young and slight or not, he obviously knew what he was doing, and for such a wiry guy he was unbelievably strong—but after two years lifting weights in a prison yard, and nearly another bucking wood and lifting logs, Tommy Turner was no lightweight. He felt the blood begin to drain from his face and yet was flooded with an odd sense of calm, as if all the days of his life had been woven into a tapestry to lead him to this very moment. Everything slowed. He stared at Matt's chin and was sure he could count the whiskers there. He smelled Dr Pepper and vanilla cookie on Matt's breath, and the sullen scent of whiskey in the background. The telephone rang as loud as the bell inside a clock tower. When it stopped, the echo carried on in Tommy's ears.

Tommy had been here before. He made himself slacken, as if he were finished, and felt Matt begin to ease his grip. In that instant he yanked one hand from his neck and used it to pull the younger man toward him, planted an elbow in Matt's face as he did. Then, with all the torque he could draw from his exhausted body, he brought the point of his elbow back across, into the soft spot just below Matt's ear.

Matt's eyes went wide. His hands fell to his sides. He went straight down, then lay stretched out on the floor making a choking sound. Tommy still had a lot more fight in him, and quickly stood and reared back to plant his foot in Matt's side.

His phone began to ring again and he stopped himself. Then Matt shuddered like a fish that had been clubbed and began to spew foam from his mouth, emitting guttural snorts like a speared boar. The phone continued ringing. Tommy stood frozen as everything changed and he began to recognize that the man was in trouble. Then his answering machine picked up and little Jamey's voice came on.

"Um, hi, Daddy, I just wanted to talk to you . . . Well, good night, I love you. I miss you. I hope you're having fun tonight." Tommy checked Matt's pulse and breathing. He pulled the mouth open, stuck his finger in, dug for some obstruction that wasn't there. He stood and pulled his own shirt off, wiped away the froth and slime, and began to breathe into the mouth. He pumped and pumped on Matt's chest as his son spoke into the recorder, reaching one hand out toward Jamey's voice when he stopped pumping on the chest to blow into Matt's mouth.

". . . and Mommy said you would get me a new baseball glove and then we can play some catch if you can find your glove . . . okay, Daddy, I'm sorry you're not home, I-I-I wish I could talk to you, I love you, good night." Tommy pumped and breathed and pumped and breathed, yet the stiffening man on the floor didn't move. By the time Tommy's sweet son had hung up the phone, while he was probably with his mother, lying in his bed and saying his prayers, Matthew Louis Bianchi was dead.

CHAPTER 3

It sounded like the ocean. He went there, with Brenda, before the baby was born. They had stayed in a condominium on the beach, at Gulf Shores. Brenda had set it all up and they went there once, for three days in early fall. It was a Thursday, and all the kids were back in school, so they had the beach to themselves and spent three days in the waves, diving in and floating on their backs until their chests grew hot from the beating-down sun.

Tommy heard that sound in his head again, as if he were back in the surf with his ears just under the surface—the low-grade roar of moving water, the constant echo of waves rolling back from the sand. For twenty minutes or more he kneeled over Matt Bianchi's lifeless body, pumped the sinewy chest, brushed away the foam and bile and opened the tiny mouth to blow in quick bursts, tasted the cigarettes and whiskey that still clung to his lips. Again and again he checked the neck for a pulse, bent his ear to the mouth and held his own breath to listen for breathing, said aloud, repeatedly, that there was something. Something. Something. Finally he fell back, collapsing himself. Then he stood, found an old bedsheet in his closet, covered Matt's body, then ripped it right off and beat on the chest and checked for breathing once more.

Again he covered the body and snorted once as he did, a wicked-sounding laugh or exclamation. Even he wasn't sure what it was. Then, as if he simply finally understood what he had done, he straightened out the legs, pushed both arms to the sides, smoothed the sheet over Matt's face, and sat down heavily in his chair.

He stared at the clock on the wall, saw in his mind the hands turning back, as if the last hour could somehow be undone. *Why did you take out that gun, Matt? Haven't I done all I agreed to do? Why are you dead? I've hit guys harder a thousand times.* He slapped his hands on his knees, tried to stand, then sat back down again.

He went to the kitchen and picked up the receiver on his phone, then slowly replaced it in its cradle. What was he going to say? *A debt collector came to my house and I killed him? His name was Matt Bianchi. Yes. That Bianchi. Carlo Bianchi's son. Yes, I know I'm not allowed to affiliate with gambling interests as part of my parole terms. Yes, I know even that can get me sent back to prison.*

Yes, I know Carlo Bianchi is a much bigger problem than the state of Louisiana.

Yes, I know.

He returned to his chair. Would *he* believe his story, if he were the sheriff? Tommy Turner, gambler, drug dealer, who tried to burn up his kid in his own house? And what if he did call the police and everyone believed him? *Here, Tommy, just tell me what happened. You're not in any trouble. I'll make sure of it.* How many police officers would come through his house? Taking pictures, measuring things, asking him question on top of question. By morning, everyone in town would know. James Lewis would know. Brenda and Jamey would know.

Carlo Bianchi would know.

Pick up that phone, and he might as well just eat Matt's pistol.

God. Those *eyes*. He couldn't stop seeing Matt's eyes. Voids. Just what Brenda used to say about his. As if a light had stopped shining behind them. No wonder she got so scared.

He stood and walked outside to Matt's car, pulled his shirt-tail out to cover his fingers, and tried the door only to find it locked. Then he quickly went back in and folded back the bed-sheet, being careful not to uncover Matt's face, and reached into Bianchi's pockets for the keys, finally finding them in the vest pocket of his windbreaker. He re-covered the body, went to his utility room for a pair of work gloves, then returned to the car, opened the doors and trunk, and went back inside.

It was against man's laws, but what could he do? He was in his own house. He was doing what he was supposed to do. He'd been going to work, visiting his son, paying his bills on time, trying to make up with Brenda. He couldn't change the past now. What good would it do? What good would be served if he went back to prison? Jamey needed him. And *dammit,* he was minding his own business in his own house. He had his rights. And *goddammit,* Tommy thought, none of this was his fault.

He grabbed a pickax and a shovel from his toolshed, then went back in for a lantern in the utility room and put them all in the back seat of Bianchi's car. Inside the house, he rolled out a six-by-eight-foot plastic tarp on the floor and, as gently as he could, lifted the body onto it and wrapped it around. He found a roll of clothesline and brought it out, but before tying up the package he remembered the wad of money Matt had left on his table.

Tommy started to count it, then felt a tingling in his jaw as if he would be sick. He pulled open the tarp, stuffed the money back into Matt's jacket pocket, wrapped the body again, and tied it together with clothesline. Then he turned off the car-port light, propped open his door, got the body onto his shoulder, and laid it as gently as he could in the trunk of Matt's car. Then he placed the shovel and pickax on the floor of the trunk also, closed the hatch, and went back inside.

He knew Miz Minter would be in bed by now, the only neighbor he had on the dirt road that ended at Tommy's house. But. No point in taking chances. He put on a new set of clothes and took the ones he had been wearing—although there was no blood or anything to show he had even seen Matt—and placed them all in a bag, which he hid under his house to deal with later. He got in Matt's car and, instead of driving out to the road, went to the cattle gate that Miz Minter's son used to enter the forty acres he owned at the dead end. He opened it, rolled across the grate, closed the gate, and sped across the field toward a similar gate on the other side, which he used to get Matt's car out of the pasture. Then he sat hidden in the brush with the lights off and waited for two cars to clear before climbing onto the highway.

As if he had planned it all along, he began to drive straight to the tract where he and Otis and James had been working the last few weeks. He cut off the highway after only a quarter mile, certain no one had seen him, and traveled the last three miles on darkened country roads, his heart roaring in his chest nonetheless. He was glad the tract was a mile or more down that road, a mile from the nearest house. He noted old man Walter's house was dark when he passed and figured he could use the track hoe they had brought out earlier that day to cut a fire line. At least to get the hole started. He knew he had to get it done, and he had to get it deep. He thought he saw a car headed toward him in the distance, so instead of turning off he continued ahead past old man Walter's place, eventually met the car going the other way, then swung around in a school bus stop, traveled back a quarter mile, and cut his lights before turning down the dirt road toward the bottom edge of the clear-cut, which he navigated completely by moonlight.

James had planned a controlled burn for the next day, something they always did after a clear-cut to open the field back up to be replanted. He had brought the track hoe out that very day. Tommy considered. A giant machine to make light work of that Louisiana red clay . . . a huge full moon . . . temperature dropping quickly to make the night almost pleasant. All this could have been a lot worse.

When he got to the track hoe, Tommy got out and surveyed things. A giant pile of brush lay next to the machine. He figured James would be looking for it by the road in the morning, so he decided he'd dig a hole where it sat, move the brush on top, and by tomorrow all this land would be scarred and black and whatever disturbance he might make at the site would be long gone by tomorrow afternoon.

He drove the car down a hundred yards or so and hid it back behind some trees. You just never knew when someone would come along. Some kids could come out there wanting to shoot off their shotguns or maybe just to have at each other. Or maybe old man Walter would hear him after all and wander down to see what was up. Tommy figured if anyone did ask, he'd just make some excuse about leaving the key in the hoe and wanting to make sure it would fire right up in the morning. And if they asked how he got there . . . well, he'd just have to cross that bridge when he came to it.

In minutes he was a good four feet deep. Then he glanced downhill in the direction of old man Walter's house and thought he saw a light on that hadn't been before.

He stopped the machine and listened closely. Sat and stared. In a minute or so he heard a truck starting.

Shit. If I can hear his truck, he can definitely hear this machine.

Quickly he fired the track hoe and positioned it to block the hole and pile of dirt from the logging road. Then he killed it, jumped out, and ran—he wasn't sure why—directly away from the direction of Matt's car.

The truck came up the road, slowing as it approached the giant machine. Tommy watched from a darkened spot twenty yards away, his heart hammering and the sound of the ocean roaring in his ears again. The window came down and old man Walter peered out. Tommy could see his grizzled gray beard by the light of the moon.

Walter pulled ahead a ways, turned around in the road, and came back to the spot, this time shining a flashlight on the machine. Then, after what seemed like two minutes, Walter drove the truck away.

Tommy waited another few minutes to make sure the truck didn't come back, walked to the car, popped open the trunk, and retrieved the shovel and ax. He stood and stared at the body once again, then worked up his courage and slipped his hand over the face to be sure.

He's dead. There's nothing else to do.

Still, he shuddered at the evil of the scene.

In his previous life, if asked, Tommy would admit to fearing nothing and no one. Yet now, in his sobriety, the idea of evil, and of evil people, scared him in a way that simply made him shake. He knew he had no time for sadness, no room for fear, and would not let the gravity of what he came there to do slow him down. The night was bright, and he set about the rest of his task with purpose.

In minutes he had found a rhythm, scooping the compacted red soil out of the hole a few pounds at a time, picking at it with the ax, and scooping it out some more. Before long his arms began to tighten and his mind began to wander, as if demanding relief from the task that lay at hand.

When Charlie Turner became an orphan in 1952, he had two living relatives. The only one he'd ever met, Uncle Vance, his father's brother, lived three houses down from Charlie and his family in Lidem, Texas, and had been the first to discover the horror his own brother had inflicted on Charlie's mom and himself. Though only thirty-five, Vance had been married and divorced twice; he had never felt the need to kill his wives when he tired of being married to them.

Vance worked as a locomotive engineer on a Louisiana & Pacific railroad run. The day after five-year-old Charlie lost his parents, Vance took the boy to the train yard, an hour earlier than Vance normally got to work. He stopped just outside the gate, instructed Charlie to crawl onto the floor in the back seat of the car, spread an old blanket over the boy, told him not to make a sound, and then drove into the yard and parked in his normal spot. He then told Charlie to crawl into a large duffel bag Vance had retrieved from his trunk, stuffed the scratchy old blanket into the bag on top of the boy, zipped it, and carried him onto the train. As Vance was early, the fireman hadn't showed up yet, wouldn't until the last possible moment, and Vance hurriedly hid little Charlie in a storage compartment in the back of the locomotive, and once again told him not to move or make a sound until Uncle Vance found him and told him to. He spread out the blanket as best he could and told Charlie to try to make himself comfortable.

Vance checked on Charlie twice during the all-night trip, each time simply touching one finger to his lips before grabbing one of three pint bottles of whiskey he had also stowed in the compartment. Charlie peed his pants on the trip, but only once, and he didn't say a word about it to his uncle.

The train arrived in Branden, Louisiana, early the next morning. Vance waited until the fireman got off to walk into town in search of some fried eggs and flapjacks. Then, without saying a word, Vance pointed the boy back into the duffel, stuffed the blanket in too, and carried him like that until they were well clear of the train yard. Then he set the bag down, unzipped it to let Charlie out, and held the boy's hand as they walked into a filling station and asked for directions to Lurleen Carter's house. Though the two had never met, Vance had heard many times about his dead brother's dead wife's sister, who lived in the dead-end town in Louisiana where Vance's train always stopped.

At the woman's house, Vance and Charlie waited on the front porch and watched the sun come up. A storm was coming in, the clouds roiling, thunder in the distance, the morning sticky and pasty, the wind not even cool when it finally began to blow. Finally Lurleen pulled her old Hudson into the carport of the tiny A-frame house just a few miles from where Tommy would be decades later. She got out, looked at the man and boy on her porch but didn't approach.

"Help you?"

"You Lurleen?"

She didn't answer, only looked with pity at the little boy with the dark spot in his pants, sitting on her porch swing.

"The boy has a letter. It will tell you everything. I'm sorry I didn't have no more clothes for him."

Vance walked down the three steps, his heart fluttering, not looking at her but knowing the woman's glare would burn a hole through him if it could.

"It's you or me, Lurleen. And I ain't daddy material." He turned back toward Charlie.

"I'm sorry to leave you like this, son." Charlie sat quietly on the porch, trying hard not to move the swing. Vance pulled the third and final bottle from his hip pocket and drank heavily from it, and didn't look back when Lurleen yelled and yelled at him as he swiftly made away down the sidewalk.

It was 2:00 a.m. when Tommy pulled himself out of the hole and lay panting on the ground, staring up at the moon. He pulled out his shirttail and looked for dry spots to use on his face. After a minute he went to the car and drove it closer, then opened the trunk and stared at the tarp-wrapped package inside.

He grabbed the trunk to keep his knees from buckling, felt

a coldness wash across his face as his eyes went black as if he had stood up too fast. *Did you ever feel like this, Daddy? The way I feel right now?* He thought again about taking the money, couldn't see any reason not to, and began to untie the tarp before changing his mind and cinching it down again.

Did you see the man who killed you take out that gun? Did you know it was coming? Did they try to put you in a tarp, stick you in a trunk, drop you in a red-dirt hole in the filthy ground?

He lifted the package, stiff with rigor mortis, carried it over, and gently placed Matt's body on the ground beside the hole. Then he climbed inside the hole, grabbed the tarp, slid the body down along the wall, and got himself out. He returned to the car, drove it back into the woods in case someone came along, hurried back, and began to throw shovelfuls of clay on top.

Did you think of me when you fell? Did you remember you said you would visit that weekend?

After an hour the hole was no longer a hole, and only a slight hump of soil remained. Then he began to lift the tops and limbs of brush from trees they had cut before and piled them on top of the mound until it could no longer be seen. He began to walk over the pile, tree limbs breaking, sticks jutting this way and that. Still, it didn't seem like enough.

He glanced back at Walter's house. It was completely dark. He jumped once again into the track hoe, fired it, and quickly began to run the tracks back and forth across the brush pile until it was a broken mess of twigs, and the mound in the soil was simply flat. He moved the machine off the debris and repositioned it by the road. When he shut it off, once again the night was totally quiet.

He checked Walter's house again, and this time it remained dark. He walked his shovel and pick into the woods—no sense throwing away good tools—and hid them both under a bed of pine needles, figuring he'd pick them up in the morning.

He returned to the pile and surveyed things one last time. He and Otis would be back in a few hours, and an hour or two after that, this whole forty acres would be on fire. He figured he would douse the pile of brush he had smashed in gasoline first, then blaze it up and tell Otis it was just for practice. Then he could toss a whole new bunch of limbs on top and do it all over again.

He started Matt's car and pulled it into the road, then left it running and got out. He returned to the pile, got down on his knees, and reached one hand in, to touch bare dirt.

With his other hand, Tommy removed his hat. He spoke in a normal voice, not a whisper or a shout. A voice made just for this time, for this occasion, for this place.

"I didn't know you, Matt. I don't know why it happened this way. I'm sorry. I couldn't be sorrier. I would do anything if I could bring you back. I'm sorry I can't. You didn't deserve this."

Then he stood and reached a hand out into the darkness, as if he could touch the departed man in another dimension.

"I don't know what's going to happen now, Matt. I'm sorry for what I did. But from here forward . . . God's will be done."

He kept the lights off again as he slid past old man Walter's house, traveled three miles down the country road back in the direction of his house. At the base of the levee he dropped the car into first gear, drove to the top, and sat looking down at the brown, murky water. The night was at its darkest now, a couple of hours before dawn, and he slipped the car into neutral, fastened the belt, cut the engine, and let it begin to roll.

He hit a wall of water at forty miles per hour. Tommy quickly rolled down all the windows, unlatched the seat belt, and waited for the force beyond description to take him into the darkness. He felt the car become heavy as it sank slowly, first up to his knees, then over the seat and his waist, and when it got up to his shoulder, Tommy opened the door and swam out as the car sank into the ooze and tried to pull him down into the darkness with it.

The night was still muggy as he pulled himself out of the current, crawled up the levee, and walked along its ridge toward his house. As the sun began to crack over the horizon, he peered in the direction of Brenda's house a mile away, but quickly refocused on traveling the last mile or so through the woods to get back to his own home. He wanted so badly to turn, move himself toward the house he used to share with his wife and son, the house that'd been all repaired so you couldn't even tell a fire had ever burned there. All he wanted to do was go inside, take a nice warm shower, and crawl into the cool cotton sheets with Brenda and Jamey, hold both of them tight and never, ever, ever let them go. But instead, as he had to, he continued through the woods to the place where he lived alone, took off all his clothes in the yard before going inside, doused them with gasoline from a can in the back of his truck, tossed them into his burn barrel, and lit the clothes on fire. Then he walked, naked, and retrieved the bag with his earlier clothes from under the house and tossed them in too. Finally he went inside, checked the living room to make sure everything looked right, turned the water on hot, and climbed into the shower.

It was better this way, he knew it. Yes, he wanted to be with them, to have them, to hold them, like the family they once had been, and he hoped would one day be again. But it was better this way. Because Brenda and Jamey were no doubt still asleep, dreaming softly with one another, and he wouldn't have been welcome to come inside and wake them up.

CHAPTER 4

After Tommy showered, he went out and stirred the burning remains in the barrel, then soaked some kindling in gasoline and dropped the sticks in to stoke the fire once more and let it burn. Inside, he once again straightened his living room, moved the lamp, the table, the sofa, spread a stack of magazines from under an end table across one end of his couch. He got down on the floor, checked under the coffee table, making sure he couldn't find any blood. Then he leaned back in the recliner and jumped out of it quickly, leaving the chair sprawling, and threw a blanket across it as if he had been sleeping there peacefully before getting up to go to work.

He made his lunch as usual, two turkey sandwiches with pepper jack cheese, sliced onion, and spicy mustard, a bag of pretzels, a banana, and an apple, and drove into town. He pulled into Bubba's coffee shop across from the paper mill, as he did every day.

"Morning, Caroline." Tommy did his best to look just like he always did.

"Hey, Tommy." She turned and poured from a steaming glass pot into a Styrofoam cup. "Y'all gon' burn today?" Caroline had worked at the coffee shop since he was small. Now, as then, she didn't talk much. This was a long conversation for her.

"We're supposed to. How'd you know?" His heart beat wildly at her question.

"James told me."

"He's been in already?"

"Yesterd'y. Dollar thirty-five."

Tommy drank his coffee as he drove the rest of the way into work. He was glad to be the first one at the shop. He filled half a dozen fuel torches, laid three saws on the oil-soaked wooden work table, and began to sharpen them, just let himself focus on the work as he removed the teeth of the chain a thousandth of an inch at a time, stooping down to inspect the chrome gleam as he blew away the metal shavings. He put the torches in the bed of the truck, along with two of the saws as well as fuel, oil, and a toolbox. He was laying in the second of two fire flappers when Otis pulled into the yard in his ancient rattling blue Pinto.

Otis opened the door of the decrepit car and emitted a series of grunts as he stood, which nearly drowned out the grinding and cracking noises the car made as he got out of it. He shuffled over and grabbed one of the flappers Tommy had just placed in the back of the truck, grinned like a tiny-eyed maniac.

"Let's do the flapper dance, Tommy!" Otis shouted, whereupon he flapped the rubber strips at an imaginary fire in the parking lot, then stood and shook his hips and yelled out, "Flapper!" Then he did the same thing again, this time raising the instrument over his head and swinging it around.

"This be a good country dance, Tommy! All we need is Willie or Waylon or one o' them big ones to cut a record!" He doused the imaginary fire again, then began to sing.

I got me a fire burnin'
I'm gonna put it out
But till I get it under control
I'm gonna have to dance and shout

As quickly as he had started, Otis suddenly stopped, leaned on the bed of the truck, and wheezed for breath. He threw the tool into the back.

"You like my song, Tommy? I'm gon' be a country star yet." Otis was dressed in a light-blue jumpsuit with a thick leather belt and pie plate–sized buckle around the middle, steel-toed cowboy boots, and a plastic cowboy hard hat. Otis fancied himself a genuine country cowboy.

"Come on, Red," Otis shouted as he opened the door to the truck and stood back before climbing in. His homely redbone hound slinked out the open window of the Pinto and walked with a sidewinder gait, lowering his eyes in shame as he passed Tommy and jumped in ahead of Otis, who slumped into the truck and tried to make himself comfortable. James let Otis bring the dog to work on Fridays, though Tommy couldn't stand the ignorant mutt. Although today he felt a certain sympathy for the animal as he tried to keep himself together.

"You got everything ready, Tommy?" Already Red was snoring on the floor of the truck.

They drove toward the jobsite through a beautiful spring morning, the air so bright it could almost catch fire. Immediately Otis fell asleep, despite the countless times James and Tommy had told him to pay attention to where they were going. He matched snores with the dim-witted hound splayed out on the floor between the two men. The dog stirred and began licking its balls, one of which hung markedly lower than the other, and peered up at Tommy with a look Tommy took for a snide grin. When Red tired of ball-licking, he lowered his head and fell quickly asleep, again began to snore, then interrupted his own snoring to whimper and run in place on the floor, once even kicking Tommy's foot off the gas pedal as he drove. Tommy stomped the stupid dog back, but Red didn't even seem to notice.

Shortly before the turnoff, Tommy pulled into a driveway,

as he had done every day for the last two months they had been working on this site. An old lady stopped sweeping the front yard with her broom—she did this every day to keep the grass from growing—and unleashed a gum smile at the approaching men.

A bright-pink apron was tied across her ample midsection. She had told Tommy before that she had shopped and shopped for an apron with the words, but couldn't find one so she had simply written it herself with a thick black marker: "If mama aint hapy, aint no body hapy."

When the truck came to a stop, Otis woke, looked ahead dreamily, and smiled.

"Mama!" he shouted. Red leaned his head back and howled in response. Fifty-seven years old or no, Otis insisted on stopping at his mama's house on the way to work every day, to pick up the lunch she had packed for him in his Spider-Man lunch box.

Quickly he tried to stuff his hard hat onto the floor.

"Better not let her see this. Mama hates me wearin' this hat."

Otis hopped out gaily, and Mama swallowed him in her fleshy arms. Otis's mama must have been six feet tall, while Otis stood no taller than five-three.

"Here's your lunch, baby." She handed him the box, then shooed him away. "Now you boys get to work. Daylight's burnin'. And Tommy?"

"Yes, ma'am?" Otis swung the lunch box and whistled as he went back to the truck.

"I put a cookie in there for you too, baby."

"Thank you, ma'am."

"You ain't got nothin' against black people's cooking, do you?" She moved in toward the truck.

"Naw, Mama, Tommy's a *good* white man, Mama!"

He began to sweat having her so close to the truck.

She looked through the window and saw Otis's cowboy hard hat on the floor, then scowled in at him.

"Don't let me see you wearin' that hat around here, Otis," she told him. "'Cause I'm gon' snatch that hat off your head if I catch you wearing it."

But Otis couldn't resist his playful nature. Rather than growing more fearful, he lit up at the prospect. He leaned down so he could see her through Tommy's open window.

"Just do it, just one time, Mama!"

Mama scowled. "Don't make me whoop you, Otis."

"Just call me Otis Bob just one time, Mama! Just one time! Just say, 'Here's your lunch, Otis Bob!'"

"Boy!" Mama shouted, then began to run around the front of the truck to Otis's side. She was so old and fat she could only shuffle.

"I'm gonna get my flyswatter and wear out your behind, Otis! Yo' daddy was Otis Robert and your name is Otis Junior! Not Otis Bob like some redneck! Like some dayum white fool!"

"Okay, Mama! Calm down. I was just having some fun!"

"I'm gonna have some fun wearing out your big fat behind, boy!"

"Yes, ma'am."

"And Tommy?"

"Yes, ma'am?"

"Don't let Otis have that cookie. He's getting too fat."

Otis fell asleep again before Tommy turned the truck off the highway, minutes from his mama's house. When Tommy drove into a pothole, Otis woke with a start, then looked all around the cab of the truck before fixing his gaze on the knob of the glove compartment.

"I don't know why Mama's so down on being country," he blurted out, more in a whine than in his normal jovial tone. Otis shook his head, and Red looked up at him admiringly. "I really don't. Black peoples has always been country. Why, just last night I saw Charley Pride on an old *Hee Haw.* And he's as black as I am."

"I used to love *Hee Haw.*"

"Why should y'all get all the good music?" Then he reached for the radio and cranked it up. An old Charlie Daniels tune had just come on.

"Hawww!! Crank it up!! Hear that, Tommy? That's some music!!"

Otis sang all the words to the song as Tommy drove closer to the track hoe and the horrible scene from hours earlier. He grew steadily more nervous as they drove, his vision beginning to tunnel, and Otis sang away merrily. Finally the song ended.

"We gonna burn today, Tommy?"

"Of course we are, Otis."

"Don't you mean Otis Bob?"

"Okay, Otis Bob."

Otis laughed. "I like working with you, Tommy. It's gonna be a hard day, though. Law, it's hot already! Law-deeee!"

"Just make sure you drink lots of water. We have plenty."

"That's hard work, that burning."

"I know, Otis. We do it all the time."

"You gotta run around a lot, make sure the fire doesn't get away. And hot!"

"Well, it *is* fire, Otis."

"Have you burned before?"

Tommy just looked at him.

"Oh yeah, I must be thinking about Terry. I get y'all confused sometimes."

"Terry? Terry was seven feet tall, Otis."

"Yeah. But he was white like you. And oooohhhhh!! Lazy!"

"Are you saying I'm lazy?"

"No, Terry was lazy. I mean, he was so sorry, the sorry just ran off of him. I mean, if sorriness had been water, it would've put the fire out!! If sorriness had been gasoline, he would've burned up! Poof!!"

"Is that right . . ."

"I mean, you gotta watch out for that fire. It's hot! It'll burn things up!"

"I never thought of that, Otis Bob."

"Oh. You quit it, Tommy. But Terry, he was always red. If it was too hot, he turned red. If it was too cold, he turned red. I don't know why people call me colored. Y'all get colored a lot more than we do!"

Tommy parked the truck and the two got out. Red jumped out and began barking at a woodpecker up in a gum tree. Tommy asked Otis to unload the tools from the truck, and he went over and moved the track hoe off the brush pile and into the road. Then he doused the pile in fuel and dropped on a lit match.

Before long only charred sticks remained and seemed to blend in with the ground underneath. Tommy asked Otis to walk a hundred yards east and run his torch on a line parallel to the road; Tommy said he would do the same another hundred yards away. He was eager to get Otis away from the grave site as quickly as possible.

"Let me just ask you one thing before I do."

"Sure."

"You know, I was thinking the other night."

"Better be careful with that." What Tommy always said.

"Aw, shoot, Tommy. I don't do it too much. Just when I'm watching TV sometimes, I'll get to thinking. Do you remember *The Waltons*?"

"Sure, way back. What about it?"

"So I was watching it the other night." Otis stopped to sniff then, and this went on for a full minute, sniffing and hawking and snorting. "Yeah, I was watching it. Anyway, I won't tell you what all was happening. There was a lot of interesting details to the show, but they not that important. It was a nice sunny day there on Walton's Mountain. Or at least on TV it was. Big John had just finished loading up some boards to take down to Ike Godsey's store."

"Otis."

"All right, all right. John-Boy had got into some trouble. He owed somebody something. I never could figure out if it was money or what. He was out driving, and he stopped off to talk to the Baldwin sisters. And you know, it just got me to thinking." At that, Otis stared into the sky, as if about to proffer some deep conundrum.

"So what about it, Otis?"

Otis turned. "Shut up, Red!" He kicked the dog, who had been lying quietly in the shade by the tire of the truck. Red lifted his head and looked at his owner, then laid it back down in the dirt.

"Those Baldwin sisters."

"Sure. The old ladies with the recipe."

Otis lit up then. "Exactly! The recipe!" He cleared his throat again, hemming and hawking up a storm. "So you got these two old ladies. They live together, always have. All the time talking about whatever happened to Ashley Longworth and what all. Making up batches of the recipe and probably sipping it when the cameras wasn't around. You really think they was sisters?"

"It was just a TV show, Otis. Of course they weren't sisters in real life."

Otis began to gesture wildly then, accenting his points with the side of one hand on the hood of the pickup. "Think about it, Tommy. Just think about it!! You got these two old biddies. Sippin' all day on they daddy's recipe. Look close and you'll see it. They wearing the same dresses! Same shoes! Same old-lady combs in their hairdos!"

"And?"

"And this!" He banged his fist now on the truck's windshield. "Sisters, my hairy black butt! Those two old biddies stayed looped up on that recipe, going into the bedroom and slipping one another's dresses on and off all day long! Only the good Lord knew what they was doing when nobody else was around!"

Eventually, Otis grew bored with his tirade on the Baldwin sisters, and the two of them took up their torches and fire flappers and got to work. The heat of the day was stifling before they even started burning. Otis walked down to the far end of the section, and Tommy started by laying a fire line that went right over the grave. He walked back and forth a hundred feet at a time, laid out streams of fuel with his sprinkler, and gave what remained of the pile atop the grave several extra doses. Then they each dropped a few lit matches and watched the fire begin to spread. Tommy continued to grab limbs and tops and throw them on the pile, anything he could do to disguise what he had done there just a few hours before.

Within an hour the fire was burning well, sending clouds of thick black smoke into the sky, desiccated organic material sprinkling the surface of the soil as it combusted. Tommy continued to disguise, throwing limb after limb on top of the burning pyre, leaves and needles crackling and exploding in sparks of orange against an indigo sky. Otis and Red wandered the site a quarter mile away, making showers of sparks of their own, the dog barking and jumping up and down each time fire encountered a pocket of pitch and set off a parade of fireworks. Around noon, James came to the site in his jacked-up truck to check on them. He had cold bottles of Coke for them, which they took and sat down in the truck to drink with their lunches. Red whimpered outside the door of the truck, begging Otis to let him back in so he could sleep on the floor.

They listened to Paul Harvey as they ate, then Otis fell into a ten-minute snore fest so loud Tommy had to get out of the truck. Then he got back in and moved the truck to get away from the burning pile nearby, to the other side of the cut where they were to spend the afternoon. Otis never woke, despite the rutted dirt road and the dog chasing behind, baying mightily. When Tommy finally shook him awake, he told Otis that if he did the little bit of work left he could take another nap down by the creek. Otis lit up at this and suddenly couldn't wait to get to work. Tommy only wanted to keep him as far from the grave site as possible, and for once was grateful his partner was so totally incurious.

After gathering himself, Otis lit his torch, then shook a cigarette from a pack in his pocket and lit it with the burning tool.

"Since when do you smoke?"

Otis sucked in and spat out a thin stream of smoke. Red cocked his head and looked at his master as if he were of another realm.

"I only smoke on burn days." Nevertheless, Otis seemed to enjoy his cigarette, leaned his head back and smiled at the smoke pouring from his mouth, laughed at it dreamily.

"We only burn a few days a year."

"That's right. I don't smoke but two or three packs of cigarettes a year."

Tommy just shook his head.

"And I only chew tobacco when I go fishing. But don't tell Mama that." He pointed his cigarette at Tommy as a warning.

"It's not her business, is it?"

"She tol' me, she quit makin' my lunch if she catch me chewin' again."

Otis flipped his cigarette into a pile of brush they hadn't burned yet, and he and Red sauntered off toward the other end of the tract. Another cigarette bobbed in Otis's mouth as he walked. Tommy set his own fire lines, and within an hour the sky was a thickening black. When it began to die down, he wandered across to check on his partner. Tommy was eager to get out of there for the day.

The older man had apparently woken from a nap when Tommy approached, and stood leaning on his fire flapper. When he saw Tommy coming, he began to dance again, thrusting the tool into actual spots of fire this time, then waving it around in the sky. Red, on the other hand, wandered the site, repeatedly poking his paw into hot spots and then pulling it back out, yowling each time, apparently growing stupider by the minute. Once he yanked his paw from a hot spot and jumped back so quickly, his low-hanging ball touched another coal, which sent him into a frenzy of barking, chasing his tail, and jumping up and down like a bucking horse. Eventually, the numerous piles of brush that had earlier clogged the site were all flattened out, the day seemed under control, and the two packed their tools and got into the truck, this time with Red on the seat between them. The dog barked a dozen times as they passed the grave site this time, and uncharacteristically, Tommy reached out and patted the beast, which made him totally quiet.

Back at the shop, Tommy couldn't wait to get going, and this time asked Otis to help him with all the equipment. Otis sulked around, muttering with his lips poked out, as he helped unload the truck, empty the fuel torches, and put everything back in its place. Red continued to nose around the yard, apparently finding a nest of wasps, which before long had him yelping and shaking his floppy ears furiously.

Only after Otis and Red were gone did Tommy notice the message indicator on his cell phone. He was back in his pickup and was about to start it to head home. He knew he would want to shower and get out of there to see his son as quickly as possible. Maybe he'd even have time to make some calls about another place to live before he saw Jamey.

Tommy didn't recognize the number. But he knew who it was before the caller finished a word. He knew well the voice. He knew well the man. He breathed out heavily.

You will deal with it. You're not going to run.

But this doesn't make sense.

"Tommy, this is Sheriff Norm. I need to talk to you. Call me right away, as soon as you get this. Before you talk to anybody else. It's real urgent."

He dropped the phone on the seat, then looked out the window of his truck at the blazing afternoon sun. He started the engine and began to back out of his space. He would go to the station. He would face it head-on.

He picked up the phone from the seat, stared at it, then dropped it on the seat again, put the truck in gear, and headed out toward Norm's office.

I'll be right there, Norm. Just let me tell Jamey myself. He still loves me. He doesn't think I'm all bad.

In the office nothing seemed right. Tommy sat in the lobby, waiting. Norm's secretary glanced at him furtively as she talked on the phone, craning her shoulder to hide her face from Tommy. Two deputies walked by, jawing. He knew them, but they didn't look at him the way one would look at a murderer. Norm was strangely unhostile when he came out after a minute, shook Tommy's hand, and asked him to come back to Norm's office. He smelled of cigarettes. In the office, Norm remained standing after Tommy sat down in front of Norm's desk.

"Tommy. You been working today?"

"Yessir. Out off Danville Road, past Mr. Walter's house. We've been out there six weeks or more."

Norm nodded for too long. "James told me y'all were burning today."

"Been there since seven o'clock."

Again, Norm nodded. “So you were out of touch all day?”

“Something wrong, Sheriff?”

“I won’t hold out on you any longer, Tommy. I’ve got some real bad news.” The sheriff moved closer, reached out his hand. Tommy took it without standing and looked up at him, uncomprehending. Norm reached out his other hand to Tommy’s shoulder. Long ago he had learned in this job, white folks don’t take bad news any better or worse than any others. May as well just get it over with.

“Some things just don’t make sense, Tommy. Something bad, bad, bad happened this afternoon.”

CHAPTER 5

"Have a nice weekend," Jamey said in his honey-sweet voice, turning back from the bottom step to face the bus driver. The brakes whooshed as the bus stopped and Mrs. Nunn cranked open the door.

"You too, baby," she answered. Late, she pressed the switches to open the swing arm in front and to turn on the hazards. "Ask your mama to call me this weekend, would you? I've got some tomatoes canned with her name on 'em." She beamed at him through a wad of chewing gum, afternoon sun reflecting off her thick glasses.

"Yes, ma'am."

"I was gonna tell her myself, but I guess her and Mamaw ain't out waiting for you today."

"You're not supposed to say 'ain't,' Mrs. Nunn," he answered, then looked to the floor of the bus.

"Well, yes, sir, you're right, Professor Turner. You're right. Maybe I should go back to second grade. What do you think?"

At that Jamey grinned, then stepped down to the ground and waved back at her through the closing bus door and began the walk toward his house. He was surprised his mom's car wasn't home, and a hollow feeling came into his chest and radiated out to his shoulders. He called for her as he entered the house, but in return heard only a spooky silence, the air damp and cool compared to the afternoon heat bearing dowı outside. Quickly, he sneezed, and looked around, confused. He never sneezed.

He called for her again as he walked through the house, opened the door to her room and even the bathroom in his search, before deciding she must have got stuck at work. She had only worked at the Dairy Queen up in Ruston for a few weeks, and Mommy had made it very clear she was planning to make a good impression on Mr. Wayne, her boss. And already twice, on days she did a really good job, Mr. Wayne gave her a little container of ice cream to take home to Jamey. So that must be why she was late. In his mind, he tasted the chocolate swirl ice cream and began to feel better.

He went into his room and smoothed his hand over the bedspread she had made up so neatly after Jamey had gone to school. He admired each of his toys, then picked up the Lego Star Wars ship Daddy had bought him, the one he put together over the weekend. He set it back down, then opened the capsule and took out one of the smiling men inside.

"My mom is gonna bring me some ice cream," he said to the little man. The figure continued smiling. Finally he put it back in its place, said hello to the stuffed cow nestled between his pillows, and went to the framed picture on his bedstand and picked it up. In the picture Jamey was still a baby, and Daddy held him in his arms as Mommy watched. Daddy had his nose upturned like a little piggy and sucked on Jamey's pacifier, his eyes opened wide. As he did each time, Jamey looked again at his father's eyes, and, as always, felt relieved to see the little specks of blue therein. He wondered once more what Mommy meant when she said Daddy's pretty blue eyes were empty by the time that picture was taken.

Eventually, he looked out the back door to see if Mr. Glenn's car was home. He saw it was, and decided he would go for a visit. Normally, Mr. Glenn didn't get home so early; in fact, usually he wasn't even back until after *SpongeBob* and *Jimmy Neutron* were over. On the way Jamey took a detour to pet Mamaw's old black poodle. She wasn't really his mamaw, but all the kids in the neighborhood called her so. Even Mommy had, when she was little.

The old dog began to whimper when Jamey approached. He could barely lift his head, but he did the best he could. Jamey saw the fleck of recognition in the dog's long, hanging face. He rested on one side under a giant water oak, lay panting between two knee-high surface roots of the tree as if in his own private room. His wagging tail kicked up little puffs of dust. Jamey bent down and spoke to him; except for the tail the old dog was as still as he could be. After a minute he managed to turn his head enough to slowly lick the boy's hand, his meaty tongue radiating the smell of decay.

"You didn't chase the bus today, Rascal," he said. Just last school year the dog ran after the school bus, barking, every day, both coming and going, morning and afternoon.

The screen door of Mamaw's cinder block house squeaked once, then slapped shut as the old woman stepped onto her porch. She doddered down and patted Jamey on the head, much as he patted the dog, breathed out loudly through her nose. "Rascal sure is glad to see you, honey," she told him. "He comes out from under the porch and lays here every day, just a few minutes before you get home on the bus."

"He does?"

"Yes, sir. I guess he feels safe in between them old roots."

"Yes, ma'am."

She stood up then, hands on hips, turned her wrinkled lips inside out over her gums. "He's had a good life. He has." Then she bent over as best she could and patted the dog herself. "I'm eighty-seven years old, going on eighty-eight, and I've never seen a dog love a little boy so much. When Rascal goes on to a place where he can chase buses again, I bet he'll picture you sitting in your seat."

"Yes, ma'am. See you later, buddy. I'll come back in a little while." Rascal whimpered once then and managed to stand. One of his front legs wouldn't bend at all anymore, and he pivoted over it in a cam-like motion as he walked. He only made it a few steps before he stumbled hard onto one shoulder. Jamey turned back, helped him up, and Rascal sulked back over to his bed between the roots.

Glenn watched the boy out his kitchen window, across the fingers of grass searching for purchase on dry, red clay. He gave himself a moment, which was rare for Glenn, who always scurried from one task to another, just to admire Jamey as he walked, timidly, toward Glenn's house. The countless things that had him distracted seemed to melt away in one deft motion as the boy approached his door.

Glenn rarely came home this early, and until he saw Jamey get off the school bus, he had been feeling sadder than normal. His four o'clock feeling, he called it, the end of another fruitless day at work, another day older, and nobody waiting for him at home. The whole day had been a bad one. One low-life helpless dimwit after another coming in to Glenn's office to apply for food stamps, welfare, relief. Every one with the same sob story he'd been hearing now for twenty-plus years. Even with Bonita and Mabel handling all the intakes that afternoon, all he could feel was the slow, steady ticking of the clock. When Louise had asked if he might make her dinner that night, he got too excited at the prospect of company and came straight home and started cooking. He should've just left a half hour early and at least got in a shortened workout. He'd been glad for her friendship, but bottom line, knowing this woman had made him irresponsible.

Glenn turned on his oven, then watched as Jamey climbed his steps and approached the closed screen door. Glenn could only see the outline of the boy on his darkened porch through the smoky screen, the wash of wavy hair surrounding Jamey's head. Glenn felt a pang of remorse again about missing his workout—not something he could do often, if he was to have a shot at the forty-and-over Mr. Louisiana contest he was hoping to enter in July. By the time Jamey knocked quietly, Glenn's worries were gone and he could only laugh. Such a polite boy.

Inside, Jamey gave him a big hug, and Glenn's world continued to improve. Jamey told him, then, about his mother.

Glenn went to the window and looked out at her driveway, felt for the phone in his pants pocket and checked it.

"She didn't call me. Did she say anything about going somewhere after work?"

"No, sir. Maybe she just had to work extra today. She said she wants to make sure Mr. Wayne, her boss, thinks she does a good job."

Glenn went down on one knee then, drawn by the hope and trust implied in Jamey's words. "I sure could use another hug. Do you have one for me?"

Jamey nodded, bit his lower lip. When Glenn picked up the featherweight boy, Jamey held perfectly still, then nestled his face into the soft spot on Glenn's neck. Together, like this, they breathed.

"You are getting so big!" Glenn set the boy down. Jamey swelled. "Would you like to help me cook? Or watch some TV while I cook?"

"I'll watch just a little bit. Then I'll come help you." Jamey headed into the other room as Glenn dialed Brenda's number and then hung up when he got no answer.

Glenn took out pots and pans, read through th[...] recip[...] again, then took cumin, coriander, and thyme fro[...] his spic[...] rack and lined them up in the order he would [...] use them. He poured oil into a bowl, then whisked in a spoon of crushed garlic along with several pinches of spice, working each into the mixture before moving on to the next. His work, like his house, was perfectly orderly. Though when he looked up from his stirring, he did notice a few spots of dust on the kitchen table. Made sense, though. It was Friday afternoon, and he did his thorough cleaning every Saturday.

All the hugs from Jamey must have turned him contemplative, so he stopped for a moment to admire the painting of the long-legged man playing a drum, which hung above his stereo, to one side of his front door. Every three months he got a new painting from the library, and unless they had added something new, he would have to restart the cycle of twelve paintings on his next visit. Of course they had all those religious ones, various paintings of Jesus with an endless blue light in his eyes, or of angels or the Virgin, but Glenn had no intention of hanging anything like that on his wall.

He went to the painting and dusted it off quickly with a towel. He surely didn't want *her* to see any dust. Then, Glenn considered how happy he was to have his house back, as he returned to his cutting boards and sliced two large carrots and a medium-sized cucumber, spread them into a circular pattern on a plate, and put it in the refrigerator. Next week would be six months since Jacob moved out, half a year Glenn had lived alone. Jacob. Just another in a long line of men old enough to be his father. Yet, somehow, another one he ended up taking care of.

Sure, he missed some things about Jacob. On the other hand, certain things were easier; Jacob liked to eat too much fat and grease, every day with the hot dogs and chips and gallons of Coke, while Glenn got leaner and tighter every year. But Jacob did have a riotous sense of humor, and he cut the grass and every night after dinner drove the trash down the parish road to the dumpster. And how things had changed. Glenn's grass was already out of hand this spring, and three bags of garbage waited in the carport for him to throw away. And if that weren't bad enough, a coon had got into one the night before, and he had spent fifteen minutes that morning picking up garbage strewn around his yard like seeds after a hurricane. Maybe he should get a dog. No, probably not. That would just be one more thing to mess with.

Glenn sprinkled more cumin into the bowl of oil, stirred it in, then opened a package of chicken and spread the parts on his biggest cutting board.

"Are you going to see your daddy this weekend?" Glenn hollered into the other room. *Tommy Turner.* That sorry dopehead and gambler. How he even thought he was ever good enough for Brenda, much less that sweet little boy in there watching cartoons. Glenn listened for a response, but the only voice he heard was SpongeBob's: *"Duh, I'm stupid, Patrick. I like karate. Duhhhhh."* Jamey didn't answer, only squealed in delight at SpongeBob's comical assessment.

Glenn continued preparing his excellent meal. He dipped his finger into the oil, tasted it, then spooned more garlic in and began to rub the concoction into every crevice of the cuts of lean chicken before placing it all onto a baking sheet and into the oven. He took another package from the refrigerator and put two handfuls of crisp green beans into a pot, added an inch of water, and began to slowly steam the vegetables. Then he removed the pot of couscous, fluffed it all out with a wooden spoon and into a flower-patterned bowl that used to be his mother's. He took out yet another cutting board and peeled two bananas, laid out some grapes and half a cantaloupe. Before cutting into the fruit, he remembered Louise didn't like cantaloupe, so he put that back and took out a dozen strawberries instead. Louise was one of the few people in this town who liked healthy food—and he wanted to keep her happy.

Glenn was feeling especially empty lately, since his mother

had died. Pointless. Forty-five years old, and what did he have to show for it? All alone, sick of his job, every day the same thing. What, he sometimes asked himself, was the sum total of his life? So he'd helped some people in his work. Maybe. Hard to say. One thing he did know. The endless stream of hopelessness and drudgery that came through his door every day had become just plain old.

There was a time he thought he could do it all. He was young Glenn Rosen, ready to save the world. The hungry? *Feed them.* The poor? *Clothe them.* The downtrodden? *Lift them up.* Twenty-three years of hearing the same sob stories had changed him. He no longer thought he could help them all. Maybe, just maybe, a few. He tried to give himself a break. Anybody would have broken by now. By enduring twenty-three years of *gimme, gimme, gimme.*

But. At least there was Jamey. Brenda and Jamey. The sweet woman who had recently moved next door and her darling little son. So what if Jamey wasn't really Glenn's son. Look who his real father was. *Tommy Turner.* So Glenn was gay. So he had no idea how to be a father. So what? He certainly wasn't scared of it. No doubt, he could figure it out. God knew he had been through enough therapy. What did he have to lose by trying something different? And just for a minute, leave Tommy to the side. He was out of prison now and seemed to be trying. Certainly, Glenn was as qualified to be a father, real or otherwise, as most of the lowlifes he saw in his work every day. Being unfit as a parent hadn't stopped any of them from squeezing kids out, or spreading their seed, all over town. But parent? *Feed my own children! Oh my gawd!!*

"Can I talk to you?"

Glenn looked up to see Jamey had returned to the kitchen, and he smiled almost inwardly. One of the many endearing things about this child: he'd often prefer the company of an adult to the television. Not to mention how polite the boy was. "Of course you can talk to me, buddy. Anytime."

Jamey smiled then. "What about at midnight?" He seemed to have forgotten about his mother's absence and was feeling mischievous.

"Sure. Come on over."

"What about at four thirty in the morning?"

"If you can wake me up. But what are you talking about? Your mommy says she just about has to pour water on you to get you up at seven to get ready for school."

"Mr. Glenn?"

Glenn checked the chicken in the oven, lowered the temperature slightly, and began to cut the strawberries into pieces. "Yeah, kiddo? What's up?"

"I got in a fight at school today."

Glenn stopped what he was doing, wiped his hands. Jamey never got in fights.

"I'm sorry, buddy. Did you get hurt?"

"No, sir. I just punched him in the arm for what he said."

"Well. What happened?" Glenn set his knife down, paid closer attention.

Then Jamey began to cry. "Oliver Evans has been picking on me."

Glenn wiped his hands on his apron and went to the boy. He went down on one knee, wiped away Jamey's tears, tried to look the boy in the eye. "You know I'm always proud of you, Jamey. If he's been picking on you, I'm glad you stood up for yourself. Good for you." Jamey tried to smile, and Glenn pushed the hair out of his eyes. He decided he shouldn't linger, and returned to the strawberries.

"He punched me back, but it didn't hurt." Jamey balled his fists. "I was so mad."

"It sure sounds like it. And like I said, you have every right to stand up for yourself. Do you want to tell me what happened?"

"He said my real daddy didn't want me and went away to jail, and now my new daddy is a fag."

Glenn started at the comment, flinched, and, somehow, stopped the knife before cutting off the end of his finger. Not at the insult; long ago he got used to being called horrible names. But rather at the idea that someone could actually think he was the boy's father. Apparently Oliver Evans's mother had seen Glenn, Brenda, and Jamey together at Walmart, and had drawn her own conclusions. "Do you know what that word means, Jamey?"

The boy hung his head and nodded slowly. "I told him you weren't my daddy, you were just my friend. But then he said it again, and that's when I punched him."

"Well, I'm proud of you for standing up for yourself, Jamey. I am. But you don't have to stand up for me. Not over some silly name."

Suddenly Jamey looked up, defiantly. "I told him don't say anything about me, about my mommy, about my daddy, or about Mr. Glenn. He's my friend."

Glenn didn't know what to say, so he poured the boy a glass of milk, checked his chicken and beans, and tried to settle himself again. The phone rang in his pocket, and he grabbed it quickly, hoping Brenda would have a good reason for being so late.

He viewed the number before answering. *Tommy Turner.*

"Just a minute, Jamey. It's your daddy." He cleared his throat before he answered.

"Glenn?"

Something in Tommy's voice made the instant rage he felt at the thought of the man disappear. For years, the only reason he even tolerated the guy was that Tommy had saved Glenn from drowning once, so he owed the asshole his life, really; he'd have been dead a long time ago if not for Tommy, as much as he wished he could forget it. God knows he had relived the moment from all those years ago a million times, the dread and panic and, finally, the sense of peace he had felt looking up from underwater at the sharp, beautiful light above before Tommy Turner had pulled him back into the living world. Just one example, really, of the shit you can't get away from when you never leave the shithole of a town you grew up in.

That, and he knew it was important to stay on Tommy's good side; prison record or no, he was the boy's father. Give the devil his due. As director of the local Family Services office, Glenn knew better than most that blood is king.

Tommy didn't kid around like he normally did, didn't make a joke or try to say something he knew Glenn would agree with. His words were a succession of staccatos, and for a minute, Glenn forgot he couldn't stand the son of a bitch.

"Is Jamey there with you?" Tommy sounded crazy—not drunk, more like stunned. His voice was dry, wheezy, high pitched like a child Jamey's age.

"Yes, he's here. Brenda wasn't home and I haven't heard from her. Jamey thought she must be working late."

Tommy began to cry then, but Glenn didn't feel sorry for him; instead he felt the tenor of his heart change, darken. He drew his breath to prepare for the manipulation he knew was coming.

"I'm afraid not, Glenn. I just got through talking to Norm. I was out on a controlled burn all day. I had left my phone in the truck, and I didn't see the message he left me until I was back at the shop and about to go home."

"Tommy?"

"It's bad, Glenn." Tommy choked the words out. "There was a bad accident out on 167. A high school kid crossed the center line." Tommy barked out one more cry, then caught his breath. "Don't tell Jamey, I'll be right over. Brenda's dead."

CHAPTER 6

They met at a dance at the VFW on a hot Friday night in June. Brenda was twenty-six then and had already been a widow for five years, after losing her high school love, Peter, to a brain tumor when they both were twenty-one. For years after Peter died she had mourned without knowing it, had never noticed the way she kept her head down when single men were around, had told her friends, in subtle ways, she didn't want to be introduced. Only really in the previous couple months had the curtain begun to open, and for the first time in years she had begun to go about her days with a brightness she hadn't even realized had been missing.

Brenda and her friend Linda, twice divorced and not quite thirty, sat in folding chairs at a long wooden table by themselves, as far away from the band as they could get. The band was made up of local boys, a group of friends twenty or so years older than she, who played nearly all original songs, not too good and not too well, and only mixed in a cover or two in each set.

Linda peeled the label from her Bud Light bottle, appeared to study its contents through the thick brown glass. Brenda tried to listen to the music, but the words meant nothing to her. Judging by the laughter of the keyboardist and guitar player, she guessed the lyrics to be an inside story, more incomprehensible crap from surely the worst band in history.

"God, this band sucks," Linda said, and downed the rest of

her beer. She gathered the scraps of label and stuffed them into the empty bottle.

Brenda nodded in agreement.

"Do you ever think about leaving?"

"Leaving! We just got here! We haven't even danced yet."

"No, Brenda. Leaving Branden." Now Linda took Brenda's beer, which Brenda had hardly touched, and began to drink it in gulps. "Seriously. Do you?"

"What are you talking about? I just started my job at Walmart."

"Sometimes I do. Seriously. My sister lived in Shreveport for a while. Sometimes I'd like to go to a big city like that. Don't you?"

Now it was Brenda's turn to contemplate. She smiled as if at something inward. She had considered leaving Branden once, right after Peter died, but she knew she never would. Sure, everywhere she went made her think of Peter. But on the other hand, every one of her good memories had been made there too.

"I thought about it once. I'm not leaving." A guy she had seen before walked by their table, smiled at Linda, and tried to catch Brenda's eye. Instinctively she looked down at the floor. "Linda?"

"Yes, I saw him. Good night, he's grown up! That's Sally Ann's little brother."

"That's not what I was going to ask you. Do you think this floor's ever been mopped?"

Linda looked at the old wooden floor then, scuffed her shoe along it as if to test a theory. "I don't know. But I'd be glad to get under this table with Sally Ann's little brother if he asked me to, clean or dirty."

Brenda watched out the window as a car pulled into the gravel parking lot and the driver sidled it in between two pine trees. She knew who was driving the convertible white Cadillac with the airbrushed painting of Texas and a pair of longhorns across the hood. She had known about Tommy Turner all her life, and had spoken exactly four words to him, only a few days before, when he had approached the jewelry counter in Walmart and she asked, "Can I help you?" Apparently not, it turned out. He had simply smiled and nodded without taking his eyes off her, and slowly backed away.

He checked his reflection in the rearview mirror before stepping out of the car and adjusting the belt on his pants, turning the cuffs on his long-sleeved shirt. Even in the fading light he looked just gorgeous with two days' beard over his dimpled chin, a pressed white shirt with pearl buttons, faded Levi's that showed the curve of his butt. He smoothed down his hair and then reached back into the car for a black beaver-pelt hat, which he placed on his head. Then he slowly made his way toward the dance hall. She followed his movements until that brief moment when she could no longer see him out the window. When she lost sight of him, she held her breath. Then he stepped inside.

Tommy shook hands with a few men as he came into the room, patted some backs, exchanged compliments and thinly veiled insults the way men sometimes liked to do.

Tommy greeted Pete Grady, a local old-timer. Pete was a short, homely fireplug of a man who had worked for just about every logging crew in town. While the skin on his face may have sagged, his arms were still as big around as paint cans. He had worked periodically on James Lewis's crew long before Tommy ever did, when his gout wasn't flaring up.

"What you know good, Pete?"

"Nothing to it. When'd you get out?"

"Aw, Pete. You know I'm not a lawbreaker. They can't put me in jail for my looks, can they?"

"Psssh. They just ain't caught you yet. I know you've broke

the law somewhere." Pete waggled his finger at Tommy, then screwed up one eye. "They'll get you one of these days."

"Well, I hope not. I'm having too much fun on the outside. Anyway, I'm gonna get a beer. It's good to see you. You're looking good."

"Psssh. I look like the north end of a southbound mule. Or the south end of a northbound mule."

Just then Stuart Johns approached him from behind, reached around, and patted Tommy on the stomach.

"What you say, little Charlie?" Stuart asked. He was a high school classmate of Tommy's father. He patted Tommy again. "When you gonna get you a gut, son? You're what, thirty now? You want a woman, you're gonna need to fatten up some. Otherwise, a woman thinks she cain't keep you at home."

Tommy smiled at the man, demurred, looked back up. "I've got my daddy's genes, I guess."

"Aw, pfff. Bull corn, son. Your daddy would have been fat as a gopher if he hadn't of played football."

"I'll catch you later, Mr. Stuart. Good to see you."

"You too, son. You stay outta trouble, you hear?"

"I'll do it."

Brenda watched as Tommy turned and walked to a table on the other side of the room. At the table sat Brenda's high school classmate Katie Winchester and a group of her friends, chatting about bridesmaid dresses. She was engaged to Clay Conroy, who had been captain of their basketball team. Clay was running for mayor of Branden. He looked like he hadn't picked up a basketball in many years. Unless that was a basketball stuffed under his shirt.

The girls all looked up as Tommy approached the table from behind Katie, who pretended not to notice him, though the rising hair on the back of her neck was visible to all her friends. Just then the band struck the opening chords for "Gimme Three Steps," their token cover for the set. Tommy quickly pulled the chair, with Katie still in it, away from the table, grabbed her hand, pulled her onto the dance floor, and began to spin her around and around. Katie's eyes remained wide and she seemed to shrug at her friends, as if to say none of this was her idea. But Brenda wasn't fooled by the craftiness of that rich little bitch. Everyone in town knew the two were having an affair.

When the dance finished, Tommy walked Katie back to her table; only now, Clay stood at the end waiting with both hands in his pockets, a cheesy grin on his face. All her friends looked away, red faced. Apparently Clay was the only one who couldn't see what was obvious. Katie scooted back into her seat. Clay approached him.

"Hey, Tommy," Clay said, offering his hand and a plastic smile. Even Brenda, two tables away, felt pity for the pasty-faced knave who didn't even have the sense to know when he was being insulted. "I haven't seen you around much."

"I've been traveling. What's happening, Mr. Mayor?"

Clay raised both hands in a conciliatory gesture. "Now, don't call me that yet. I've got an election to get through. But that's what I wanted to ask you about. Can I count on your vote?"

Tommy did a double take, then reconsidered. "Of course you can, Mr. Mayor. You can count on me for lots of things."

Tommy Turner had been a gambler all his life, and he didn't seem inclined to switch his passions toward anything safe anytime soon. Brenda had heard stories about him for years, from different people who knew him. She heard he worked off-shore, building the derricks, fixing machines, feeding pipe, the kind of work most people in their right mind would never do. She also heard he had quite a hand for cards, and that at times he made a living that way. For the last year or more, he had made it playing poker.

Clay walked away and another man approached Tommy; Brenda didn't know his name. He wore flat-soled boots in the manner of a roughneck.

"You still workin' offshore, Tommy?" the man asked.

"I think I'm done with it," Tommy answered. He held up ten fingers.

The man held up his own hands then, eight whole fingers and two half thumbs. "I didn't do too bad myself," he answered.

Tommy knew not to show up at these events too often, to always be the one people wondered if they'd see. And it seemed everyone wanted something from him, wanted him to like them, Tommy Turner, the outlaw child of Branden's most famous son. All the good ol' boys liked him. But most of the church people were happy to see him too. The women said nothing, only stood close and didn't move away when he moved closer. Often well-dressed men approached him, intelligent, respectable, some he barely knew. They smoked cigarettes and drank beers, smiled at him through clouds of smoke, nodding in an exaggerated way with one eye shut as if they shared some secret, as if they needed to know him in case they ever needed to know someone like they thought he was like.

All Brenda could see was his beauty. Maybe he had money; who could know and, really, who could care. Her father, may he rest in peace, had a saying about many people who had nice things. *Their bank statements are printed in red.* Who could say. And then, as he stood two tables away from her, who could care. All she could see was the depth of his eyes, the longing so clearly unhidden there. He caught sight of her and walked straight toward her as if she had willed it.

She was filled with something then, something she told him about a hundred times over the years, which she had never felt before. She was no longer anxious as she had been when she watched him, no longer envious, no longer curious, even. She felt simply complete, as if she knew exactly what he needed and was utterly certain of it. She could sense Linda's eyes on her, but didn't dare look at her friend. She felt a tingling below the waist, and tried quickly to remember what panties she was wearing.

Tommy just stood there for a minute, smacking his gum and smiling at her in much the same way men stood and looked at him, as if begging to share a secret.

"Hey, girl." He finally spoke. He didn't even bother to say his name, or to ask hers. He just kept chewing that gum and smiling, without a care in the world. He took off his hat, held it across his chest, as if to guard his heart. "You mind if I sit down?"

Tommy hadn't gone to the dance to see Katie. He was just feeling lonely that Friday night. He had spent the last several weekends in New Orleans playing cards, and decided on his way out of town to turn around and stay home this time, see if he could catch up with any old friends. Tommy was thirty-one years old then and had been on his own since he was fifteen—the state had tried to put him in foster care for a while after his mother died, but he ran away so many times they finally quit looking for him. He figured Katie would be there, that he'd dance with her and try to get her out to his Cadillac if he could get her away from her friends. And if he couldn't, there would probably be some other girl that would like to go for a ride.

A lot of these girls just figured him for a bad boy. He had been told more than once that he was heartless, cold, inhuman even. Just as often, he felt the same way about them. They were like spoiled children, some of these girls—manipulative, dramatic, attention horses, always wanting to throw themselves at him and wail, then pull apart and slap him in the face before throwing themselves at him again, as if self-consciously acting out scenes in some bad pornographic movie. The winter before, one woman had asked to take him to a party in Shreveport, wearing only a loincloth and a mask over his face, which he was under strict instructions never to remove. Heartless? With all he had lost, at least he had a good excuse to be heartless.

But this Brenda—he knew he had seen her before, but until that night he hadn't really paid attention. Certainly she was no beauty, though she did have some gleam in her eye, like a little fleck of some precious metal that bounced the light back at him in an unusual way. It was the way she looked at him. Like she didn't want anything. Like maybe she had something to give. As if that little speck in her eye somehow looked right through him. In his quiet moments, he allowed himself the truth. On long drives home after a good few days at the table, he would let his mind go wherever it wanted to go. When times were bad he kept it damped down with whatever he had, benzos or opioids or even alcohol if he didn't have anything else; when times were bad he didn't let the truth he had studied so thoroughly show its head. Loneliness was such a part of him he almost considered it a friend, someone to talk to, lying down or rising up, early morning or late at night. His longings by then were ingrained so thoroughly, he rarely felt them himself.

They dated. So she wasn't the most beautiful. She wasn't psychotic. She was levelheaded. As their relationship grew, Brenda fawned over him so much, and never even seemed to have a negative thought about him. She never asked about his time in New Orleans, how much money he'd won or lost, where he'd been, didn't mention the other girls she had to know he'd been with.

They found out she was pregnant, and hastily got married, just as his luck ran out for real the first time. By then Tommy hadn't had a regular job in over a year, and had gone soft on her steady stream of attention. He went back to the oil rigs, but didn't have his mind on things. After a couple months back he tripped on a cleat and broke his ankle in two places and had to take disability for six months.

Brenda, widening daily, continued to work at Walmart, struggling home at the end of each day to find Tommy passed out on the couch from the medications he received in steady supply. When the baby came, they thought at first maybe he could be the stay-at-home parent, and Brenda went back to the jewelry department three weeks after Jamey was born. But the diapers and the magnitude of it got to him quickly, and within a few more weeks, Brenda shared the parenting with her mother while Tommy willed himself to stay sober enough during the day to work for James Lewis. James paid him to hobble around with a chain saw and drop big trees into spaces way too small. And each day, by nightfall, by the time Tommy pulled his truck into the driveway of their decrepit rental house, Tommy was sure to have his head fixed up for the evening, enough to fend off the love she constantly poured on him like the coolest, freshest water, and the chore of rolling around on the floor with the baby.

There was only one problem with all of it. Tommy had learned, and he knew, never to be bested in love. He had discovered, young, that for all their differences in appearance, all the words they learned to use, women were interchangeable. Every time was the same, no matter the players; he said what he said, her face flushed, the two of them carried things forward and got into a rhythm that brought on a rush and an upsurge and, finally, a crushing sense of all that never was, all for maybe five whole minutes of pleasure. By a young age Tommy had learned it was easier just to pay a little bit for it; one way or another, he ended up paying. At least that way they didn't expect him to stick around and pretend.

But Brenda. He searched and searched for the words. All he knew was, she was different. Keeping her at a distance required a stronger drug than any he had ever used. Then came Jamey, and the pain in the center of him every time he looked at that boy. For Jamey, there was absolutely no drug. They just didn't make anything strong enough.

CHAPTER 7

Tommy had learned to gamble when he was eight years old. They were living back in Branden then, after Charlie had blown out his knee and been cut by the Saints. He was only twenty-seven years old, and was working hard to rehabilitate and get himself back into football. He had every intention of returning to football. But he didn't have a contract, his knee wasn't improving as fast as he would have liked, and they had ended up living in the same house Charlie grew up in. He didn't really want to do it, but to help make ends meet while he got in shape again, Charlie had joined the union and taken a job at the paper mill, where lots of other guys were glad to do his work for him. After all, he was Charlie Turner.

The house needed a lot of work, but Aunt Lurleen had finally married at forty-five and moved to Baton Rouge, and offered it to Charlie and his family for free. Though her own family had never lived in a house, instead taking up shelter in a variety of trailers and shacks and tents in the woods when she was a child, Tommy's mother hated being back in Branden, and began to drink more and more as she watched Charlie's hopes of getting them out for real dissolve. Charlie had a permanent day-shift job—much to the consternation of many longtime paper workers, who never stopped putting up with graveyards, weekends, and holidays, but despite the favoritism he received, he still despised the work. Half the guys looked at him cross-eyed and laughed behind his back, and the other half constantly asked him to reenact moves he had shown in football, their clear implication that his career as an athlete was behind him. Tommy, then a third-grade student who was bullied daily, did his best to avoid both parents at night, when the slightest provocation could set his mother into a drunken rage, and his father passed out early on the sofa, an ice pack on his knee and an open bottle of pills spilling out on his lap.

One frigid night in the fall, his father's first without football in twenty years, Charlie and Angie argued.

"I want to do it, Angie," Charlie pleaded. "I can't do this shit. I can't. I want to go to California."

"It's over, Charlie. Face it," Angie answered, pouring herself another glass of gin as she did. She shuffled to her spot on the sofa, then returned to the kitchen, grabbed the bottle, and went back to her spot. She was almost tucked in for the night. She stared at her glass, then slowly looked up again. "You're not going to make it back. You can't even walk without a limp. It's been eight months now."

Charlie stood up then, paced the room. The yellow incandescent light gave his unshaven face a pallid glow, made him look forty years old. He breathed hard. "I'm telling you, Ange. California's my best bet. Three different guys have told me about a miracle healer there. Thornton—the halfback I played with last year—he went to this guy. Two years ago everybody said he was done. I'm telling you, Ange."

Angie breathed out. "You're done, Charlie. Time to find a real job. Maybe you should've paid better attention when you were in college. Maybe you could get a real job, then."

"I'll coach if I have to, Angie. I don't want to stay here either. If the surgery doesn't work, I can get a job coaching. Easy. I know a dozen guys out there."

"You want another year's worth of prescriptions, Charlie? Is that it?"

"I can borrow a little bit of money to leave y'all. Just let me go out there, have the surgery, get set up. I'll call the doctor out there tomorrow. I'll send for you as soon as I find a job. Even a temporary one."

"You're not leaving me stuck in this shithole with *him*," Angie answered. Tommy got up to leave the room. The phone rang as he did.

"Yes, this is the Turner residence." Charlie stretched the receiver away from the green rotary phone. "Yeah, this is Charlie."

Suddenly Charlie's face lit up. He beamed. His teeth had never looked so white in the dim room. Charlie lit a cigarette and the smoke swirled around him. "Uncle Vance. How you been?"

"Charlie. It's been a long time, brother."

"Over twenty years, Uncle Vance. You brought me right here to this very house."

"Yeah, I'm sorry about . . ."

"Don't worry about it, Uncle Vance. Dang, it's good to hear from you."

"I heard you were back in Branden."

"Yeah, it's just temporary. Trying to get my knee fixed up. I'll be back, next year I hope. How 'bout you? You still runnin' those trains?"

"I wouldn't know nothing else, son. I've got a little side business, but . . . So listen, Charlie, what are you doing for money?"

"Oh . . . I got on at the mill. It's just temporary, for now. So what's going on in Texas?"

"Well, look, that's why I called. I'll get right to it. I'm branching out, a little bit. You're the first man I thought of."

"For what, Uncle Vance?"

"Look, Charlie. I don't want to talk about it too much on the phone . . . What are you doing this weekend? I thought I'd drive over and we could take a trip to New Orleans. You busy?"

Charlie laughed then. "Naw, Uncle Vance. This weekend's good. What's happening in New Orleans?"

"I'll tell you about it when I see you. You got any money? Five hundred maybe? I bet you could bring a lot more than that home."

"Money's not too good . . ."

"Aw, don't worry about it, son, I'll stake you. Let me just ask you something. You ever play poker?"

"Poker? Can't say I have, Uncle Vance."

"All right, well then, let me just say it like this. How'd you manage to avoid getting tackled as much as you did?"

"Well, I don't know, Uncle Vance. I guess they just didn't know where I was going. Probably because I never knew where I was going."

"*Ha!!* That's just what I hoped you'd say, son. Poker won't be much different. Besides that, you'll be a big hit. The great Charlie Turner!!"

Later, as Tommy was brushing his teeth, his father came into the bathroom, happy. He insisted Tommy put on socks and a coat with his pajamas, carried his son outside on his shoulders in the still, frigid night. Charlie held one of Tommy's hands and, with his other, pointed up at the sky.

"You see the light from those stars, Tommy?"

Tommy warmed at his father's touch, bent forward to nestle around his daddy's neck. "Yes, sir."

"The light you see from those stars shined years ago. That's how long it takes for the light to get to earth. Can you believe that?"

"So when we see them shoot out of the sky . . ."

"They shot years ago. Sometimes hundreds of years ago. And we're just seeing it now."

"Wow!!"

"It's a big place, this world."

"It's huge!"

"And all these problems we've got down here. They're tiny. It's all going to work out for us, son. One day we're gonna jump on one of those stars and ride across the sky!" In one swift move, Charlie swung Tommy off his shoulders and held the boy tight, carried him into the house like a football, and tucked him into his bed.

Charlie won back Vance's five hundred dollars that weekend, and Vance let him keep the extra five hundred he won to spare, which was more than a week's pay from his job at the mill. On his next trip down, Charlie won a thousand. Still, Angie doubted playing cards was any way to try and raise a family, and drank even more heavily when Charlie was away, while reminding Tommy, more than once, that they only had him because his daddy was too broke back then to buy a pack of rubbers. Tommy, wisely, avoided her when his father was gone, and even slept out in the woods a few times. Angie, too drunk, didn't notice.

Charlie figured it was beginner's luck, and wondered if he didn't somehow deserve some good after what had happened with his knee, and everything else he had been through. But at the same time he knew, and wondered if other players did, that his talent for deception was his greatest tool. When the all-night games wrapped up on Sundays, in the country house in the small town close to New Orleans, eight or ten or more big spenders had lost most of their money to the football-player-turned-gambler, Charlie Turner, the Miracle Man. Vance, for one, seemed to understand why his nephew was such a natural; he had many talents besides the ability to drive a train. Outside the house, before driving Charlie home, Vance shook his nephew's hand.

"Charlie, you don't give away nothing. I've been playing this game a long time. I can tell a man's cards by the way he holds his eyes. But not you. I have no idea what you're thinking. It's just like I predicted. You've got the best poker face I've ever seen."

Charlie did as little as he could to hang on to his day job. He used his vacation and sick days every month, convinced whomever he could to do as much of his work as possible, and spent as many weekends as he could manage playing poker in the country house of the man named Bianchi, away from the law, in the little town down south.

But though her husband was bringing home good money, more than he ever made in football, being back in Branden and spending weekends alone with Tommy didn't agree with Angie, and she drank more and more. Eventually Charlie figured the best thing for their son was to take up weekend travel with his dad.

At first the boy was well received. The men who joined these secret games, held in the sprawling country house in Des Allemands, were often lonely men, who left wives and children of their own at home when they ran away to gamble, hoping for a good string of luck every time they went. Many of them were glad to have a kid around, to joke with or wrestle during breaks in the game, as if he provided some familiar relief from the giant odds of ruined life at stake. From his father, Tommy had learned a sense of decorum, how to offer a firm handshake to the men, ask how they had been, speak to them by name, answer yes, sir, no, sir. Tommy spent much of those weekends watching television in a back bedroom of the house, reading a book, or playing with a dog some of the men sometimes brought with them. He wandered in and out of the card rooms through mazes of empty bottles and clouds of acrid blue smoke. At times, maybe late on a Saturday, or Sunday morning before things wrapped up, when his mind began to go hazy from pills and beer and exhaustion, Charlie invited his son over to look at his cards. Even as a boy, Tommy shared his father's head for numbers. *Come and look at these cards, son. Whisper in my ear. Tell me what to do.*

Tommy loved the feeling as he looked at those cards, the clarity like a faint blue light that came into his core, the sense of purpose, his heart beating as if it would explode. When they won, when the boy's advice made a difference, Daddy even let him drink half a beer. But then, at other times, there were long drives back home when Daddy didn't speak to him at all, only muttered to himself and periodically pounded the steering wheel as he drove through a haze of self-flagellation.

On the good drives back, Daddy couldn't stop smiling, laughing, joking. *I love you, son. It's so much fun taking you with me. I wish I'd had more time with my daddy.*

On the others, his father said nothing, only glared, pounded, swore.

Tommy began to get in fights at school, first monthly, then weekly, then daily. The words were always the same. *Your daddy used to be a hero, now he's a bum.* Some kid's uncle or father or older brother had come home with stories they repeated around the table, which quickly made their way to the schoolyard. *Your daddy's the laziest one at the mill. My daddy (uncle, brother) said he sits on his butt all the time.* More than once, Tommy heard the word "dopehead." Charlie won enough to keep them going back, but fortunately he somehow managed to keep his day job. For a while, he did.

It wasn't long before Tommy's presence was no longer welcome at the games; apparently some began to think Charlie used him as a spy, a decoy, a ruse in some form. For a month he left his son behind at home, and often came home with his whole week's pay blown. Vance refused to stake him any more money; to raise some, Charlie began to sell the painkillers he had in abundance. But before long he was arrested, pled, and spent three nights in jail. Burned, his doctors no longer offered the prescriptions. When he was fired from the mill the following spring, Charlie Turner made a follow-up call back to Texas. *Uncle Vance? You still need help with those collections? What's that? Yeah, I can do it. I can carry a gun.*

CHAPTER 8

"You don't have to be somebody great. Just take care of the little people." That was the last piece of advice Glenn's father gave him, when Glenn was ten. It was three days before he left for the last and final time—Glenn could say the exact date if he chose to think about it, which he preferred not to—and it was the last time his daddy ever spoke to him when he wasn't yelling.

Samuel Rosen was a community college dropout who left New York in 1964 "to teach those racist bastards in Mississippi a lesson," as he liked to tell it. He found Mississippi hot, ugly, and stuck in feudal times, and his uneven temper and general whininess made him unable to get along with the other righteous hippies down there changing the world. After a few months, with no idea what to do with his life, he headed west in his Volkswagen bus, where he stopped on a Sunday afternoon at Mae's coffee shop in Branden, Louisiana. A skinny waitress with a name tag that said "Darlene" approached the unshaven man and asked if he'd like to try Mae's famous peach cobbler. A year later, Darlene gave birth to a skinny baby boy named Glenn.

Samuel spent most of his time away when Glenn was small, traveling to other small towns in the South for union organizing or back to New York for resistance training and to visit his perpetually ailing mother, whom Darlene was never invited to meet. He showed up at Darlene's house two or three times a year, talking about how much he missed his son or Darlene's beautiful smile, often wearing threadbare clothes and without a dollar in his pocket, hungry for food, warmth, her touch.

Though Darlene asked him each time to settle down and stay, after a week or two Glenn's father always went away again, and Darlene was left to work at the diner, the grocery store, and the chicken plant, and for friends and neighbors, sewing and repairing clothing, to help them get by.

When Glenn was nine, his father showed up again, driving the same beat-up Volkswagen, its rear stuffed with dirty blankets and pillows. This time he stayed. Darlene and Samuel had talks late into the night, slept until noon, drank coffee in their undergarments at the kitchen table into the afternoons. Glenn sometimes found them back in bed when he came home from school in the afternoon. After a month, the two of them sat Glenn down to tell him Daddy was going to be staying forever. Glenn's father spent his days writing, getting fat, and getting high. Still, Glenn began to love having him there, especially when he was able to coax his father outside in the afternoons to take a walk or throw a ball with him.

Samuel Rosen stayed a year before giving Glenn his second-to-last piece of advice: get out of this place as fast as you can.

The night Glenn's father left, he was screaming at the television. It was a hot spring night in April 1975. The three of them crowded around their snowy black-and-white television as marines stuffed helicopters full of fleeing Americans on the roof of the embassy in Saigon.

"Where are you, Lyndon Johnson? You craven redneck! You should have your own bourgeois ass there!" Outside, a neighbor yelled back a muffled response, privy to every word spilling out of Darlene's tiny cinder block house. The neighbor's Catahoula bayed along with its owner's shouts. Glenn so wished his daddy would just stop it, settle down, write in his tablet, something. *Please, Daddy. Please just get the pipe.*

Samuel paced the room, shouted at the television, stepped outside to yell up at the heavens. When he came back in for the final time, Darlene looked at him once and bawled, then fell into a chair with her face in her hands. Samuel went to her, then asked Glenn to sit down beside his mother. He put a hand on each of their knees.

"Brother Eldridge said if you're not part of the solution, you're part of the problem." He bent down to look Glenn in the eye. "You're part of the problem. Both of you. Darlene. Glenn." He held a hand out to his son to shake. Glenn took it, awkwardly.

"What can I say. It's been nice knowing both of you." He pushed hair out of his face.

Darlene exploded in a flurry of shouts, and Glenn grabbed at his father as Samuel walked out the door toward his Volkswagen and didn't look back. The two stood looking at him in the muggy night. Glenn's father stared straight ahead in the driver's seat, then finally shook his head once as if to dislodge the thoughts in his mind, started the van, and slowly went down the dusty road as Darlene wept silently and Glenn bawled openly in the night, his mother holding on to him with both arms lest he be sucked into the void that followed him wherever he went.

After the man who came from a world altogether different from her own left for the last time, Darlene returned to her roots. She began to take Glenn to church, squeezing herself into one tight dress or another each Sunday morning as she expanded with age. "Just some little thing I picked up somewhere," she always said when the husbands asked her about it after service as the wives pretended not to listen. She dressed Glenn in suits from Sears, tried to make the two of them a respectable family in town. But the things they talked about in church made no sense to Glenn, just a collection of abstractions about a man who got nailed up to a cross, died, and magically, three days later, came to life again. And yet somehow, later that same year, he was a baby, born in a barn once again with the smelly animals. It just made no sense. Yet well-dressed, respectable people—doctors and lawyers and schoolteachers—seemed to believe, nodding their heads along with the message, sometimes falling down on their knees and wailing, shouting out horrible things they had done or merely imagined they'd done, begging for mercy from this magical man-child called Jesus. Glenn told himself, as he grew, that he was blessed with his father's natural doubt, and only went to church with his mother until she just could not force him into the car any longer. The whole thing, Glenn told her many Sunday mornings, was just ridiculous.

Darlene cycled through her share of men, eventually marrying three of them, somehow bringing them out of thin air in this tiny little town. Apparently, after her drawn-out affair with Glenn's offbeat father, Darlene had matured; after Samuel, she always went for the traditional type, blue-collar men with their own kids they had screwed up beyond recognition. And in Glenn, they seemed to see another chance to be a father. Yet, though she may have matured in her *perception* of men, her relationships, in form, were exactly the same. The men ignored her, did what they wanted, let her play the victim. Glenn hated each one more than the last, and by the time he was in high school, he spent as many nights at friends' houses as he did at his own.

Glenn moved into a moldy apartment with a rotten staircase when he went to college in Ruston, where he studied some history and psychology and dabbled in philosophy and the classics. His piecemeal approach was fine for a while, but by junior year he began to seriously wonder what he was going to do. He settled on something practical, a degree he knew would keep his mind free of someone else's clutter and at the same time would let him help the little people, that would make him part of the solution. With an undergraduate degree in social work, he applied for an intake position with the Branden Family Services office, a building he had driven past a million times in his life.

When he got the job and moved back to Branden, Darlene wasn't married at the time, so Glenn shared a duplex with his mother. She never seemed to think it strange when Glenn told her a man named John would be moving in with him; she just seemed happy her son was happy. John was a traveling salesman who spent much of his time out of town, always returning with gifts Glenn knew came from the airport, but which he welcomed anyway. They lived together for two years until Glenn found out John had a wife and four kids in Monroe. Then Joe-Joe, who had been away from Branden thirty years and had worked as an exotic dancer in San Francisco, only returned to Louisiana to "retire" and find a younger man. Apparently his retirement consisted of sitting on his widening ass all day in the living room and waiting for Glenn to get home and cook him supper. Even Robert, who came along five years ago, seemed interesting at first, told Glenn on their first dates how much he liked to travel and was saving for an RV. Glenn figured out fast that Robert only liked to travel to the liquor store and back and had only been out of Louisiana once, for a pipefitters' convention in Little Rock. He had never even been to New Orleans. What kind of a gay man has never even been to New Orleans? Glenn, ever hopeful, waited two years before finally sending Robert on his way.

Glenn seemed to be spending his mid-forties mostly alone, daily going to work, ceaselessly lifting weights in the gym, and going home. And lately, in his work, he had simply had enough. That rose-colored belief that he could help the little people was long gone; now, far from being the town's token liberal, as he was considered for years, Glenn had begun to wonder if Reagan didn't have it right. Day after day he saw the same thing, and it had worn on him with a quickening pace. People came into his office, applied for food stamps, welfare, Medicaid. Though precious few wanted to hear it, still every day he did his job, tried to talk to them, counsel them, help them come up with a plan to get back on their feet.

Yet the excuses never stopped. They never stopped. They kept getting better. Just last week a man had come in and applied for everything. Why, Glenn had asked? The man said he had returned to church and been saved, and couldn't make a living selling drugs anymore. Not two days later another man came in for the same thing; his wife had left him, and he just didn't have the heart to get up and look for a job. Adults these days were so immature. And Glenn's patience was way beyond thin. If he had to hear it one more time: *I just need some help. I just can't make it. It's too hard. I need somebody to take care of me.* One of these days, it was going to happen. Glenn knew it was coming. He was going to tell one of these screwups just what he was thinking: *I have some help for you. It's right here in my fist, and if you care to step outside, you pitiful son of a bitch, I'll be glad to deliver it.*

Four years ago Darlene married Fred, her third husband. She had known Fred from town for many years; he was one of the many who had ogled her in high school. Fred's father had won a thousand acres of worthless land as settlement of a lawsuit back in the seventies, but when she began to hear rumors that natural gas had been discovered on Fred's land, Darlene sought him out in public, always talked to him after church. His wife had run off with a dentist from Shreveport. Fred had chased Darlene for years earlier, and she had told Glenn the man was so stupid he could barely button his shirt. But when she heard about the money, her feelings changed, and when he asked her after church one Sunday if she would think about marrying him, she accepted quickly. Dumb or not, Fred was sweet, and was often heard describing Glenn as his gay stepson, never even hinting that the two hadn't met until Glenn was almost forty.

On their second anniversary, Fred dropped dead and left Darlene everything, including the house they had built on Caney Lake. Then, though nearly sixty, she joined every women's group in town. She visited old people at the nursing home, helped make quilts and prayer books for shut-ins, became secretary-treasurer of the VFW Ladies' Auxiliary, started a garden, gave away tomatoes all over town. She was welcomed in all these endeavors with open arms, as one who had finally returned to the flock. No one ever mentioned all her years astray, the strange, tie-dyed beauty that had defined her through the seventies, the effect she still had on husbands all over town, her longstanding bid to be Branden's leading succubus, her ways as a common slut in high school.

A year ago, though she was way too young, though she still carried the sloe-eyed hunger and wanton appeal that didn't even have to be named, Darlene died one spring night in her sleep. Ever since, Glenn had felt like he was floating, and had lain in bed in the morning's first light many times, half dreaming, half awake, with no idea what he was supposed to get up and do. A dozen times or more, though he had worked there over twenty years, Glenn had taken to driving past his office in the mornings, half a mile down the road, before realizing he had missed his turn. He had even wondered more times than he cared to admit about his father. His father . . . good riddance to him.

Until his mother died, Glenn had always been able to keep his head on straight about his work. When he couldn't keep anything else straight, his work, he could. Sure, Glenn had wanted to punch somebody before, and had seen his share of scrapes in bars with guys who were just as gay as he was but didn't want to admit it, guys who acted like they were just there to see what a gay bar was like, who rode along with their gay pals, who maybe thought they could say whatever they wanted to, who seemed to assume that because Glenn was gay he couldn't possibly kick their stupid redneck asses. Just last month in Monroe there was that guy, he was gay too and had no problem admitting it. But he wanted to fight Glenn because Glenn wouldn't agree that George Bush was an imbecile. Glenn only replied how much he was grateful to George Bush to be protected from people in other parts of the world who wanted to kill Americans. "What kind of a faggot are you? You don't hate Bush?" the guy had asked. "If you care to step outside, I'll show you what kind of a faggot I am." But all Glenn had to do was take off his jacket and show his massive biceps, and they never wanted to step outside.

At forty-five, Glenn had found himself all alone. And though for years he stayed awake nights worrying about how his mother would face old age and whether she would have a dime left to her name by then, instead she had left him a pile of money big enough that he didn't even have to work anymore, if he didn't want to.

But what would he do if he didn't?

Brenda and Jamey had come into his office a couple years back, when her worthless excuse of a husband went away to prison. She was one of the few clients he didn't despise immediately. He saw it right away, as he watched her sit out in the chairs with that gorgeous little boy scribbling into a coloring book. *Here are people I can actually help.* When they came back to his desk, little Jamey closed the book and sat with his hands folded in his lap, as his mother sheepishly asked Glenn how to get things started. Her face flushed red as she spoke.

He knew it was bold, but he was tired of being careful and just tired of feeling alone. He placed his hand over hers on the desk.

"I know your husband," he told her. "I've known him all my life." The boy seemed to perk up at this news and smiled for the first time. Glenn felt faint then, at the beauty and the trust in that little boy's face. His heart raced at the sight, and for an instant he imagined he was looking at his own son. Before he could stop himself, he got onto his knees and took both of Jamey's hands in his other.

"We can help you," he told the two of them. Then, looking at Jamey, he continued. "I know you miss your daddy, don't you?"

Lately, Glenn has wanted to tell himself to just give himself a break. He has told himself it's just a phase, life will make sense again soon, just go to work and go to the gym, drink some wine with Louise, enjoy your friends, and it will all be better soon. He has told himself again and again, all the little problems, all the loneliness, all the doubt, just let it all go, just do the things you know you need to do, and the rest will take care of itself and good things will happen to him. Still, he has taken to lying awake at night; now that his mother is gone and he doesn't have her to worry about anymore, everything else comes on him at once, dark little thoughts darting into and out of his mind like trout in a shallow stream. When he thinks about his mother, he wonders where she is. And if she is happy. And he wonders, in a way he has never wondered before, if there is something else besides . . . this.

Just let it go. That's what he tells himself, lying in his bed, alone, at night. *You can't go back and make a perfect childhood.* Let it go. *You won't always be lonely.* Let it go. *Yes, there is a point to your life, and you will figure out what it is, and soon.* Let it go. *You don't have to know exactly what your life is going to look like, Glenn.* Let it go. *Just keep doing what you're supposed to do now, and the rest will be revealed to you.*

You can do better, Glenn. You can always do better. It's never too late.

But one thing he does know: Jamey. All he knows is that every time he sees Jamey, if only for a minute, he stops wondering. He stops asking questions. Every time he looks at the boy, Glenn feels a sense of things wash over him like an emptiness being washed away. All the doubt and boredom and angst and worry, washed away like a bad old habit he doesn't need anymore.

He wondered if that was how Christians felt.

CHAPTER 9

In Jamey's closet, Tommy found the navy-blue suit Brenda had just bought him for Easter and helped his son get dressed in it. Jamey clipped on a muted gray tie and looked at himself in the mirror. The two barely spoke to each other as they had their breakfast, showered, and brushed their teeth in the bright spring dawn. Jamey had begged to sleep with Tommy in Brenda's bed, as he had every night since his mother died; not sure what else to do, Tommy had been staying there in Brenda's house, getting up each night after his son fell asleep to sit at her small kitchen table, where he drank coffee and worried himself until nearly dawn. It was better than lying in fitful sleep, staring at Matt Bianchi's lifeless face.

Twenty-three members of Brenda's family were there, and a similar number of friends and work mates. The minister's remarks were short, and the mourners filed forward, laid hands on her casket, spoke to the perfected corpse therein in susurrations of grief. Her mother, long widowed, walked with two canes, leaned them against a railing when she took her turn. The others stood back, gave her plenty of room with Brenda's body, through some unspoken arrangement. She didn't cry, didn't say a word, but simply ground her jaw and breathed out heavily, shortly, as her one and only child lay before her. Tommy was next in line. Finally she moved to one side, didn't completely move on as all the others had done, and Tommy took this as his sign to haltingly approach. His eyes were on the body. Brenda's mother, kindly, waited until he was done, but didn't look at him when she asked if her grandson would have to go to foster care. Tommy didn't respond. He didn't blame her for hating him.

She shuffled sideways on her canes away from the casket, never averting her scowl from Tommy. He took it as a sign to follow her, which he did.

"I hear you found God in prison."

"Yes, ma'am. God found me, I guess. I asked for His love and mercy. Even though I don't deserve it."

"No, you don't." She pounded one cane on the floor. "No, you don't! You didn't deserve my daughter either."

"No, ma'am, I didn't." He had expected this from her, and he fought hard not to cry. Jamey would need him to be strong.

"You didn't deserve anything about that sweet girl. Or that sweet little boy either." She nodded her head toward Jamey, who stood in the back of the church with Glenn.

Brenda's mother sucked in her breath. "Well. God can have you now. I don't have no more use for him after this." She repositioned her canes and walked away.

Most of Brenda's friends and relatives avoided him, but a few offered a hand and smile, expressed their sympathies. Several complimented Jamey in his suit, told him how grown-up he looked, how proud his mom would be of him, but most didn't seem to know what to say to him, and after a while, Tommy began to take him out the door.

"We'll be over in just a little bit, Glenn," Tommy said, holding one of Jamey's hands in his.

"Okay. Everything's ready."

After the burial, Tommy and Jamey drove in silence. Jamey, the strong one, asked his dad if they could go to Dairy Queen. Tommy agreed instantly, relieved to be given direction. Inside, he told Jamey to order anything he wanted. In the child's temperate fashion, he said he didn't feel like having ice cream. He wanted to sit on the same side of the booth as his father, and proceeded to eat every bite of his food, chewing carefully, folding the hamburger and french fry wrappers into neat silver squares as he finished. He brushed the crumbs away from the table, wet a white paper napkin with a piece of ice and wiped off the table when they were done eating, as if the two had never been there.

Tommy could tell his son wanted to talk. He had been noticing things lately, learning the simplest notions of his child. The discoveries had been, as Brenda's mother used to say, the saving things. Many times since his return to the world, Tommy had marveled at the ease with which he had come to understand something about the boy; at times, something as little as a turn of his head or a dip of his shoulder spoke volumes.

When Jamey was a baby, in that first magical year before Tommy completely lost himself, he and Jamey had worked out a language. Brenda was the steady one, of course, the one who always knew what to do with the child, who could invariably read the endless expressions and infinite emanations babies give. But sometimes, when it wasn't just an earache or gas or a plugged-up nose, when the baby's discomfort left him wailing in the face of all Brenda's efforts, Tommy's touch was the magic potion.

But today Tommy was itching, distracted, couldn't think straight. Every voice he heard in the Dairy Queen sounded like Matt Bianchi's, every face bore some great or tiny resemblance to the dead man's swarthy face.

Jamey had changed his mind about the ice cream, and devoured a chocolate-dipped cone without leaving a drop on the table. He licked his fingers.

"Daddy?"

Tommy looked at his son like a total stranger at first, then pulled the boy toward him. Jamey was pliable, a rag doll; a minuscule twist of his head in Tommy's chest told him the boy was eager to be held.

"Yeah, buddy?"

"Am I gonna get to live with you?"

It came over him then, this tsunami of things. He fought it down, stalled, took a napkin and blew his nose to give himself a minute to think. He felt a tingle in his jaw, an unmistakable sensation, but fought it down.

"Jamey, the people who have been with us when we have our visits—they won't let you live with me just yet. I already asked them. You're going to stay with Mr. Glenn for a while. They said because he hasn't been to jail and because he was a really good friend of yours and Mommy's, that you can live with him for a little while."

A whitened look of resignation came over the boy's face, a barely perceptible flattening of his cheeks Tommy had seen more than once. A flood of tears came into his own face in response. He wiped them away quickly.

"But you could come and live for real in our house. And sleep in Mommy's bed." Jamey bent now and looked under the table, picked at the gum hardened there. Tommy reached out with a napkin to wipe away the ice cream moustache, then took his son's face in his hands.

"Daddy wants to live with you so bad. And I think we'll be able to soon." Jamey's face flattened further. A bile that felt like the substance of Tommy's pointless life rushed into his throat. He swallowed it down. "But I'll visit you every day after work, I promise. And you can spend weekends with me. And maybe they'll let you stay with me some nights."

Jamey continued to pick at the gum under the table. Tommy knew his son didn't believe him. The boy's face went further blank, so much so that even Tommy couldn't read him. After a few minutes of silence he tried to hug his son again, but Jamey was stiff, indifferent.

"What do you think if we get another dog to play with Rascal?"

Jamey shrugged. He didn't look up from the hardened gum.

"Maybe we could get a girl dog and you could be the preacher and we could have a wedding for them. What do you think?"

He shrugged again.

"Maybe that's just what Rascal needs to make him feel better. A dog wife to bring him his slippers."

"I want Mommy back."

In an instant, the tingle returned to Tommy's jaw. This time he couldn't stop it, and was relieved to make it to the toilet before losing the lunch he had barely eaten.

Tommy spent the afternoon moving Jamey's bed and some of his things into Glenn's house next door. Glenn invited him to stay for dinner, which he gratefully accepted, and afterward watched cartoons with his son while Glenn cleaned up. Eventually, he helped the boy into his pajamas, watched him brush his teeth, and tucked Jamey in for the night, promising to return after work the next day.

He drove toward his house. It had been four days, and the shock of what had happened was expanding, the complications growing greater with each hour removed from the act itself. No doubt, Matt's family and friends were looking for him. No doubt, plenty of people knew he had been in Branden Parish, and was last heard from there. It was even possible someone knew he had gone to Tommy's house. Granted, they couldn't come in and spray that stuff around Tommy's place that shows where blood had been spilled, but Matt's fingerprints would certainly be there. And what was going to happen if that car floated up or if someone, somehow, figured out where to dig?

Not to mention who must have been worried sick about him, with no idea what happened to their son, their brother, their man.

At least Matt didn't have any kids. Not that Tommy knew of.

Driving home, he was scared. He watched for lights in his rearview mirror. He felt a disconnect, as if he were watching his life in the road behind him and now it was unfolding, in slow motion; all he could see was faces. First his daddy's, then Brenda's, then Matt Bianchi's. He parked in his driveway and was sure someone was watching him when he got out, whether from the woods across the road or from his own bedroom window, waiting to strike with an unseen fury.

Inside, he turned on the television and couldn't sit still, felt himself being filled with a vast, empty feeling as wide as forever. He woke with a start after falling asleep on the sofa, then shuffled into his bed and dreamed. He fought the covers over and over, woke up from his dream sweating and tortured, sat up and shouted at the darkness, and beat with both his fists on the mattress and wall. The night was hot and sticky; it was the middle of the night, and he got up and went outside hoping for relief from the heat but simply couldn't find it in the windless, inexorably stagnant darkness.

He stared at the television again until the infomercials began, starting with an ad featuring nearly naked women exercising with a contraption that looked like a thick, bendable snake, which they squeezed between their thighs while moaning. He turned it off, went back to his bed, tried again to sleep. He thought once more about his beautiful son, tortured himself with dark imaginings, his own misgivings, the unassailable regret that he and Brenda had not been able to reconcile. His eyes were open as he pictured Brenda and how at first she had seemed so plain to him, neither beautiful nor exciting, and how much she had grown on him. She was always doing the little things, though her nose was crooked and her eyes too close together and her teeth a little off center, she took such good care of him and then the baby when he came; Tommy never once saw her even *look* angry at him, or at the baby. She never asked where he had been, though he wondered if she knew about the others; they were nothing, they meant nothing to him, but still he had been with them while his wife and then his wife and baby were home waiting patiently for him. He tried to close his eyes, but they wouldn't stay that way and he wasn't going to fight it anymore. He lay perfectly still, poured more sweat, didn't try to stop the tears when they came. He simply beat the mattress and cried for all the things he did and didn't do, all the ways he didn't love them, all the times he was out there rooting around with his snout down dark alleys through all the filth and all the nothingness and all the shit strewn around like the incorrigible swine that he was, and no doubt would always be.

Maybe they would take Jamey away. Maybe it would be for the best. That way Jamey could live with some good, upstanding people who would take care of him and love him, and then Tommy could just stop worrying and put all his screwups out of his mind, and whatever happened would be out of his hands. And what did he have to teach a little boy anyway? How to be a worthless pig like his daddy?

He was still awake at six o'clock, tired and stiff as motel sheets. *Just one drink. Only one.* The thought itself was enough to motivate him upright and on to the telephone.

"Sorry to call you so early, Rob." In the background he heard Rob's television.

"Aw, hell, son, you know I don't sleep. I haven't slept a good night in fifteen years. That's the only thing I miss about drinking." The television kept getting louder.

"It's good to talk to you, Rob." Rob didn't ask why Tommy was calling, and Tommy didn't offer a reason. Tommy knew not to say anything about Bianchi.

"You're doing a good job, Tommy. A real good job. Just keep coming back. Worst thing you can do is be alone."

"That's the truth."

"Hold on." Rob set down the phone, went and turned down the television. Tommy could hear the rustling pages of a book. "Hold on, here it is. Yep. That's exactly what it said."

"What's that?"

"Something I was reading yesterday. Basically, I'll paraphrase what I read; it reminded me that sometimes, the prison we make for ourselves is worse than the one they can lock us up in."

"You're a good one, Robby. I'm grateful to know you."

"Aw, brother, ain't nothing to it. You just hang in there. The big man upstairs is writing the story of your life right now as we speak. And you're the star of the show. But that don't mean you get to know what's gonna happen."

"I know that's the truth."

"Well, listen. I've got to get on to work. Y'all staying busy in the woods?"

"You know it. Trees keep on growing."

"Yessir, that's true. Nothing can stop things from growing."

CHAPTER 10

"Where did you get this apple?" Louise asked, her mouth still full of the dangerously scrumptious fruit. Never one to forget the manners drilled into her by her mother, Louise immediately put a hand to her mouth and tried to hide her embarrassment over her outburst. Glenn watched her, giddy in his own right, as if studying some new exotic pet. Nothing she could do would hide the dreamy look of pleasure washed across her face.

"Do you like it? I get them from a small produce stand on Government Street. I picked them up when I was down at Whole Foods in Baton Rouge last week."

"Like it? It's like heaven. Only crunchier." She approached Glenn, reached a hand out to his muscular shoulder, then squeezed it again to confirm what she thought she had felt the first time. "I can't believe I've met someone who appreciates good food as much as I do, in this cute little town. I've driven by that fruit stand a thousand times down there."

"Oh, I do, darling," he responded, then watched for her reaction. He sensed no dislike for his words, and felt himself relax even further. "We all spend our money somewhere. I really enjoy eating well and feeling healthy. It's more important to me than lots of things."

"You know how much I love your cooking, honey. When am I invited over again?"

"The door's open, Louise. Anytime."

"Ooooh, I'm so excited to meet a man who can cook. And so handsome!"

Glenn blushed at that, and Louise turned partially away. Miss Mabel came into the break room then, dragging her feet as she always did, *tssh-tssh-tssh*. She removed a plastic container of greens from a paper sack, along with a quart-sized box of potato salad with chunks of hot dog in it, placed the greens in the microwave and began to smell up the place. Louise offered her the plate of apple slices; Miss Mabel looked at Glenn with a smirk, took a slice, smelled it, then licked it and considered. Though only two years older than Glenn, she insisted that Glenn, boss or no boss, call her Miss Mabel, though the other ladies in the office called her Big M.

Miss Mabel was wary of Glenn and his fancy foods, which he often brought into the office to share with the ladies in a perpetual effort to get them thinking healthy. He constantly harped on the three women with whom he shared the office, all of them overweight to one degree or another, on the importance of looking fit. "Our agency's clients look to us for guidance." That was his favorite saying. "When they see us, they see the government. We are the government! No one likes the idea of an overweight government."

Finally, Miss Mabel bit into the apple, and to his surprise she smiled and nodded in agreement. She reached for another slice and ate it.

"How much do these apples cost?"

"Good food is not cheap, Miss Mabel. I believe those were three ninety-nine a pound."

At that, she momentarily choked and nearly spat out what was left in her mouth. "Four dollah a pound, I keep buyin' applesauce in the big jar," she answered. "My kids wouldn't eat the peelin' anyway."

"Growing foods organically, without poisons and the like, costs a lot more," Louise retorted. Miss Mabel took her greens from the microwave, eased her ample frame into a chair, and laid into the greens and potato salad.

"Four dollah a pound," she tsked. "Mmmm, mmmm. It do taste good, though."

Louise was new to Branden, placed there as part of a traveling position, which she had transferred into six weeks before. Branden was the first placement in her new job, in which she set up work training programs in rural communities. She understood she would probably be there six months. For the first fifteen years Louise had worked for the state, she held jobs similar to Glenn's, most recently in charge of a Family Services office in a middle-class section of Baton Rouge. But when her husband left her, without warning, for another woman last fall, she took this new position, eager to get out of her old life, even if only for a little while.

Glenn and the ladies made space for her in an office they were using for storage, and she set about her tasks with youthful passion. Since she seemed to comment each time on the foods Glenn brought in to share, he took the bold step of inviting her over one night to eat with him.

Within minutes of arriving, she asked why he had never married. Glenn simply continued nibbling on the habanero pepper in his hand at the time, and tried to stall before answering.

On her second visit he told her about Jacob, and all the others before him. Though her words passed no judgment on him, the look on her face clearly did, and all she had to say was she never would have picked him for gay. Then she quickly changed the subject.

The two enjoyed those nights together, and she even tried to cook for him once in her plain little apartment. They quickly agreed that the atmosphere of her place paled compared to the little Garden of Eden that Glenn had built in his backyard, complete with three birdbaths and a miniature waterfall. Over the next several weeks she had helped him cook their luscious meals twice a week. And each time, after they ate, they sat quietly in the garden and watched the birds. When it rained, the two sat on the porch and listened to the patter on the roof, raindrops fallings softly from the heavens.

They talked a lot about work, different things they had done for the agency, funny client stories from over the years. He couldn't help but notice the unguarded way she sat, the light reflecting from her long, wavy hair. She liked to sit with her chest out, arms at her side; *vulnerable,* Glenn thought. *Nothing like a man.* Invariably, the conversations turned to her husband, soon to be ex.

"He's not a bad guy," she always began, looking at her fingernails as if she might find answers there. Glenn had heard that comment at least a dozen times. How he could feel such venom for a man he knew he'd never meet was a giant surprise to him.

"He's just not ready for aging," she continued. *No,* Glenn thought, *he wants to remain a child.* "It's like, I waited so long to marry, and now this." *Now what? Now he's a fool? Most men are fools, honey.*

But Glenn didn't say these words; instead he went to her and massaged her shoulders. She turned quickly into his touch, pulled his hand deeper, to the crevice of her neck. "Dammit, Glenn," she said as she began to cry. "I told myself I wasn't going to talk about this tonight."

"It's okay, honey," he answered, rubbing her shoulders some more. "I'm your friend. You can tell me anything."

"I think he just feels like he missed out on something. I mean, we talked about kids. It was always 'two more years.' Then another year would pass and it was 'two more years.'"

Glenn heard himself shouting before he even knew how angry he had become. "Of course he has! He's missed out on the chance to spend his life with a phenomenal woman. If he were here right now I'd spank his butt for him."

She grew quiet then, bit her lip. A single tear rolled down her face. She didn't look back at him, only reached for his hand and whispered "thank you," then pulled it toward her supple lips.

"It's like, I've just created the same situation over again. It's like my father is still with me everywhere I go, sitting on his fat ass in his chair, drinking one goddamn beer after another and ignoring me. And my mother, she's there too. Fluttering all around him like Edith Bunker. Always dressing me up in these cute little dresses and telling me not to make a sound or else I might upset him. All the same shit I talked about for years in my counseling. Gary just made so much sense at the time. I swear to God I thought I was past all that rejection."

"We are amazing creatures of habit, I agree," Glenn retorted. "And not just in the good ways." He paused, considered her words, squeezed her shoulders again. "Sometimes it seems the very thing worst for us is the one we want the most."

She broke down then, turned to smile at him through the tears, then reached up and pulled him into a hug, shuddering all the while. She buried her face in his chest.

"You're a great listener, Glenn. I mean it. I'm really starting to see that I've surrounded myself with people who don't want to listen to me. Just like neither of my parents did. Just the same things, over and over."

"I'm sorry, honey. I enjoy listening to you. You're such an interesting person."

"People who said they loved me, but really didn't give one good shit about me." She came to the edge of things then. He reached for her hand this time. She pulled his finger to her mouth, lingered with it against her lips. Then she stood up straight and sighed, as if drawing her first breath in a new, different world.

"Don't worry, Glenn. I'm not going to ask you if you love me."

CHAPTER 11

There was a time. Tommy and Brenda and the baby had gone to the lake on a quiet Sunday afternoon. It was fall, early fall, one of those balmy October days when the rain had gone away for a while and the air was golden, crackling, so infinitely bright it could combust.

They had argued that morning. Brenda and Tommy never argued. Brenda rarely pushed her husband, made minimal demands on him. If she wanted him home at five, she asked when he'd be home. When she needed help with the baby, she asked what he might be doing later. She had planned a picnic, put a ham in the oven before taking Jamey to church that morning. She didn't even ask for Tommy's help when they got home, with cutting up potatoes for potato salad or rolling out dough for her pie crusts. He banged his way around the kitchen, hamhanded, tried to figure out how to be helpful. He finally just asked what was bothering her.

"I want to buy a house, Tommy." She poured the blueberry-and-sugar concoction into the pressed-in crust as she spoke.

"But Brenda . . ."

"Tommy. Maybe you haven't noticed, but we have a baby now." She slammed two pies in the oven, turned, and set her egg timer.

"I'm making good money lately."

"Tommy." Brenda slapped both hands on the counter. "What do you want to do, Tommy? You can't gamble forever."

"But."

"You know what Brother Stuart said in church this morning? 'Don't build your house on sand.' I'm sick of paying our bills with money we stuff in shoeboxes, Tommy. I mean it. I have a regular job. You can too. People keep their money in banks, Tommy.

"That's what people do, Tommy." She went and picked up the baby from the other room when she said it, held him up for his father to see. Jamey's head twitched as if about to fall asleep.

"If you can't do it for me, do it for him." She pulled the baby close then, kissed his cheek. "Everything you need is right here."

Tommy got into his car and drove away, rode around town with his windows down, breathed fresh air, watched people go into and out of churches. *That's what people do.* He didn't stay gone long. When he went inside she grabbed the picnic basket in one hand and the baby in the other and went out the door. Tommy followed without a word.

At the lake she laid out a blanket in the dappled shade and positioned Jamey on his back with his head in the lee of the basket, where he went right to sleep. Tommy and Brenda avoided each other at first, didn't speak, limped away from each other like two boxers who have to share a ride home after a fight. Tommy lay down and watched the baby, who woke after a few minutes to chew on his rattle and shake it in turn.

Brenda, always forgiving, put her arms around Tommy and pressed her ear to his back, seeming to lose her thoughts in his heart's rhythmic beating. They kissed for a bit in the shade as the baby oohed and cooed. Finally they both laid back, closed their eyes, and drifted off to the echoing birdsong in the pine tree that shaded them, a burning summery smell in the air.

Tommy awoke to find her on one elbow, staring at him dreamily. She smiled.

"Would you like some pie?"

Tommy had always loved sugar, anything sweet. Brenda cut a slice and slid it onto a plate, the gooey blueberry filling bulging out both sides of the wedge. She didn't ask before piling a cloud of homemade whipped cream on top. Tommy's heart thumped. He never ate anything so decadent, as much as he would've loved to. He was way too vain about his washboard stomach and, besides, sugar clouded his mind. If Tommy Turner had learned one thing in his life, it was the strength to deny.

But as Brenda had apparently done with her feelings that morning, this day he let everything go. He devoured the substantial wedge of blueberry pie, even adding more of the airy whipped cream on top, then asked for a slice of the pecan, much to Brenda's delight. He ate it, then laid back down.

"Wait," she said. Tommy stopped. Brenda reached and unsnapped the front of his cowboy shirt, untucked it from his pants, pulled it off, and laid it gently to the side. She pushed him onto his stomach, then took each of his arms and spread them out above his head and began to rub his back. Jamey had fallen asleep and Tommy all but passed out himself as Brenda's sinewy hands rubbed forgiveness into his muscles.

Tommy fell asleep. He dreamed he was climbing a tree for a treasure he knew was there, then partly awoke and lay in a half-lucid state, a sheen of sweat on his face from the afternoon heat and the hot blanket on his skin. He looked across the lake at the large boulder sitting half in and half out of the water, then smiled as he felt himself fill with a rare feeling of absolute contentment.

When Tommy was a boy, a local man named Peterson had moved that rock onto the far bank of the lake, two hundred yards if an inch from the nearest road. Peterson refused to tell how he had moved the three-ton rock in there, or even where it had come from. He would only say he wanted a place to sit when he fished in the lake, longed for something to remind him of his days as a boy in West Texas. "Back," Peterson often said, "when life was purely kind." Men in town speculated about it for years, made a variety of bets over who could get Peterson to tell how he did it, once and for all. The local paper even ran a story about it every couple years, but Peterson never told. By the time the three of them had their picnic by the lake, the rock had settled into place so thoroughly no one wondered about it anymore, and although Tommy saw it every time he visited the lake, he hadn't really noticed it in years.

In his half sleep, Tommy heard Brenda talking to the baby in low tones, Jamey muttering and making satisfied sounds as he lay in his mother's arms and drank his bottle, urgently. Tommy mumbled something, and he felt Brenda lean over him to listen. Tommy came fully awake then, looked up to find her smiling down at him like an angel, a contented softness without edges in her face in the muted light, the air around her veritably popping with electricity.

"My god, Brenda." She leaned in closer. "This is it, Brenda."

She splayed a palm on his back again, the knots of muscles in a thin layer of sweat relaxing at her touch.

"What's that, honey?" She held the bottle for Jamey with her other hand. The baby continued to drink with unquestioned abandon.

"Didn't I ever tell you? This is where I brought that boy back from the dead." Still groggy, he reached out to rub Jamey's tummy, much as Brenda touched him.

"You did tell me that, sweetheart." She leaned in to kiss his cheek. "I like that story."

Tommy moved on one side, a cheek pressed flatly into his palm, and cupped the baby's face in his other. Jamey spat out the nipple long enough to show his dad a toothless grin.

"One day I'll tell you a story about a boy named Glenn. He wouldn't be here if it hadn't been for your old daddy." Jamey grabbed his finger then, his own tiny hands sticky from the milk. He smelled of plastic from his diaper and the dry, sweet scent of baby powder. Tommy grinned proudly down at him.

"I bet you'd like this, wouldn't you, little boy?" Tommy rose then and took off the baby's diaper. Jamey's eyes opened wide at the feeling of the warm, golden day on his skin. He began to kick his legs and shout, then grinned a gummy smile with a thick milk moustache and reached two fat arms out to his father as he begged for a hug.

CHAPTER 12

Glenn sat on Peterson's rock on the shore of the lake, looking out at the water. It was a crisp spring day in North Louisiana, and Glenn had gone to the lake with his mother and her latest beau, Mr. Tupelo. The late afternoon wasn't exactly cool, but a bank of clouds had formed in the west and periodically blocked out the sun, and the roiling sky had begun to darken prematurely as bursts of wind ruffled the surface of the water and the temperature plunged for minutes at a time. Warm rays had been shining strong when they arrived an hour earlier, lifting Glenn's mood and his sense of the future, but the cold, threatening light that had grown all around him in the last hour served to heighten Glenn's sense of emptiness.

Mr. Tupelo—unlike most adults, he had asked Glenn to call him by his last name and not his first, which made Glenn think he was classy—owned a timber company and was down for the day from Monroe. Glenn liked him. He was friendly to Glenn, eager to talk to him about school, sports, other interests he had. But he didn't try to be too friendly. He told Glenn as they drove that a handsome lad like himself must be very popular with the ladies. Glenn liked that, even though he had never given a thought to a girl in his twelve years on earth. He couldn't say exactly why, but he thought Mr. Tupelo might be married. Mr. Tupelo had explained to Glenn and his mother, as they drove, many features of North Louisiana tree farming:

the stalwart longleaf pine, the vicious pine beetle, the dreadful creeping kudzu, the pink-blossomed wisteria.

After their picnic he asked Glenn's permission to take his mother for a nature walk, to give her a refresher course in the birds and the bees. As they slipped into the woods, Mr. Tupelo dabbed sweat from his face with a handkerchief, his hand already well below Darlene's waist. The tan line on his finger and the perfumy smell of his car were Glenn's clues he was married. But in truth, Glenn didn't care. That was their problem. As long as Mr. Tupelo left her with two crisp fifty-dollar bills, like he always did.

Glenn sat on the rock and wondered what his dad was doing right then. They had come here once, just the two of them, to jump off the rock and go swimming in the lake. Dad seemed distracted then, which he did almost every day, but he had stood right here on this very spot. Glenn couldn't think of another time when the two of them had done anything together, other than watch cartoons at home while Dad smoked his little pipe and giggled uproariously at the television. Where did he live? Did he ever plan to come back? Was he married again? Did he have any other kids?

Glenn stood up on top of the rock. They had swum together that day, jumping in and getting out, then doing it again, each time swimming a little farther out, judging their distance by counting strokes away from shore. Ten at first, then twenty, thirty, forty. They got as high as eighty, eighty strokes straight out from shore before they turned back. Dad must have told him a dozen times that day how proud he was. Glenn couldn't remember much about his dad, but he was a very strong swimmer. That much Glenn remembered.

Finally, he jumped in, swam the ten strokes out, then returned to shore, climbed the rock and did it again. Then twenty, thirty, forty, fifty, sixty, seventy. He felt a little tired standing on the rock for the eighth time, but his mom and Mr.

Tupelo weren't back yet, and there really wasn't anything else to do. So he dove in again, swam the eighty strokes out and then back in with ease.

Not bad for twelve, he thought.

He climbed the rock again and sat and looked out. The water was growing colder, and a cool, choppy wind had begun to blow. The breeze was really stiff; also, a heavy shade had fallen on the edge of the lake where he swam, blocking off the slanted afternoon light. In fact, on his last swim out, he could see he was reaching the edge of the shadow, and was looking forward to treading water there in the sunlight for a minute before swimming back into the shade.

Boy, Dad had been proud that day. Some of it seemed silly even to Glenn; he was after all ten years old at the time, and it's not like ten-year-olds are just beginning to swim. Maybe Dad just didn't *know* how well Glenn could swim. Maybe he was just surprised. That made sense—he had probably never even *seen* Glenn swim. Surely, he never would have taken the eighty strokes out by himself; he only did it because his dad was there swimming with him. But what would he think now? If Glenn could make it to *ninety,* wouldn't he be so impressed? *Maybe Mom has his address somewhere,* Glenn thought. *If I make it to ninety, I can write him and tell him.*

Glenn felt great when he surfaced from the dive, kept his strokes tight and counted them out loud as he went. Around fifty he began to feel stronger, sixty even more so, started to tire by seventy, felt good again by eighty, and cut through without hesitation on toward ninety. At eighty-five he broke out of shade into the sun, an incalculably glorious feeling, and felt the warmth on his skin as he took his last few strokes. When he made his goal he felt great. He spun back toward the rock, treaded water, and basked in the sunlight. By then the breeze had picked up to something strong, and he felt the blowing coolness on his face, watched a jillion sparkles on the water all around him, and was as happy as he had been in a while.

On the third stroke back, he was finished. Suddenly both shoulders and all of his chest constricted in a cramp so strong both elbows shrank to his sides and he could only tread with his hands. He saw a figure on shore, then standing on the rock—he couldn't tell who it was. It took all his will to raise one hand and wave as best he could. Then the arm shrank to his side again, his legs kicked harder, and all he could do was try to dog-paddle.

When the wind dumped a large drink of water in his mouth, he coughed once, hard, and then, that was it. He felt himself sinking, fighting, coughing, pulling his hands in closer against that pain in his chest and the rushing, metallic taste of panic. Just like that. He held his breath and kicked with all his might, ignored the pain, got his head back above the surface for a massive gulp of air. And then he went down. He forced open his eyes as he sank, saw only the bright round light from above refracted a thousand different ways through the water. He couldn't breathe. But the sun. It spread in all directions, touched everything, reached the top and the bottom and the sides of the water and was perfectly bright no matter which way he looked. It. Was. So. Beautiful.

Tommy waited at home all that morning for his dad to show up. He dreamed about the fun he knew they would have. The weekend before, Daddy had come home for a visit, a short one for sure, but he had stopped by on Saturday a week ago, and promised he'd come back this weekend and spend more time with Tommy.

Mom was gone to the store when he arrived. Tommy was home alone, watching a rerun of *Flipper*, when his father walked into the house that day. Daddy didn't look the same.

He had some new clothes; they were pretty nice and he was as handsome as ever, that bad-boy grin on his face and one little lock of hair always flopping down over his forehead. But he looked older. His cheeks were different, hollow, his eyes wide, as if his face had somehow been pushed and pulled, reshaped, like a ball of dough. There was something fake about it when he smiled. He went into their bedroom and Tommy heard him banging around in there. He was sweating when he came out, mopped at his head with a towel.

"When's your mother coming back?"

"Pretty soon. She just went to the store."

Daddy scanned the room, end to end, up and down, wiped his face again. Then he turned back to Tommy, gave that plastic smile once more. "I can't stay, son. I gotta be on my way." Tommy felt washed in sadness. Nothing mattered. Daddy must have seen it. He bent down on one knee.

"I tell you what. I'll pick you up next weekend. There's someplace nice in Texas I'd like to take you. Every time I drive past there I think about it. What do you say?"

Tommy's heart jumped. "Where are we going? Is it a card game? Can I start going to the card games again?"

The two turned, then, at the sound. His mom stood in the door, holding a brown paper bag. Her face was red.

"Let's talk in the room," Angie said.

Tommy stood at the door and listened to the words she said to Daddy. He wondered what Daddy was doing. Daddy said nothing in response to her screaming.

Still, Tommy couldn't make out what she was saying. He heard only a garbled collection of outbursts. Then she lowered her voice, and the next words came through clearly.

"I never should have let you touch me. You piece of shit."

"Angie."

Tommy imagined his father in there, fumbling, digging his

hands into his pockets. He heard a scuffle, pictured her pulling away from his touch. "No, I mean it. Then I wouldn't be stuck here in this shitty town with your kid."

Daddy was silent for half a minute, made no sound at all. Then he said, "You got any money?"

"What!"

"Jerry told me what you've been doing. I'll get it back to you. I promise."

She slapped him. Nothing else could have made that sound. "Does that make you happy, Charlie? Does it?"

"No. No, baby. I'm sorry. I'm gonna get right. I am. I promise."

"At least it's honest, *Charlie*. At least I sell something people want. Not *drugs*. Just . . . just get out of here. Please. We don't need you. You're no good to either of us anymore. Just go."

In two steps he threw open the door, stumbled over his crying son on his way out. Charlie stopped, picked Tommy up, went back down on his knee. He bent himself to look into Tommy's eyes.

"I'll be back. Next Saturday. Be ready. I'll take you someplace you'll like."

Tommy was nervous all week. He wondered if their weekend together would be like the last time he had seen his daddy. It was months before, back in the winter, right after Christmas, before he had moved away to Texas.

Daddy seemed happy then.

The last time Tommy saw his father happy was their last poker trip. He had started playing periodically in Texas, after things had dried up in New Orleans. Until then, Tommy was still allowed to go with him. Even as they loaded the car for another weekend away, Tommy could tell it was going to be special. While normally she would have ignored them as they drove away, Tommy's mother actually got up this time, came to the car and greeted them. Tommy watched her through his father's open window.

"Good luck, Charlie. You boys have fun this weekend."

"We're gonna bring home a pile this time, baby. I can feel it."

Daddy was animated on that gorgeous late December drive over to Texas in a rare way. They sang songs as they drove, told jokes and stories, and Daddy lit one cigarette with another. There was a nice campground along the way, and Daddy had promised him they would stay there on the trip back, if the weather held.

Four other men were already playing by the time they arrived. Daddy had told Tommy on the way over that these men were high rollers, and he'd be playing for a lot more money than he normally did. Uncle Vance and two of the others greeted them both as they arrived, shook first his father's hand and then his own, before Tommy retired to a corner and watched them all begin to play.

Vance was in charge of the deck at first, repeatedly adjusted the short-billed engineer's cap he was never seen without, and talked about his days running trains. He dealt the deck in his usual manner, throwing a card in front of each man and tapping his finger once after the first round, twice after the second, then back to once after the third, noting only odds or evens as if he couldn't keep the full numbers in his head.

A man who called himself Captain Sullivan lifted his cards first. Uncle Vance said he was a retired field commander of multiple engagements in Vietnam. He spread his fingers wide, as he only had a thumb and two fingers remaining on each hand. He talked to no one in particular about being taken prisoner with five of his men, how he had survived for forty-three days on bugs and rainwater, how his captors cut off four of his fingers piece by piece and fed them to the goddamn rats running around, until he finally decided it was do something or die. He took long sips from a tall brown glass, muttered to himself, and tapped on the table with a freakishly long middle finger as he threw in chips. He told them all how he slipped out of his bindings one day, his hands being so much smaller without those fingers, and strangled the friendly little man who came in to feed them every afternoon, how he held the man's neck tight and how his ratty little smile never faded, how his eyes eventually turned to glass. Then he freed his other men and they rounded up half a dozen machetes, slicing those little commies into a spray of blood and bones as they made their way out of the village.

"Sullivan, you say you're from Waxahachie?" John Adams asked. He seemed unmoved by Captain Sullivan's gruesome story. Adams was a small-plane pilot, and he'd done it all, from crop-dusting to dragging banners to county fair aerial shows. Sullivan pulled his drink from his lips long enough to nod yes.

"I was in the army with an old boy from Waxahachie," Adams added. "Paratrooper training. He wasn't the sharpest knife in the drawer, let me tell you. I can't remember his name just now, he had three or four names, I do remember that. Billy Joe Jim Bob or Johnny Ray Robby Bob or something like that. Tell you what. Let's just call him Waxy. 'Cause he was from Waxahachie."

Sullivan nodded again, seemed to be slightly interested now. He scratched his neck with that oblong finger.

"So we go up in the plane for our first jump and the sergeant gives us all the instructions, you know, right hand on left shoulder, count to three, if that doesn't work then left hand on right shoulder. Basic stuff we already knew. The last thing he said was 'Enjoy the ride down, boys, and trucks will be waiting to take you back to base.'

"All the way up, Waxy was telling everybody he was scared to death. Saying maybe he'd just ride the plane back down, go home to Texas and get in the grocery bidness or something.

Raise pigs. Sweep the floors at the goddamn high school. Said maybe he'd fulfill his life's ambition and become a full-time drunkard at the VFW hall. Anything besides this crazy shit, jumping out of an airplane like a man that didn't have the common sense of a chicken snake. Anyway, Waxy was the second to last out the door. Well, I had already jumped, but the way the last guy told it, he just about had to pry Waxy's hands off the doorframe with a prising bar. So finally Waxy jumps out.

"Well, he didn't count to shit. No one, two, three, cord. No way. He reaches right for it. Nothing. Then he reaches for the backup cord. Nothing. Next thing I know, I'm floating down to earth, enjoying the view like I was supposed to, and here comes Waxy. I hollered at him, I said, 'Waxy? What happened? Your chute didn't open?' And you know what he said?"

Sullivan smirked now, ready for the line he knew was coming. He took another drink and waited, didn't fall for the bait. Adams was undeterred.

"It was like it all slowed down. He said, 'Hell no, it didn't open. And I bet them trucks ain't gonna be down there, neither.'" Adams almost dropped his cards as he fell forward in laughter, though no one else seemed to find the story funny. Finally Mr. Finch halfway smiled too, though likely he was just smiling at some picture in his mind.

Mr. Finch, the fifth man and oldest player there, was an accountant who was living on the run. According to Vance, he slept in his van in a different town every night. Several months before he had surprised everyone he knew, including his own wife, when it was discovered that he had stolen a hundred thousand dollars from his employer through creative bookkeeping. Finch never spoke. Each time the cards were dealt he picked up his hand, studied them over the top of his glasses, squinted, then looked up quizzically from one side, his mouth open and one eye nearly shut. But he never asked a question, never even spoke.

Tommy spent most of the weekend in the other end of Captain Sullivan's house with Sullivan's hound, Buster, who was the picture of lazy. All the dog did was lie in one place, yawn, and lick his lips. Periodically Tommy returned to the poker room, where Daddy's pile of chips was steadily growing. Daddy was hushed but each time more animated, rubbed Tommy's shoulders with one hand, whispered in his ear, showed him the cards in his hand with strict instructions not to respond in any way. *Those are good cards, Tommy. Don't you think? Let's win us some money.* Some of the cards were good, other hands nothing special. Once he held nothing but a pair of fives.

But Charlie drew them in this way, at times animated when his cards were bust, at others completely sullen when he held a winner.

Sullivan and Adams, and even Uncle Vance, were all losing their money rapidly, and would be long finished before Saturday night. Close behind was Mr. Finch, who looked at Tommy with his mouth open and one eye closed each time he came into the room. Sullivan asked Charlie about football, asked if he missed it.

"I was lucky," Charlie answered. "Nobody can even explain how I ran a hundred and seven yards that night. It's a miracle I even got out of the end zone."

Finch clicked his chips together in a steady, rhythmic pattern but didn't say anything.

Later, Tommy watched television with the dog. Buster yawned and licked his lips again and again. Buster's ears perked up when he saw a dog on TV.

"Tommy!"

Tommy returned to the poker room. Daddy was sweating now, looked exhausted beyond measure. Sullivan and Vance and Adams were all cashed out, and whispered among themselves. Daddy smiled at him when he entered the room, beckoned him over with a head wave. Daddy took a bottle from his shirt pocket, sucked down some pills, put the lid back on with his one free hand.

"What do you think, Tommy boy?" He smelled of cigarettes, sweat, whiskey. The others ignored Tommy this time. Finch looked at him again that same way, pushed the remainder of his chips into the center of the table. Daddy showed Tommy his cards, smiled slyly. Tommy's heart began to pound. Daddy pushed the mountain of plastic into the center. Finch screwed his eye closed even harder and dropped his cards face up on the table. Tommy felt it all flood into him. Daddy dropped his own cards, raked in all the chips.

"This is no place for a boy," Mr. Finch said then, pushing his chair away from the table so hard it tipped over backward. "No place."

"What do you think, son?" The two drove back late that evening. "It'll be nice to be home Sunday for a change."

"Yes, sir."

Daddy lit another cigarette, cracked the window slightly in the deepening cold. "You think your mom will be happy?"

"Yes, sir. She'll be glad you won."

"*We* won, Tommy. You're a big help. You're a great partner. Whoa! It's getting colder." He tossed his cigarette out, closed the window tight.

"It's too cold to camp. We could get a motel room. You want to?"

"No, sir. Can we just go home?"

"Sure we can." Tommy glowed inside. Then, Daddy began to sing.

I've been working on the railroad
All the live-long day
I've been working on the railroad

Just to pass the time away
Can't you hear the whistle blowing
Rise up so early in the morn
Can't you hear the captain shouting
"Dinah, blow your horn!"

Daddy leaned forward then, as if to see through the old truck's windshield into the night sky. He opened the window, stuck his hand out, then pulled it back in quickly.

"Do you see that?"

Now, Tommy leaned forward and looked upward himself. Sure enough, he saw it. Snowflakes. Daddy began to laugh, softly at first, then harder and harder as it began to come down in a blanket of white. The closer they got to home, the more the snow built up.

"I can't believe it! I've only seen it once before."

"I've never seen it."

"That's right. We're almost home. Let's just pull over here for a minute." Daddy eased the truck to the side of the road. The two got out, stood in the falling flakes, listened to the whisper as the fluffy bits of ice slammed into them, the truck, trees, the ground. They stood together, hand in hand, and watched it fall.

"Look at this. Would you look at this. It's the most beautiful thing I've ever seen."

Tommy opened his mouth, caught flakes one by one. Charlie took the wad of cash in an envelope from his pocket, showed it to his son.

"Actually, this is the most beautiful thing I've ever seen." He kissed the money. "Two thousand dollars. Thanks again for coming with me, son. You really know your cards." Then the two got back into the truck and drove the rest of the way home, where they found Tommy's mother passed out on the living room sofa.

• • •

Tommy waited in front of the house all morning that Saturday. Was it another card game where Daddy was going to take him? Or could it be Six Flags? Early on, that morning, before the wine and the whiskey took her completely away, before she laughed and then snorted at him for his question, he had gone to the door and asked his mother if Daddy had called. The rest of the day, he just waited out in the yard, avoided her, and dreamed about Six Flags. Daddy had promised years ago that one day they'd go to Six Flags. He said they could ride all of the roller coasters, even that big one they called the Thriller, the one they showed in the commercials on TV that turned you upside down and all around eleven different times. A kid at school told him he had been on the Thriller; he swore he was never scared but did admit he had puked at the end. Tommy knew he wouldn't be scared either; Daddy would put an arm around him, pull him in close, and he'd never be scared.

Finally, at four o'clock that spring afternoon, Tommy convinced himself he must have got the day wrong and decided he'd go down to the lake. He went to the door to tell his mom, but she was nodding off in her chair in front of the television by then, so he didn't bother. He walked through the woods in that direction through the strangely crisp day, dreaming of his first dip in the clear water.

He was sure he heard a sound as he approached the shore, from somewhere out there in the lake. Just where the shadow ended and the sun began, there was some commotion. He stared in that direction—a steady wind had turned the water's surface into constant chop, plus the angle of the sun on all that bouncing water blinded him. But then he saw it. Yep, he was sure of it now. A hand in the air. And then nothing.

Tommy knew he was there alone, but even if he hadn't been, he would have done nothing different. He was never one to hesitate. He pulled his clothes off, jumped in, swam until it hurt, and he kept on swimming. He was thinking about

Flipper. That's what he was watching the Saturday before when his daddy walked into the house. Some people had jumped out of their boat and were swimming. Mr. Ricks approached the boat. A lady was screaming. She couldn't find her husband. He was down in the water somewhere. Then Flipper found him. He dived down below, nudged the lifeless man toward the surface. Flipper broke through and jumped out of the water. Then Mr. Ricks pulled his shirt off, dove in and found the man, turned him on his back, swam with one arm to the swim step of the boat. The lady helped pull her husband onto the boat. Mr. Ricks pumped on his chest. Then the man spat up water and began to breathe.

Tommy stopped to tread when he reached the edge of the shadow, stared from above into the darkened world below the surface. He could just make out a flash of white, a shrinking glimpse of skin below. He dove, just like Mr. Ricks had done. When he grabbed the arm, he kicked with all he had for the surface, flipping the boy onto his back when he entered the world again. The boy was lifeless, cold, a stranger.

The boy's parents waded into the water as Tommy worked his way to the edge. The boy's mother was screaming, crying. His father was so old. The old man pulled the boy the last few feet and laid him down next to the big rock, slapped him, pumped the water out of him. The boy's mother stood there screaming, jumping up and down in a weird way, slapping both sides of her face.

"Winston! Winston!" Darlene yelled at the old man. "Help me!"

The boy began to cough. His mother fell on him then, weeping, wailing, pushed the man out of the way; the man wore a seersucker suit and fell onto his side in the sand. Tommy lay on his back, gasping, burning, exhausted.

"What happened, Glenn? What happened, baby?" The boy

was making a sound, gurgling, trying to speak. She rubbed on his chest, arms, fingers. "Oh, I'm so sorry! I'm sorry we left you. We just went for a little walk!"

Tommy began to catch his breath then, and the boy tried again to speak. He began to cough in a fit, and his mother turned toward Tommy. She came to him quickly, began to rub on Tommy's chest and arms. "Who are you, little boy? What's your name? Where did you come from? You're a hero!" She kissed him on the cheek. Tommy wanted to lie there forever, breathing, have her kiss him again and again. She went back to her son when he made another sound.

"What! What's that, honey?"

"Scared," the boy gurgled. "I wasn't scared."

His mother threw herself on him then, and wailed until the ambulance arrived.

After they took Glenn away, Tommy told the story three different times. He told two deputies, separately, how he had approached the lake from the other side of the rock, how he had an eerie feeling, how he thought he saw something in the water. How he dove in and swam out just to be sure. Did he stop and think about it before he went in? No, sir, he didn't think at all. Did he look around for help? See if anyone else was at the lake? Think about running to find a phone and call the police? No, ma'am, he didn't do any of those things. He knew what to do. If someone was out there, Tommy knew he had to swim.

The man deputy asked if he could shake Tommy's hand, but the lady didn't ask anything. She just took him into a hug and held him for a long, long time. Tommy felt her shuddering against him and knew she was crying. The boy's mother had done the same thing before she went away in the ambulance, told him thank you so many times. She had told the boy's father to go home. "Just go back to your wife," she said. Tommy had no idea what she could mean by that. So many different people said so many different things. He was so, so tired. And starting to feel confused.

Finally, Sheriff Norm approached. He was big like Tommy's daddy. Charlie had told his son many times that he had gone to school with the sheriff, and that when they were boys he had played pickup football with Norm, even though black kids weren't allowed to play on the high school team. The sheriff wore a black felt cowboy hat and chewed on a toothpick.

"Tommy?" The sheriff held out his hand. "I'm Sheriff Norm. It's nice to meet you." He threw his toothpick down on the ground. Tommy watched as ants covered it quickly.

"Nice to meet you too, sir." Tommy shook the sheriff's hand. Daddy had showed him how to. The sheriff's hand was so strong.

"Can we get you anything? I've got some Cokes in the car. Some cookies." Sheriff Norm hooked a thumb over his shoulder. Tommy nodded yes. The sheriff yelled back at the man deputy.

"Do you know the boy you saved?" The deputy handed Tommy a can of Coke. Sheriff Norm took it back, blew a sharp breath to clean the top, then cracked it open for him.

"No, sir. I don't think he goes to my school."

"Well. You're a real hero, son. Your parents . . ." He looked away then. "Will be real proud. I'm going to make sure you get an award for this. Get your picture in the paper. I'm pretty sure that boy would've drowned if you hadn't come along and acted so quickly." Norm clapped him on the shoulder then. "I mean it, son. I'm real proud. I know grown men who don't have the balls to do what you did." Tommy didn't respond, only swelled in his presence.

"So you just came down here by yourself?"

"Yessir. I was at home most of the day; my daddy was

supposed to come see me this weekend, but he hasn't got here yet. I might've got the day wrong."

Norm looked away again, this time for way too long.

"Was your mom at home when you left?"

"Yes, sir."

"Tommy. Tell me the truth. Was she drinking?"

Tommy hung his head then. "Yes, sir."

"Let's get you home. I'm going to give you a ride. I need to talk to your mom."

Angie was sitting on the porch when the two arrived, a full glass and a mostly empty whiskey bottle on the floor beside her chair. She studied them both with wary eyes, her motions slow, exaggerated. She dragged on a cigarette, her hands and lips trembling, eyes half closed. Norm took off his hat, held it over his chest.

"Angie."

She dragged deeply on her cigarette again, as if waiting to respond.

"What the hell did he do now?" She spoke slowly, caught her breath. "Don't tell me he's turning into a screwup like his daddy already." The words were slurred.

Norm glared at her then, bore into those icy blue eyes that had wilted grown men since she was twelve years old. She stared back herself, indignant—*Come and get me*—before going for another drag on her shaking cigarette. Norm had learned long ago not to give white people who bucked him even an inch. With those in his own community, at times he offered a bit more sympathy . . . but with white folks, he gave nothing. He was the duly elected sheriff, chosen by both black and by white. And he had a job to do.

She reached for her glass and, when she did, Norm took a quick step forward and slapped it away from her, shocking them both when it shattered on the concrete steps.

"You son of a bitch!" she shouted, and began to stand up. Norm moved like a cat. He thrust himself in close, clamped a hand over her mouth, and shoved her back into the chair. Her eyes opened wide. Finally, she was paying attention. Norm lowered his voice, spoke evenly, a notch above a whisper.

"You meant to throw that drink on me, Angie. That's what you were going to do. Don't try to deny it. You listen to me. I've got something to tell you."

Angie melted then, began to cry. She didn't struggle. Norm turned to Tommy.

"Tommy. Come here and sit down, please. I've got something to tell both of you. Angie? I'm going to take my hand off your face now. You keep your mouth shut. You hear me?"

She nodded. Norm removed his hand haltingly, took a handkerchief from his pocket, and wiped off his fingers. Then he squatted down in front of the two of them. Tommy watched on, rapt. Angie looked down, her face red hot with shame.

"I was on my way over here when I got the call about the boy nearly drowning in the lake. Your son's not a *screwup,* Angie. He's a hero. I'm real proud of you, son. I'm going to make sure you get an award for this.

"Tommy saved Glenn Rosen from drowning, *Angie.*" Still, she looked to the side.

He wiped his face with the handkerchief. "And now, I'm afraid I've got some bad news. We just got a call from Dallas about an hour ago. The deputy who called me knew who he was, and knew he was from here. I'll fill y'all in as soon as I know more. I really don't have any information yet." Angie turned to him now, and Norm could see an altogether different tear beginning to form on her face. Tommy looked about wildly.

Norm reached for his hand, held it, squatted all the way down on the floor of their porch. He bent to see into Tommy's face.

"I'm real sorry, son. I've got terrible news. There's only one way to say it. Your daddy's dead."

CHAPTER 13

All his guys had called him several times apiece over the previous week, left a variety of messages dealing with different matters of business. Every hour, and for the previous two days more than once an hour, he checked his messages, waded through the coded words, and felt with each passing moment less and less attached to any of it. Without exception they used the language they had developed, a system Bianchi and several others worked out years ago when those meddling government assholes were tapping his phones. Each of them had special instructions for the previous week that all of the normal rules were off. Any word from Matt, even a rumor about him, warranted a call to Bianchi, in the plainest language, any time of the day.

Late in the morning, Bianchi stood in his bedroom, two of the little white pills in one hand, his phone in the other. He stared first at one hand, then at the other. Finally he swallowed the pills and returned to staring at the phone, as if willing it to produce a sound. As he did, a call rang through, from a number he didn't recognize. He answered it hurriedly, his voice a shade higher than normal.

It was Ernie. Big and dumb, but steady. He must have changed his number again.

"Hey, boss, I wanted you to know, the guy we were talking about yesterday? He's gonna deliver fifty *LARGE* bags of the concrete mix to the jobsite this afternoon. Fifty *LARGE*." Ernie accented the word just that way. Bianchi pulled the phone away from his face, looked at it with irritation. Everyone knew he owned a construction company, and of course they used a lot of concrete. As usual, Ernie took all of it a bit too seriously. Normally a fifty-thousand-dollar collection would be good news, but this day it meant absolutely nothing.

"Good job, Ernie. Have you heard from Matt?"

"Who?" Big and dumb.

"My son, Ernie."

"Matt? I talked to him about a week ago."

Bianchi hung up the phone without further ado. He had no energy for such bullshit.

Maybe Matt was off camping. Bianchi had never cared for sleeping outside, what with heat and bugs and snakes and all manner of creatures that had no fear of him, unlike most humans who knew him, who most certainly did. But Matt had always done things his own way, and as much as the two had in common, there were a few things his son enjoyed that Carlo Bianchi didn't. Plus, Matt had done this before, disappeared for a couple of days when he just needed to get his head clear. Matt was well into manhood—he'd be twenty-seven on his next birthday—and Bianchi took the greatest pride, more than from anything else he had ever done in his life, from his absolute knowledge that his youngest son felt certain of things. Carlo had worked all his life to control the people around him—Matt's two older brothers sure needed it—but Matt had never taken to any of his father's controls, and in the end, Bianchi had figured out Matt would do just fine on his own. Sure, Matt still looked up to him, still wanted to keep his old man proud, and he seemed to know well enough by now, most of the time, how much his father loved him. It was good. It's what is supposed to happen. So he knew he could disappear for a few days and still have a job when he got back. But still.

Bianchi understood the pressures, sure. He had been

young himself once; it could take a lot of years to learn how to deal with this business, how to keep it from taking over absolutely everything. Bianchi knew Matt had a stripper over in Dallas. Maybe he was spending some time with her, just laying low for a little while. If so, that was fine. Bianchi wasn't worried about the girl. Only the drugs. Those girls were always on drugs. And Matt did not need to start messing with that shit again. Please, God.

But Bianchi had to face it. No doubt, his son was on drugs again. He knew it the last time they spoke. Matt had a downcast look in his eyes then, and Bianchi recognized immediately what it meant. He knew his son was ashamed, was worried his father would be angry with him. And how much Bianchi had wanted to reach out to his son then, tell him he wasn't angry, he wasn't even disappointed. He was nothing but proud, yet still worried for his son. Worried, yes, angry, no. When Matt had been young, yes, Bianchi was angry most of the time. But age, and time, and the settling of things had stripped that seething anger away from him, and left a heart-sized hole in its place. A hole that only his family, what was left of it, could fill.

He had never wanted his son to go into this business. Bianchi had tried to send the kid over to LSU, thinking maybe a little education would be good for him, help him train to become an engineer like the old man had dreamed about as a child, building bridges with sticks and houses with that foul-smelling mud down by the river in Algiers. But Matt didn't really have the smarts for college, although he was smart enough to figure out he could never make the kind of money playing straight that he could make working for his father. On top of that, he was always jumping into things way too fast; he never thought for even a second before he dived right in. The kid couldn't go a week without getting into some kind of fight at school, whether at a frat party with his pals, or with one of those tie-dyed pussies wandering around the campus in sandals reading poetry, high on marijuana. Matt was an equal opportunity fighter. He'd punch anybody if he thought the guy had it coming.

Matt Bianchi was cut out for thug work, that's for sure. Talk about a kid who knew how to take care of himself. Once in high school, he had somehow separated from his friends down in the French Quarter. The way he told it later, he went into the can, and, when he came out, all his friends were gone. Only later, after wandering out the door and into the mayhem, drunks of all varieties up and down the street, did he find out they were still inside. He didn't make it half a block down Esplanade when three black kids jumped him, probably figuring him for some drunk white tourist with a pocket full of money. Matt left two of them on the pavement with their faces smashed in, and the third limped away screaming with a separated shoulder. Yet the next weekend, he was down there again.

Thuggery. That's what everyone else called it anyway. Where his son was concerned, Bianchi thought of Matt's talents as just a natural extension of his personality. Point of fact, since Matt had finally given up on college and come to work for his old man, the boy hadn't punched a guy once, not that Bianchi knew of. It wasn't necessary. A guy just had to be sure of himself. That's all. Bianchi just paid his son to be sure of himself. People made a deal. They wanted money, or credit at his casino. He lent them money, or gave them credit. They knew the terms. Then later, maybe they didn't have the money to pay him back, or decided they regretted the whole thing, or they had a gambling addiction and it was all his fault, or whatever other excuse they had. Whose problem was that? All Matt did was remind them of their obligations. That's all. He didn't have to be a thug. He just had to make sure they understood that he would be, if he had to be.

Bianchi hadn't sent his son up to North Louisiana to deal with the Turner guy. He was only supposed to be looking in on a paving project between Branden and Ruston. Matt had called him that afternoon, told his dad he didn't like the way things were going on the project, and that he wanted to stick around and do some more observation the next day. Then he mentioned he might go see the Turner guy. That was all on his own. Turner was one of Matt's accounts, and Matt knew how to deal with his accounts. He had mentioned it in passing, that's all. Why Matt wanted to go see the guy, who knew. Turner only owed them maybe twenty thousand, no big deal, really. Turner was a long-term customer. He was even making his payments, on time, every time. But Matt said he was going to talk to the guy, and Bianchi figured there was a reason for it. Micromanagement was not his style. Matt knew how to manage things. Yet, when he said it, something in Matt's voice made Bianchi think there was more to it than that. Like somehow he was trying to go an extra mile to please his father. As if Bianchi could have been an inch more pleased with that boy. He always thought he showed it as clearly as it could be shown. But who knew. Maybe Matt didn't know how much his father loved him, after all. It was easy to second-guess himself when the boy wasn't around to ask.

Matt never asked for any favors, never looked to take the easy way out of anything just because he was the boss's son. In fact, the paving project up in Jackson Parish had been Matt's deal entirely, Matt's way of showing his father he could begin to take on more responsibility, maybe one day take over things entirely. Of showing his dad something Bianchi knew already, that Matt was more than just a tough guy.

Bianchi managed to pass time until noon. The nausea had kept him from eating a thing that day, and he felt like absolute hell, a maw of hunger eating a hole inside his stomach that echoed through every inch of him. Finally he ate some toast with a little butter anyway, brushed his teeth, and got himself dressed. He couldn't sit around and wonder anymore.

He made it to the far side of Metairie before he needed to pull over and throw up. He wouldn't let it slow him down, though, and got back on the road for the rest of the four-hour drive to North Louisiana. He looked for a radio station, but it all just sounded like noise. Instead he tried to enjoy the scenery as the road carried him through the mucky swamp of South Louisiana into green and rolling hills as he traveled north.

Matthew was his youngest son. Mark and Daniel were much older, and from a young age they both seemed to want something completely different from their father. Matt was an asthmatic child, until he was eight or nine, was nearly debilitated by it. He had sneaked up on Bianchi and Marilyn when they were forty-four years old, when the other boys were both in college and drifting away. And he couldn't blame them, really. He never paid attention to either of them. When Mark and Daniel were growing up, all Bianchi was doing was trying to run down a dollar.

No doubt, Matt was the most loyal child a father could hope for. Being sick as a boy, he just clung to both his parents, physically and in every other way. The doctors said it affected him; maybe he lost enough oxygen enough times that it had an effect on him. They said maybe that's what made him so impulsive, why he didn't do well in school. So they got him tutors, leaned on him night and day to do his homework, to put school first. It never worked. But hey. There was still no way Bianchi could have been any prouder.

Law school. That's what Bianchi really hoped for. Before they realized for sure that he wasn't cut out for college, Bianchi liked to imagine his son with a degree in engineering, then a law degree and a big office in downtown New Orleans. Then, not only would he actually know something, have some real understanding how things in the world actually worked, but then as a lawyer he could make the big money and stay on the right side of the law. Bianchi paid the lawyers that looked after his interests three hundred dollars an hour. And people said what *he* did was illegal.

The guys were just leaving the paving project when he arrived at four o'clock, walking to their trucks carrying lunch boxes and hard hats. Several said hello to him, looked back over their shoulders when he passed, but he didn't acknowledge them, just went straight to the foreman's trailer. Inside, the foreman was sitting at his desk, looking at a computer screen. The look on his face made clear to Bianchi he wasn't expecting this visit. Bianchi had met the guy once, years ago, but hadn't spoken to him since then. The foreman hurriedly shut down his computer and stood.

"Hey, Biggun." He approached Bianchi with hand extended, an ingratiating smile on his face. "What brings you to the north country?"

"When's the last time you saw Matt?"

"Matt?" The foreman sat on the edge of his desk. He was a tall man, with giant hands, and seemed to be counting on one of them. He had aged since Bianchi met him that one time, and when he smiled he showed a set of dentures, though he couldn't be much past fifty.

"Thursday last, I think it was. He stopped in and we talked about things. Said he'd be back Friday, but he didn't come back."

"Did he say where he was going Thursday night?"

"He said he was staying at the Holiday Inn in Ruston. Asked if I knew where he might find some company for the night. Said a few things about small towns, hicks, et cetera, et cetera. I told him he couldn't find that kind of stuff up here, he had to go back to New Orleans to find a woman that rents out."

The foreman laughed. "I told him if he did ever find a hooker up here, to make sure she really *was* a woman. I'm telling you, y'all've got some of the craziest shit I've ever seen down there in New Orleans. I'm just a country boy, myself."

"Nothing else?"

"No, sir, Mr. Bianchi. He said he'd be back Friday. That's the last time I talked to him."

"Here's my number. You call me the minute you hear from him. Or even if you hear anything about him. You got it?"

"Sure, be glad to. What's . . . what's going on?"

Bianchi felt a rush of things, heard himself talking before he even knew what he was going to say. Something settled into him, into his center, and he suddenly didn't care that he was letting everything out with this stranger.

"He's never disappeared this long before. I'm starting to worry about him. We're very close."

The foreman shifted nervously. Bianchi was suddenly embarrassed. The foreman's face turned red, he looked away.

"He'll turn up, Mr. Bianchi. Probably just got a girl somewhere. He'll get tired of it and get back to work." Then he looked up again with that ingratiating smile.

Bianchi bristled, thought maybe he'd punch the false teeth right out of that fool's head. Instead, he just turned and went to his car.

The nausea came on again full steam when he got back into his car and plugged Turner's address into the GPS. The guy obviously lived on a country road, one of these little blue highways miles away from the next one. It wasn't that far of a drive, and he was definitely not going there until after dark. He drove into Ruston to the Holiday Inn. He carried a picture of Matt in his pocket, along with a couple fifties in case the manager didn't want to talk.

He rarely went anywhere alone anymore, and this jaunt was

the longest he'd been away from home in at least a year. It wasn't that he thought he couldn't handle himself anymore, just because he was an old man now. People didn't really interest him anymore, true. But things just seemed to work out that way.

He left his piece in the car when he got to Turner's house. He couldn't imagine any need for confrontation. He just wanted to know if the guy knew anything.

Tommy cracked open the door enough to see him and knew instinctively not to take too long before opening it. He took some breaths before inviting Mr. Bianchi in, shook his hand, offered him something to drink or a place to sit for a minute. When Bianchi declined, he went to the sink himself, slowly filled a glass with water, drank half, then filled it again as he kept his back to his guest, all the while fighting the fear in his chest and arranging his face for the moment he turned around again. Bianchi spoke before Tommy finished drinking.

"Was Matt here?" Bianchi picked up things from Tommy's shelf, pictures, books, decorations. He pretended to show interest in them, but Tommy knew by the glassy look in his eyes that he had none. Matt had done the same thing when he was here. Just trying to show who was in charge.

Tommy nodded as he drank, then turned around to face his guest. "He came by here. Yes. One night last week. I wasn't sure why, I've been making all my payments."

"Did you pay him the twenty thousand?"

Tommy knew he was in fertile territory, but something told him not to lie. "No, I don't have it all. I told him that. I didn't even know why he came. I've been making all my payments. I told him I could pay five hundred, but he just wanted the points. I paid him. Why are you asking me all this? I've been doing everything I'm supposed to do."

Bianchi studied him, for a full minute didn't say a word. "You don't have any idea why I'm here?"

Tommy shrugged, hoped his manner was convincing.

"No idea?"

This time Tommy spread his hands, widened his eyes, shook his head. Bianchi seemed to back down, but maybe he was still just controlling things.

"He told me he was coming here last Thursday. He checked into the motel Thursday afternoon. But he never went back there Thursday night, he never slept in the bed. And I haven't heard from him in a week."

"I'm sorry, Mr. Bianchi. He was just here for a few minutes, like I said." Tommy felt a biting urge to look around the room, convince himself everything was in place, that he hadn't missed anything. Yet he continued staring straight at his guest. Then Bianchi himself looked around the place, stopped his eyes on the television, the refrigerator in the kitchen, the picture of Tommy and Jamey from years ago.

"But Mr. Bianchi?"

"Yes?"

"Matt was really high when he was here. I hate to have to tell you so, but he was really on something."

Bianchi moved toward the door. "Here's my number. You let me know if you see or hear anything."

Two hours later, halfway back to New Orleans, Bianchi called Tommy. Tommy was almost asleep with the television on.

"I think there's more you're not telling me."

Tommy sat up straight. Now, he was wide awake, and didn't have to worry how he looked. "Mr. Bianchi, I swear. I told you everything. He came here. He left. He took my two hundred bucks. I intend to pay everything I owe you. He told me I had to pay it all at once. I'm saving every dime I can."

"One word. Call me if you hear a single word."

Bianchi hung up the phone. He'd been watching faces for a long time, and Turner's was one he just couldn't read. Just like Charlie Turner's was. He continued driving in silence. Outside Baton Rouge, as the massive steel bridge first came into view, he switched on the radio. Still, everything he heard was nothing but noise, and he returned to his thoughts in the silence. Later, almost home, he headed north along the lake. Something wasn't right. Maybe he needed to get this Turner guy down to New Orleans, get him onto Bianchi's own turf. Just to see if he had anything else to say. He dimmed his lights and turned into his driveway, then waited for a second while the big metal gate opened to let him back into the house he had owned for forty years, the place where now he spent all his nights alone.

CHAPTER 14

Glenn's stomach grumbled with displeasure before he hung up the phone. Purely hopeful when he made the call, afterward his head buzzed as if he had had too much coffee. He walked down the hall to talk to Louise, dabbed at his forehead with a handkerchief. Instead of her, he found a note taped to her door: "You were on the phone. I went to the grocery. Be over at six."

He returned to his own office. Miss Mabel and Bonita, the receptionist, were looking at him, whispering to one another; they each waved and smiled like little girls when he caught them staring, Miss Mabel's glistening makeup reflecting the overhead light.

He had spent over an hour on the phone with Child Protective Services, with their statewide office down in Baton Rouge. Sure, he could have called one of the regional offices, but he felt better telling a completely fabricated story to someone he didn't know at all, not to Maggie from the Area 3 office. Maggie from the Area 3 office would certainly have asked too many meddling questions and might have even insisted on driving over from Monroe that afternoon, just to get more facts. Or, more likely, to get out of doing the real work that no doubt was piled on her desk.

He figured it wouldn't hurt to get more information about custody. The idea had come to him as he was tucking Jamey into bed the night before. He knew he better stay on top of this thing, rather than just letting things settle comfortably into place.

"No, ma'am. I've never seen him in our office before. He just came into our office for the first time this morning, wouldn't tell me his name. He was alone, said the kid was in school."

"Not someone you recognized?"

"I've never seen him before. No one else in the office had either. He just asked his questions, then turned and walked out. I really don't even know if he was telling the truth. He could have made the whole thing up."

"And why didn't you report this to the Area 3 office?"

Glenn was prepared, and he waited the right amount of time before answering. "Well, I tried, but I couldn't get through for some reason. The line just kept ringing. I called you because I wanted to talk to someone right away." *This isn't so hard,* Glenn thought. *Making up stories.*

"He may have fabricated the whole thing, I don't know." Glenn backtracked then. "I've never seen him before. It's highly unusual for our office." He stammered, searching. "It's a full moon. People do all kinds of crazy things."

"Well. Why would this strange man just come in and make up such a story?" The lady on the other end tried to laugh, but it was forced. Then she collapsed into a fit of coughing. Glenn was nervous. He took the moment to recover himself, dialed the story back quickly.

"All he said was that he had supervised visitation as part of his parole. And then the child's mother . . . passed away."

"And where is the child now?"

"He said a friend of the boy's mother was taking care of the child. Apparently he, the father, was the only family left. But he didn't really feel capable enough at this time, so he had asked this other . . . woman . . . if the boy could stay with her.

And now he's worried your agency will make the child go to foster care. Because he doesn't feel like he can really take care of his child right now."

"Well." She breathed heavily into the phone. "The obligation of CPS is always to look out for the best interest of the child, as you know. We probably should check into it. We really should be notified by the proper authorities."

"Meaning the sheriff's office."

"Right. The sheriff's office."

Glenn felt things close in on him, and quickly excused himself from the conversation with a promise to try to find out more. He even asked for her direct number and promised to call her back with more information. When he couldn't find Louise, he returned to his office and called Sheriff Norm on his back line. When that didn't work, he dialed Norm's cell phone.

The transition from being a middle-aged man who lived alone and spent most of his personal time alone, to the life of a temporary parent, had been surprisingly easy. Certainly, he missed his lovely friend Brenda, and more than once a day he found himself tearing up at a sudden memory of her, at the sight of the charcoal grill behind her house that she loved so much, at the roses she babied by her front door that were beginning to bloom. Yet, as the saying went, life goes on. In the mornings, Jamey got himself ready, even made his own breakfast and dressed himself in the clothes he had laid out the night before. Glenn had been going to work early, following the bus as it pulled away, and it hadn't been hard for him at all to get his work done each day, and get back in time to meet the bus when it dropped Jamey off at four o'clock.

Even his workouts hadn't suffered. Jamey loved going to the gym. As Glenn pumped his iron, pushed himself ever harder and harder, the boy read comic books on the sofa in the manager's office, did his homework, or if it wasn't too hot, just relaxed on a bench out on the sidewalk under the Big Al's gym sign. And when Glenn got to his cool-down work, lifting the lightweight dumbbells over and over to give his arms and shoulders those fine little cuts, Jamey liked to join him, working his own set of five pounders, bent forward side by side with Glenn in front of the wall-to-wall mirror. Just the day before, a man had come in, a newcomer to Branden who didn't know Glenn, or anything about him. The man smiled as he watched them, side by side in the mirror, doing their repetitions. "Nice boy you've got there," he said. "Looks like you're getting him started early." Then, he turned to Jamey. "You keep this up and you'll have arms bigger than your daddy's one day."

Glenn was too amped up to sit at his desk and pretend to be doing something productive, so he went outside and waited for Norm's arrival. On the phone, he tried not to sound too desperate; "something important," he had told Norm. The sheriff had said he was ten minutes out.

Glenn thought of the first time Norm had come here to see him. It was just after Glenn had been promoted to manager of that office, when his predecessor had died at home one night after managing the branch for nearly thirty years. Norm had stopped in many times to talk to her, but this time he came just to see Glenn. The two offices had regular dealings with one another, and as sheriff, Norm thought it pertinent that he get to know the new man in charge at Family Services.

Glenn had always been fond of the sheriff, who was utterly likeable for a small-town Southern sheriff. Granted, he'd had his own hurdles, as an African-American peace officer in a small town with a racist history. But Norm was always uncommonly courteous to everyone in Glenn's office. When he would stop by to see Marjorie, Glenn's predecessor, Norm was usually affable and liked to joke around a bit. Maybe that was just because Marjorie was an attractive woman, but still. Norm obviously had a good nature, just to be able to joke around the way he did. But the day Norm stopped by to see Glenn for the first time, the sheriff seemed somber.

When Norm stood up to leave that day, Glenn knew there was a problem. Norm fumbled with his hat, put it on backward at first, then took it off and looked at it for a long, long time. Glenn decided to take a chance.

"Sheriff?"

Norm looked at him then, seemed confused. His face was as blank as a tabletop.

"You feeling okay?"

Norm sat back down, then quickly stood, closed Glenn's door, and began to cry. After apologizing several times and composing himself, he told Glenn his brother in Houston had recently died.

"Oh, Norm. I'm sorry. Here, sit down. Can I get you anything? Water? Coffee?" Norm returned to the chair.

"I'm sorry, Glenn. I didn't come over here to bawl like a baby in your office. Look at me." Norm dabbed at his face with a handkerchief. He removed his hat again and set it in his lap.

"Shit, Norm." Glenn looked at the older man, then searched madly on his desk for a box of tissues. "I'm glad you feel comfortable here. You're welcome to cry in my office anytime."

That did the trick, broke all the tension in the room. Norm laughed loudly then, leaned back in the chair. Glenn was pleased with himself. He had been lucky, and he knew it. He'd never been one who knew what to say.

"I'm grateful, Glenn. I'm just . . . sad. I'm grateful my brother forgave me for being such an asshole. That's the only word for it, really. I mean, I tried to reconcile with him in recent years, but only in the last few months, when he knew he was dying, did he forgive me." He held his hat in his hands, turning it repeatedly.

"See, we never had much in common. Well, Glenn, he was . . . gay. That's not what they called it back then, when we were kids, but that's what he was. And that type of human nature wasn't very well accepted in my community, any more than it was in yours. Some of the boys called him . . . terrible names. I caught him once with another guy, we were in high school . . . and I wouldn't talk to him after that. Even though he was older, I felt like it was my job to look out for him. And then we didn't talk for fifty years." Norm blew out then, shook his head at the memory.

"But you finally got back in touch recently then."

"I'm grateful for that, Glenn. I am. I just can't believe Ronnie's gone."

This day, Norm arrived in his patrol car, parked, stood and positioned his hat, brushed lint from his shirt. He didn't see Glenn at first as he approached, walking with his head down and whistling. Glenn's heart pounded. Norm broke into his finest *how y'all doin'?* smile when he finally looked up. Glenn, despite his blatant physicality, melted like a child at Norm's strong handshake.

"Hey, fellow, it's good to see you." Norm glowed, as much the politician as personal friend. "I came as fast as I could. I was just about to go home. I had a late, late night last night. Everything all right?"

Glenn told his friend everything. Norm nodded along.

"I was hoping you'd call me, Glenn. I have to admit. I knew Jamey was staying with you, otherwise we'd have stepped in already."

"Tommy asked me the night she died."

"I knew that already. You know I did."

"Nothing gets past Sheriff Norm, does it?"

"Not much. That's why a fellow who looks like I do keeps getting elected. But Glenn." He turned toward the younger man then, squeezed his shoulder. "Truth is, I'm in a tight spot. I've got to be careful. It's up to me to notify CPS."

Glenn turned toward the roar of the paper mill, the foundation of Branden, half a mile away, belching its incessant steam into a beautiful, bright azure sky. "And then they'll take him away."

Norm, too, watched the lovely white excrement from the mill, churning and churning with its low-grade roar as it did hour after hour, day after day, month after month, year after year. Together they watched it rise from the stacks in frothy columns until it flattened, scattered, became a part of the sky. "I don't know, Glenn. I don't know what they'd do. I'd make my recommendation, of course. Here's what I want you to do. Keep doing what you're doing. Keep taking him to school, get his homework done, keep his clothes clean, make sure he has lunch money every day. I'm not going to make the call. If it comes down later, I'll take the heat. But I need to tell you something serious. I need you to forget this conversation. We did not talk about this. You got it?"

Glenn cried then, there in the parking lot, a sudden burst of tears. All he could do was cover his eyes with one hand. He was twelve years old again, lying on the edge of the lake, gasping for air. Norm didn't shy away, in fact he moved a step closer, spoke in a low, steady voice.

"I wish he was your son, Glenn. You're the best father that child could hope for." Glenn just nodded, his hand shielding his eyes.

"Brenda was good people, except for her judgment in men. But . . . it's best I don't judge. Hell, Tommy never had much of a chance either, not with the mama and daddy he had. Charlie Turner in particular . . . god, what a shame that was."

Glenn collected himself, eager for the talk to continue. "I've heard a little about him. I don't really remember Tommy's parents."

"Did you ever see him run?" Glenn nodded, but Norm held a word on his tongue so Glenn didn't speak. "I mean,

Glenn, I swear his feet didn't touch the ground. The man was barely human when he held that football. They never knew which way he was going. Sometimes he'd run straight at the defender"—here Norm demonstrated as best he could with his large frame—"then if he didn't see a hole he'd go straight back three, four, five yards and take another run at it. Left, right, spin one way then the other, over the top, anything." Norm was winded then, stopped talking for a minute.

"He wasn't even that bad of a father, what I saw. Until he started owing money to the wrong people and got real bad on those damn pills."

Norm stopped, spat on the ground, disgusted. He reached in his pocket, lit up a cigarette, and took a few long pulls before stamping it out with the toe of his boot. He hitched his pants, then adjusted them so his gut hung over the belt.

"Looks like I've lost this battle." He smoothed down his shirt, patted a few times on his stomach. "Anyway, it was early in my career as sheriff. He was burned out by then; he'd already broken half a dozen rushing records at LSU, was tearing up the NFL, but his knee blew out and that was the end of that. He ended up back here, working right over there with half the other people in this town. Watching that steam pour out all day long. It was too much of a letdown for him, I guess. All this was after his own daddy killed his mother and himself, back when Charlie was about Jamey's age. So the guy had a hard life. Like I say, it's best for me not to judge.

"He must've got hooked on those pain pills when he played football. But being out of football didn't get him unhooked. He was running a pharmacy scam, doctors here, pharmacies here, Ruston, Winnfield." Norm pointed in all directions. "Then selling the pills. I mean, Glenn, picture this. Here's this guy, he's the hero of our high school, a couple years older than me. He was so good even the black kids cheered for him even though they wouldn't let us play. He marries Angie Jones, her people were trashy but *god,* what a beauty. It was like the sun shined on her no matter where she went. Here's Branden's hometown hero and I'm having to take him away in handcuffs for selling pills. And then later . . . that same day Tommy pulled you out of the lake . . . I had to tell him and Angie that Charlie was dead." Norm lit another cigarette then, smoked this one all the way down to the butt without saying a word, the smoke shrouding him in mystery. Finally, he stamped it out as he had the first one.

"Charlie Turner started with nothing, and ended up with nothing. Same deal we all get, if you think about it, I guess. But . . . it's the in between that's a lot worse for some than for others.

"I swear, Glenn. I can count on one hand the times I've had good news for people in this job. So, yes. Hell yes, I'll help you." Norm pursed his lips as if satisfied. "We never had this conversation. But do this. Get your lawyer to write up a temporary custody order and get Tommy to sign it. It's generally good for a year, and he can revoke it if he wants to, though he probably won't. He can't raise that boy, not after what he's put himself through. Hell, at least he knows it. Will you do that?"

"I'll do it, Norm. I was thinking about it last night. That's exactly what I'll do."

"I'm glad you called me."

"So, Norm?"

"Sir?"

"Cynthia's been gone almost a year now?"

Norm only nodded. "Week from Tuesday. It'll be a year." He became wistful.

"It's been an adjustment, I guess."

Norm only nodded again. "That's one way to put it."

"You're a good friend, Norm."

"You are too, Glenn. We've each had our own battles, but we're doin' all right." Norm turned toward him, then.

"Norm?"

"Sir?"

"Have you met Louise Andrews? She's been working here in our office?"

"I haven't met her, but I know who she is. I saw you coming out of the grocery store with her last week." Norm gave a little smirk, which Glenn noticed but ignored.

"She works out of Baton Rouge, but they've got her traveling to different communities. She'll be here a little while longer. Anyway, we have similar tastes, we both like to cook. She comes over once or twice a week to cook with me."

Norm still wore that smile, but looked straight ahead with it. Glenn knew he had to be careful. "It can be hard to make new friends, when you're much past eighteen."

"Well, her husband left her. She's trying to make a new life. She's been a good friend, just somebody I can talk to about things. Especially with Brenda, and Jamey. It's a lot of changes. But she wants to know different things about me, I don't know. It's confusing, really. I'm awful old to be so confused."

"You want to know what I think?"

"Yes, Norm. Please. Tell me what to do."

"We never know what's happening to us until later. We never know what the hell's going on right when it's going on. Hell, man, you're brave. You're just willing to admit to being confused. So here's this woman you just met. You enjoy her company, but . . . you haven't . . . spent a lot of time with women . . . you're not quite sure what to make of it. You know, it's funny. Even just seeing her from a distance. She makes me think of Darlene."

"My mother? You think so?"

"Just a little. Something about her. Way she stands, maybe."

"Maybe."

"You know, I was at home the other night. Just relaxing. It wasn't that late, ten, ten thirty. Old Western was on. Cynthia loved Westerns."

"Cynthia did?"

"You never met a black woman who loved Westerns?" At that, Norm leaned back and laughed. "She loved NASCAR too. I'd rather watch hobos picking scabs off their arms than watch a bunch of cars racing around a track, myself. But I do like Westerns. Anyway, I was watching the show. Volume down low, just relaxing. And I looked over, and her chair was empty. And I thought, my god, man. Cynthia sat in that chair, or in that spot in our living room anyway, for thirty-eight years. And now she's gone."

He lit another cigarette then, again smoked this one all the way down without a word. He contorted his face madly, his eyes pained by the memories. "And I thought, my lord, she's gone. How many times did I sit there with her, arguing over what to watch on TV? If we were talking at all. Half the time I wasn't even there, staying late at the office, not talking to her over some perceived slight. I was always trying to play tough with her, I drank too much, shut her out. *God* I hated to lose an argument. She wanted me to appreciate her more; I wanted her to love and respect me more. I'd wake up in the middle of the night thinking of things I wish I'd said to make my point. And now . . . I wish I'd just told her how I felt. How much I loved her. How much sunshine she brought into my life. I wish I hadn't needed to be right all the damn time. I wish I'd just told her how much she meant to me." He shrugged. "But now she's gone, and I can't."

He turned to Glenn, dug his massive hand into Glenn's shoulder, seemed calmed by the human contact. "So Glenn, here's some advice from an old man. Just tell her how you feel. Just go with it. If you two enjoy each other, what difference does it make where you've been? Where she's been? Right now, both of you are right here."

"I've never heard you talk so much, Norm. Thanks, though. It means a lot."

Norm laughed. "I've been thinking a lot. About life. Just yesterday I was out at Pine Hill Manor visiting Daddy." Norm shook his head. "Daddy was a working man all of his life. Hauled pulpwood, truck-farmed, you name it. He used to punish me and Ronnie by making us go out in the backyard and dig up stumps. Daddy, he could dig a stump out of the ground with a pocket knife, I swear . . . And now look at him."

"Not the same strong man he used to be?"

"Psssh." Norm shook his head. "Life is one cruel son of a bitch, Glenn. Simple as that. So anywhere you can find some happiness, take it. I mean, how long is it before you and me are just a couple of old men, messing our drawers and slobbering?

"But I've been spending time with a few different ladies. They all want to bring me food, then eat it with me. They're all talkative. Makes me more talkative, I guess."

"Is that right?" Glenn asked. "You scoundrel. Anybody I know?"

Norm blew out. "Rachel Peters is coming over tonight. You know her?"

"Pretty lady."

"Son!" Suddenly Norm left the ground, threw both arms up, and kicked both legs in a jump for joy. "You should've seen her in high school. Man, she was hot as a ten-dollar pistol back in her younger days. Her daddy was a foreman at the paper mill, and I was just a son of a pulpwood hauler. She wouldn't've looked at me if I'd've paid her to. Now fifty years later she's bringing me gumbo."

Norm bent and picked up the butts he had dropped earlier in the conversation. Then he took out another cigarette, looked at it, shook his head, and put it back in the pack.

"No, I only get four a day. Rachel's quite a cook. I better save that last one till tonight after my gumbo."

CHAPTER 15

Tommy tried to make everything normal. He went to work, visited his son, washed his truck, shopped at the grocery store, did everything just as anyone who paid attention to him would expect him to do. The only thing he couldn't do was sleep. Each day he went to work tired, after a fitful night spent waking and waking, beating the mattress over and over until he was so tired he fell asleep again, only to wake once more, defeated.

Otis annoyed him even more than usual. Tommy had no patience left for the overgrown baby and his unceasing tales, childish lunch box, and shameless laziness. Tommy asked him to turn down Paul Harvey one day as they ate in the truck, then slapped his hand on the dashboard when Otis refused. Otis gave Tommy a cookie from his mother's kitchen one day driving home, and Tommy threw it out the window. He stuffed earplugs into his ears and wore them everywhere he went, tried anything he could think of to drown out the noise all around him. At work they were cutting a new tract with a logging crew of Guatemalans who spoke no English, which suited Tommy perfectly. He spent day after day on the skidder, rolled across the land dragging logs back and forth, back and forth. He wore muffs on top of the earplugs and it was loud but he couldn't hear a thing, could only feel the vibration in his chest, and he let it draw him in and hold him there in that safe, humming place. Then at lunch he left the earmuffs on as he ate in the truck, Otis yakking away about *The Waltons* and baby

Jesus as Tommy stared straight ahead and didn't say anything at all.

Several days in a row, driving home from the yard, he thought he would stop for a drink. Just one drink, maybe a shot of something, anything, then he'd start to relax. Maybe he'd stop in Mikey's store on the way home, he wouldn't even buy a whole six-pack, he'd heard Mikey tell guys in there not to break up the six-packs, but he'd let Tommy do it, it wouldn't be a problem. They'd been friends for a long time. Maybe just that one can, or one tall bottle of Budweiser, would shut down the film reel playing in constant fast-forward in his brain. Just one little drink. He had almost two years sober now, but knowing that didn't seem to help anything. Surely he didn't have to worry about going back down that dark road.

Because, *goddammit,* he deserved to feel better than this. He was doing everything he was supposed to do. He was going to work. He was going to meetings. He was taking care of his son, as best he could. He was eating right and trying to sleep. He was going to church. He wasn't running from his responsibilities. He was paying off his debts.

What in the hell was he supposed to do? No, Matt didn't deserve to die, but he screwed up. Plain and simple. Tommy went through it again, for at least the thousandth time, in his mind. Matt walking in, insulting him. Acting like he owned the place. Playing tough guy. Then that gun. That completely unnecessary gun. *Dammit.* A man had to protect himself. *Dammit.* What he wouldn't do for just one drink. Or one little snort or *something.* Even a cigarette. But no, no, no. He was not going back down that road.

The only time Tommy felt safe was in the daylight, when he was at work. Each day, when he was done, he stopped off at Glenn's to see his son. Some days he brought over food, and some days Glenn would cook, then they'd eat some dinner and maybe watch a few minutes of TV. Some nights he took his son on a walk or a drive while Glenn went and did other things. But each night, by eight, Jamey was tucked safely in his bed, and Tommy was driving home to try and sleep himself.

The drive home at dusk was lonely, vast, with Tommy constantly scanning the horizon, or the rearview mirror, for anything different. Maybe he'd stop at the grocery, maybe the coffee shop for some pie, or maybe he wouldn't. He drove under the speed limit. He didn't smile too much, or too little.

Since his supervised visits were over, he and Glenn agreed they would keep the same visitation schedule he had planned to share with Brenda. Glenn didn't ask if he was ready to take Jamey into his own house yet, and Tommy was glad for it, relieved not to have to say the words out loud. In fact, Glenn asked him to sign a temporary custody order. Tommy didn't really see the point of it, but he agreed. He didn't worry about Jamey living with Glenn, it wasn't that; he just didn't know what to think of it, not being able to care for his own son. Yet, he was totally grateful the social workers didn't take his son away, and Glenn convinced him that he had a lot to do with that. Of course, Tommy knew how Glenn felt about him; he'd been nicer lately, but he was never one to hide his feeling that Tommy had done his best to ruin everything for Brenda, and for that sweet little boy. To hide his feeling that if only Tommy had been a decent husband they never would've divorced, then Brenda wouldn't have been working that job out of town, driving that dangerous road every day. But Glenn took good care of Jamey; as a temporary father, he wasn't too bad, especially for a man like him. One who could never have kids of his own.

Already, Glenn had found Jamey a counselor. Tommy tried to pay him for that, but Glenn said he had somehow arranged for his office to pay. Still, Tommy offered Glenn the money. At first Glenn refused, then after thinking it over a day, he talked it over with Tommy, and they decided he would just pay Glenn his normal child support. Tommy didn't discuss it with Glenn, but he didn't plan to give up; he hoped to be able to get things together so Jamey *could* come and live with him at some point. Maybe in a few more months. At some point, things would have to start looking better. But these nightmares . . . Let him stay where he was for now.

Finally after far too many sleepless nights, Tommy was able to sleep and, when he did, began to feel the faintest hope. He told himself over and over again, each time he went through the fight in his head, two or three fewer times each day than the day before, that eventually this would pass, that one day he'd be a full person again. Not half a man so haunted by one miserable mistake after another. He couldn't begin to imagine how Mr. Bianchi could connect him with the disappearance of his son, but he figured someone would be calling on him again, so he did what he could to get these people out of his life as quickly as possible, and saved every dime. One night he stopped by Mikey's store for a Dr Pepper, and asked Mikey for a copy of *Playboy.* Mikey handed one over, a lopsided grin on his face. Tommy handed the magazine back without opening it. *Put it back. Gotta save my money.*

He drove home from a meeting on a full-moon night, the shapes of trees and houses and horses inside fences by the road clear enough to see, his mind full of wisdoms. All the sights he saw brought back memories of his mother, his father, his youth. Over and over, he checked the mirror. *Not everything is wrong. Look at this beautiful night.* He opened the window, the smells of pine and loam and warm black asphalt settling into the truck with him.

We'll make it through this. This is hard, but it isn't a prison.

Tommy had been through prison, the real thing; whatever bad he lived with out here was a picnic compared to life in there. He remembered what a terrible day it had been when he first went in, bigger men jeering at him, their steely eyes, the thought of years locked up in that dank hole. Having to sleep behind bars, sit on the toilet for everyone to see, the constant clanking of metal, echoing footsteps, the nighttime moans of the brain-dead and the half dead as their darkening minds relived traumas of every variety.

But he got through it, and nothing he had to suffer on the outside even compared to anything on the inside. Granted, he had drugs of all types in there, narcotics and uppers and downers and things he never heard of on the outside. But at least he wasn't out trying to kill himself every day.

It was a long time before he began to see any advantage to getting sober. But it happened there in prison, one day when he finally just got tired of running away. People constantly talked about God, about a higher power, of the saving power of Jesus, just like his father used to when Tommy was a boy out under the stars, in the years before the drugs and the pain and all his mistakes took him away. There was no other explanation for it really, he didn't have any sort of near-death experience or anything. He was just lying in his bed early one morning, hurting, wanting more, scheming for how he would get his next high, and there it was. *I'm going to lie here until I don't want it anymore.* He lay in bed for five days then, puking and cramping, praying for it all to go away, until he was simply emptied out. Until the man he had always called Tommy was gone. Then he got up, put on his baggy prison clothes, and Tommy Turner went to his first Alcoholics Anonymous meeting, a hollowed-out shell of the man he had been before.

For all Tommy's faults, he wasn't a fool; he knew from day one that it wouldn't be easy. That he'd have to do the work. Only then, a year into prison, did he ask Brenda to bring his son to visit him in that place. And when Jamey came, a scared little boy, Tommy reassured him it was temporary, that soon enough Daddy would be free, free to be his daddy again.

All the boy wanted to do was sit on his lap and hug him.

And he felt little Jamey burrow into him, in a way he couldn't stop. It hurt, but he didn't want to stop it. And he knew that, if he did stay sober, he'd never be able to stop it, that ache right down in the center of himself that pushed everything else aside.

"Hands on my shoulders." He remembered that expression from his first meeting. One of the men inside described his feelings that way. "My higher power has his hands on my shoulders. He leads me where he wants me to go." Tommy drove through town, closed the window against the heat and humidity. He was almost home. He slowed in the straightaway before that last turn, loosened his grip on the wheel. *Jesus, take the wheel,* he thought. He removed both hands entirely. *Lead me where you want me to go.* And what would happen to Jamey if things didn't work out for Tommy? he wondered. *Have to put it all in God's hands.* The truck stayed true, continued to slow, kept itself between the lines. Eventually he took hold of the wheel again, once more checked his mirrors, then turned the truck down his road, hoping this night would be a good night for sleep.

CHAPTER 16

Jamey stepped off the bus, then stood and watched as it rumbled around the curve and past his old house. His best friend, Jack, waved at him from the back seat, then stuck out his tongue and made a face. Jack slid open the window and craned his head out, yelled, “Bye, Jamey-amey-amey-amey, see you tomorrow-orrow-orrow.” In a minute the bus was out of sight, and he heard Mrs. Nunn downshift as she turned the bus back onto the highway.

Mommy used to meet him when he got off the bus every day after school, every day in kindergarten, every day in first grade, and almost every day in second grade. She had told him last summer, before he started first grade, that she would have to go back to work soon, that she wouldn’t always be there to meet him every day. It was okay, though; he was getting bigger, and didn’t need his mommy to be there with him every single day. On the days she worked late, he went to Mamaw’s house for a little while. Her house smelled like dust, but he liked it there; she must have had a million channels on her television. She liked kids’ shows as much as he did, and was always leaning back to cackle and slap her knee at something SpongeBob or Flapjack said. Mommy always told him in the morning when she wouldn’t be there in the afternoon, all except, well, that one day. That one very bad day.

Mamaw had some chairs set up underneath her oak tree, and a lot of times she would be sitting out there with his mommy waiting for him, when the bus let him off. The two of them were always laughing when the bus rolled up. Not just little girly giggles either; sometimes they'd be laughing so hard they'd both be red in the face, grabbing at their chests trying to catch their breath. Mamaw was always telling some story about different things she had seen or done, or different people she had known, and his mommy thought her stories were so funny. Mamaw was old, so she had lots of stories. Mommy liked to say, "That Mamaw's a real *character.*" Jamey thought that meant she worked in books or movies, like the characters he read about in books or movies he saw on TV. It didn't really make sense to him, though, because she never seemed to go anywhere, and besides that, people in books weren't real people anyway; they were just imaginary people the authors thought up so they could tell stories. But on those days, those golden days that came in the spring or fall of the year, when the air was perfect and there was no rain in sight, the best part of Jamey's day was the moment he stepped down off the bus, when he saw his mom there with her shiny brown hair and her twinkly gray eyes in the shade underneath the tree, laughing at something Mamaw had said as the old woman rubbed her giant swollen knuckles and wrinkled her old purple nose. And without fail, Rascal would be sitting there too, lying down in the shade with all four legs splayed out underneath Mamaw's chair. And he always jumped and barked like crazy when Jamey stepped off the bus.

This day, Jamey sat down in one of the chairs before going in, just looked around for a minute and thought about things. He was glad to see Mr. Glenn's car was home, so he'd be inside waiting with a snack or maybe just a big glass of milk. If Mr. Glenn wasn't in too much of a hurry, maybe he'd have time for just one cartoon, then they'd go lift some weights so he could grow up and get big and strong too.

Rascal lay in his usual spot, in the little doggy room he had found between the giant roots of that tree. His tongue hung out of his mouth; it lolled all the way down into the dirt. It was coated with dust. His eyes were open wide, a little more so each day, and Jamey wondered if he just wanted to see a little better, to see as much of the world as he could, while he still could. Rascal panted and panted, like he just couldn't get a deep breath. This day, he could barely lift his head. He followed Jamey with his eyes as the boy got closer, pulled his tongue to the skyward side of his mouth and licked at the air, searched for Jamey's hand, radiating breath that smelled like eggs. His tail twitched too, though Jamey guessed he didn't have the energy to flop it up and down at all. He whimpered once, then seemed to sink even farther into the dust. Just the prior fall Rascal had still chased the bus, and mauled Jamey when he got off; once not even a year ago, Rascal had darted ahead of Jamey as he walked home and pulled a water moccasin out of some lilies right in Jamey's path, shook the snake back and forth and bit it in half before tossing both sides of the writhing body onto the ground. But Rascal could only dream about doing those things anymore.

Mamaw opened her screen door and stood silently on the stoop watching him pet the dog, her old eyes sparkling. She doddered down and patted the boy as he patted the dog. The door squeaked when she let it go, hit the frame with a *thwap!*

"Come see me, honey." She stood with her arms out. She wasn't much taller than Jamey. He gave her a big hug.

"I've been thinking about you all day, honey."

"Yes, ma'am."

"You know, I lost both of my grandparents and my daddy to the flu when I was just a little girl. So I know what you must feel like, losing your sweet mama like that."

Jamey just looked down.

"Ooooh, and mean! My mama was so mean after that! After my daddy and her mama and daddy were gone. It was just her and me and my two brothers." The old woman stopped talking and seemed to consider as she watched a group of grackles shout and dart at one another in the top of her tree. "I know she loved me, she always took good care of me and fed me good . . . she was just mean after that. But they didn't have all the medicines back then like they do now to make people feel better."

"Yes, ma'am."

"Is Mr. Glenn taking good care of you?"

"Yes, ma'am."

"Is he feeding you pretty good?"

"Yes, ma'am."

"What do y'all eat?"

"Usually chicken and rice and green beans."

She paused, put one finger across her lips. "Ohhh, pfff! You tell him you need a hamburger sometimes!"

"Yes, ma'am."

"You come back and see me in a minute if he doesn't have any cookies for you. I know he likes all that *health food*. Pfff! You tell him Mamaw said little boys need cookies to survive!"

"The goal, of course, is to get them trained for real-life situations. I mean, that's the problem with a lot of schooling, you know? I mean, if you're fourteen, and you're smart, or studious, or both, you might enjoy doing division and algebra and science experiments. But if you're in your twenties or thirties or forties, and you've already shown you're not interested in school when you dropped out, how much good will it do to learn algebra? Geometry? Going to college when you never finished high school is, frankly, silly for some people. But that's what a lot of these so-called training programs are. Just sending people back to school. Instead of teaching them how to do something."

"I can see you're passionate about this. So much of our

work at Family Services is just putting out fires. We rarely get to actually help people improve themselves."

"Like how to use a computer, or better yet some sort of trade. Especially for women, most of them in these situations have no practical skills. Not skills that make money anyway."

Glenn ran water into a pot, while Louise relaxed at the counter with a large glass of wine. She had had two already, and was feeling dreamy as she watched him clean up. "It's so nice to know a man who can cook. Not to mention one who washes dishes.

"Right now I'm setting up the two sewing centers, the one out south of Branden and the other this side of Ruston. We hope to get other centers going later this year, but that's all the money we have right now. They're not hard to set up—all you need is a space and some machines. Which, might I add, the State of Louisiana has lots of, I can assure you."

Glenn reached out an arm swollen from dumbbell curls to pat Jamey on the back. He was so quiet that Louise had forgotten he was there. The three glasses of wine may have been to blame.

"We don't mean to hog the conversation, Jamey," she told him. "I bet it's not much fun to listen to adults talk about adult things, is it?"

"No, ma'am, it's fun. I like listening to y'all."

"You're a sweet boy, Jamey." He blushed. "Did you enjoy your dinner?"

"It was good. Mr. Glenn cooks pretty good for a man."

Louise laughed out loud then, covered her mouth with her hand out of instinct. Gary had always told her she had crooked teeth. She went and hugged the boy from behind, kissed him on his cheek, tousled his downy hair. He tilted his head back to look up at her and gave her a giddy smile. His permanent teeth were just coming in strong, blocky chunks of ivory with random spaces in between. He was just what she always wanted. A little boy. She told herself not to, then put her nose right into his hair anyway, breathed in the scent of a rubbed penny.

She and Gary had talked about kids, but that's as far as it ever got. He always wanted two more years. She was nearly thirty when they married, so the first few times he told her, she agreed it made sense. She was certainly young enough. The "two years later" eventually turned into eleven; at some point she flat-out told him never to say the words "two years" ever again.

She could have had a couple of them by now, as big as the one in front of her, and bigger.

"Jamey, what's your favorite meal I cook?"

"I bet I know," Louise answered. "Baked chicken."

"No, ma'am, that's not my favorite."

"Macaroni and cheese."

"I'm asking Jamey, Louise."

She gasped. "Have you made him those shiitake mushrooms? Those are incredible."

Jamey began to speak, but she finished downing her glass and answered for him. "How about pot roast?"

"Just give him a minute to answer, Louise."

Suddenly, she was embarrassed, a white-hot point of shame burning the end of her nose. "I'll do the rest of those, Glenn." Now she was dying to make herself useful, lest she trip and fall into one of her poor-me traps.

"No, you two talk. I'll do them. Jamey's probably tired of talking to me already. And he knows I won't let him watch too much television. What's the rule, Jamey?"

"No TV until all the dishes are done," Jamey said dutifully.

"Usually Jamey helps me with the dishes, don't you, buddy?"

"I always did them with my mommy," he told Louise.

"So Jamey, how is school?" She felt it a foolish question, as soon as she said it. She wondered if she should mind her own business, but pushed forward anyway.

He shrugged. "It's okay."

Glenn had told her Jamey was seeing a counselor. She knew it was none of her business, but as soon as she heard that she asked about credentials. MSW? Psychologist? Psychiatrist? State school? Private school? How old? *Do you know anything about her?*

Glenn wasn't the only one looking out for this boy.

Maybe it was the wine. One thing she could count on with wine. She could tell herself a hundred times not to do something, but once it was in her head, it was as good as done. Especially after three glasses of wine. Besides, what was the harm of asking? Glenn said he was talking to Jamey, but any way you look at it, he was a man. Surely Jamey could use a woman's voice. She was a social worker, trained to help people with their feelings. It wouldn't be right to ignore what was obviously going on. Or to miss a chance when it was right there in front of her. She moved her chair closer, pulled his hot little head into the crook of her arm.

"I bet you miss your mom, don't you?" Through her shirt, she felt his face getting hotter, then the shudder and then the growing dampness spreading onto her chest. Glenn turned and looked at her blankly. She gave him a wan smile. A dish towel was draped over his shoulder.

"I know, baby. I know. I lost my mommy when I was little too."

Eventually, Jamey pulled out and looked at her with a mottled face. "You did?"

"Mmmm-hmmm. I was eight. I just missed her so much. My mommy was always so nice to me. She loved me so much."

He began to cry again; Louise knew it was for the best, that a certain magical number of tears would have to fall before this beautiful child could even begin to heal. Glenn moved closer, but all he could do was stand and watch, that towel draped over his shoulder.

"What do you miss most about her?"

Jamey began to sniff now, on the way to collecting himself. He didn't answer quickly; Glenn had told her this about him. A contemplative boy.

"I miss the way she combed my hair."

Louise was overcome by this revelation, exactly what she remembered most about her own mother. Then she was crying, and poured herself another glass of wine.

"My daddy never combed my hair. He and my grandparents were so critical. I wish I'd had someone like Mr. Glenn to take care of me."

She pulled Jamey's face into her hands. "Has Mr. Glenn been combing your hair?"

Jamey looked at Glenn then, who had taken the towel off his shoulder. "I will anytime you want me to, buddy. Anytime."

"Would you like me to do it?"

Jamey nodded at her.

"I'll go get a comb," Glenn answered. Louise thought it was so he could feel useful.

She took the comb when he returned, ran it through the boy's fine hair. He melted into her.

"It's good to miss people we love. One day you won't feel so sad anymore, but only if you let yourself miss her now." She continued combing his fine nest of hair as Jamey tried to catch his breath.

"I miss my daddy too." Jamey's eyes were downcast, his breath hot on Louise's hands.

Glenn cut in. He didn't want to say it, but he knew it was the best thing Jamey could hear. Someone needed to take up for Tommy.

"Your daddy's working really hard to make himself better. So you can go and live with him when he gets everything fixed." He moved his hand to dry Jamey's tears.

"He's working really hard. He wants you to come and live with him so bad."

Jamey buried his face in his hands. He nodded over and over. "I miss both of them."

Glenn bent down to try to look into Jamey's face. Glenn was more surprised than Louise was when he heard what came out of his own mouth.

"Your mommy's safe with Jesus now," Glenn told him as he pushed the boy's hair out of his face. Jamey nodded over and over. When he finally looked up, his face red and glistening, all Glenn could see was a beautiful, sad, red-faced Tommy Turner.

CHAPTER 17

Jamey was pretty glad he didn't have to help with the dishes. Most nights, after dinner, he helped Mr. Glenn do them. But Mr. Glenn didn't like Jamey making a mess, he liked the house to stay really clean, so it wasn't as much fun as it used to be with Mommy. They had some of their best times washing dishes. Mommy always had him put just a little bit of water into the sink, put that plug thingy into the drain, then squirt the green gooey soap out of the plastic bottle into the sink before he filled it the rest of the way. That way, the soap got mixed up real good and made lots of suds so the dishes got really clean. Then, after he filled that side of the sink, he would fill the other side with just plain water to rinse the dishes off after she washed them. Jamey's job was to rinse them and stack them in the stacker. Sometimes, Mommy would let him put soapsuds on his face and make it look like he had a beard. If she was in a really good mood, which she was a lot of times, she let him put suds on her face and make her a beard too, or sometimes ball them on the ends of her ears like earrings. He liked doing them, too, at Mr. Glenn's house. But tonight he was happy just to enjoy the lady's company.

He got into his jammies and decided he'd lie in bed and read a book for a few minutes before he went to sleep. He had a new book from the library. The story was about some cowboys who were riding their horses while a bunch of cows walked all the way from Texas to Kansas. The characters in the book, they weren't really people, they were just imaginary, they were supposed to live way back in the old days, back before people had cars or trucks or anything. He was pretty sure it was after the dinosaurs lived, but not completely sure. It wasn't fair at all. The cowboys got to ride on horses, but those poor cows had to walk all the way there, and it was almost five hundred miles! At night they all liked to sit around the campfire and sing songs. One of the cowboys had a big puffy beard and he liked to play his fiddle while some of the other cowboys danced. The cows must have liked the music too, because in all the pictures, they were smiling.

Then they started to tell stories. One of the cowboys said he couldn't wait to get back home and catch some fish in the little stream behind his house. Another said he didn't ever want to go home, but wished instead he could just ride his horse and sleep out underneath the stars around a different campfire every night. Then the cowboy with the big puffy beard put down his fiddle and started to cry. He said he couldn't wait to get back home. He said he missed his family.

Jamey turned the light off and settled into his bed, wondered if he would dream about Mommy. He'd had a few dreams about her. Usually she was waiting for him in her chair, talking with Mamaw out there by the bus stop. He missed her a lot. But he wasn't too sad. She had never once said a mean thing to him, never yelled at him, not even one time. His friend Jack, who lived down the road, he was in second grade too, his mother yelled at him so loud sometimes they could hear it through the woods all the way from the next road over. But even though Mommy was gone, and he missed her, Jamey knew she was looking down on him, and loved him even more than she did when she was with him. He felt sure of it.

She would want him to be strong. Some days, since she'd been gone, he just wished he could stay home from school and play with Rascal all day and do nothing. Maybe Rascal would feel better if Jamey could spend a whole day with him, and they could take a walk in the woods. But he knew Mommy wouldn't want him to do that, and every morning when he woke up, he thought about her and thought about what she would want him to do. And each day, he got himself dressed and went to school. He'd been talking to the lady after school about Mommy. She told him, next time he came, they were going to do a project to help Jamey remember her. The lady said she would bring some old magazines, and she would help Jamey cut out some pictures that made him think good things about his mommy. Things he wanted to remember. Then, she said they would say a prayer, they'd send all their good hopes and thoughts and wishes up to heaven for her to have with her.

He put his book down, went to tee-tee one last time, got back in bed and lay there thinking. Lately Mommy had been taking him to church. There, they learned that when people die they go to live with Jesus and have all the good things they want, and they're never sad again. Mommy loved chocolate, and he smiled at the ceiling, wondering if she was up there eating a pile of it right now, she could eat and eat and eat and didn't have to worry about getting fat anymore. He learned that, in heaven, people never argue or fight, life was just perfect, and you could have your own dog or cat or whatever pet you wanted. You could keep it in your room to live right there with you every day, and if you had a dog it would even go to school with you and wait outside for you all day. You got to watch cartoons all day on Saturday, not every day because that would be bad for you, even in heaven people still had to go to work or to school and get smart and strong.

Finally Jamey got up, kneeled down beside his bed. *God, bless and take care of Mommy, make my daddy better, bless Mamaw and Mr. Glenn. And please help Rascal so he doesn't hurt too much. Mamaw says he'll be coming to see you soon, and please make the rest of his life good for him.*

He got back into bed. He felt so glad Daddy was out of jail and could visit him again. He wished they could live together now, but Mr. Glenn said his daddy was real sick and something went wrong in his brain so he couldn't take care of himself or Mommy or especially not a little boy. Because when you're a grown-up and you have kids, you have to make money so you can buy food and clothes and all the things they need. But Mr. Glenn said Daddy was going to keep getting better, and soon they'd be able to live together again. Daddy even said he deserved to be in jail, he did some bad things but he was really sorry for them and he was working really hard so he didn't do bad things anymore. Daddy said he was so sorry he hurt Jamey and Mommy, that he wouldn't drink beer anymore and there were places he couldn't go now. He said he learned his lesson in jail, just like kids learn lessons in school. Mr. Glenn was pretty good as a practice daddy, he tucked Jamey in at night, read him books, sang him songs. Then, each night before bed, he kissed Jamey on the head and said, "Good night, little boy, dream about all the things you love."

What the lady said after school, that's what Jamey thought he would do. Mommy had a bunch of old magazines in the house. He didn't have to wait for his next meeting. He just needed to look through some of those magazines and find some pictures that made him think about her when she was happy. And even if he couldn't find anything that was perfect, there was always that one picture he had already. He liked that one the best. Jamey switched on the light and picked it up, stared at it again for the millionth time. It was that picture of the three of them, the one where Daddy sucked on Jamey's pacifier from when he was still a little baby. Jamey reached into the drawer next to his bed and took out a blue marker. Just so nobody would be confused, he took the marker and colored in his daddy's eyes. Mommy was already perfect but, though

Jamey never did understand it, she used to say Daddy's eyes were empty by the time that picture was taken. He colored his daddy's eyes the brightest blue. That soft, soft color that made Jamey feel so good in his heart, that color that was way back beyond everything, way back like the giant sky where Mommy lived now in some peaceful place people here on earth can't see.

CHAPTER 18

Bianchi struggled to sit up in bed, a wall of pain and exhaustion pressing him back into the mattress. Another night without sleep. He reached for the bottle of pills on his bedside table, but before he could get it open he felt everything come forward in a rush of things and was relieved to find himself next on his knees by the toilet as his torso convulsed and the whole inside of him turned itself out. He squatted there awhile, not quite relieved, then when enough time had passed, stood and rinsed his mouth, brushed his teeth, and shuffled back to his bed to lie with a forearm over his eyes as the overhead light pulsed brighter.

He reached for a bottle of water that the pretty young blonde had left there the night before and took a drink, wishing only after he did so that he had wiped away the waxy residue of her lipstick from the bottle's mouth. Then he sat and stuffed his pipe with a pinch of the dried green weed, lit it with a stiff wooden match, and took in a long, slow drag, then another, felt it settle into him and begin to push down the wave of nausea that would otherwise drag him out once again into a cold, choppy sea.

Bianchi had never been one to lie in bed; until just the last few months, every day of his life he sat straight up the minute daylight peeked into his room. Even a week after Marilyn died, he was hopping right up in the morning, ready to keep on going. What good was it going to do him to lie around? So he'd never again have love like the love he had with his beautiful wife. So what? How was staying in bed all day going to change that one inexorable fact? It wouldn't. It absolutely wouldn't. It wouldn't change anything.

But ever since Christmas, he could tell he was slowing. All Carlo Bianchi's life, even when he was just a greenhorn out picking up collections for his uncle, he had known one day would be his last. Everybody has a day. We all have our time to go. Carlo believed there was a place for what he did—the law had its place, and what he did had its place. Neither he nor anyone who had ever worked for him forced anyone to do business with him. They came because he had something they wanted. How was it his fault if they took too much? If they wrote a check they couldn't cover? But . . . he would always have his detractors. The work he did, there would always be those who opposed it. It would always be . . . of questionable value. He knew he wouldn't be blessed with life and health forever. Look at Marilyn. Nothing but an angel from the day she was born. And poof! Just like that. One day she was gone. If that's the deal she got . . . he certainly couldn't expect anything better.

But this nausea . . . The day before Matt had disappeared, he was feeling hopeful. He and his son had had a good talk that morning. Matt had called him early—he woke up with the sun too, just like his father—and asked if he could take his old dad for brunch at the Frenchmen Hotel. They didn't talk about work at all, only enjoyed the clear spring morning, speculated on the Saints, made plans for a fishing trip out on the salt, and put away a breakfast like those Carlo used to eat in his younger days. They didn't talk about Matt's drugs either—Carlo had learned better than to approach that delicate subject directly. Bianchi had gone home late that morning with a good feeling in his heart. He had called his doctor immediately and made an appointment for the next morning.

The minute he walked out of that office the next afternoon,

he was sorry he had gone. And sure enough, they'd been calling him ever since. "Doctor would like to see you again. There's something on the scans that isn't quite clear." Those lying sons of bitches. That was the problem with everybody anymore. Nobody had the balls to just tell the truth. It isn't clear? Of course it's clear. The cancer was back. It was eating up his insides like the cancer it was.

Maybe he'd get to see his beautiful girl again after all. No one ever loved him the way she did. But not yet. There's Matt. He needed to fight this, for Matt. Maybe he'd go back and see that lying son of a bitch after all. Even doctors were good for something.

He finally stood and grabbed his chest. His heart was pounding, which at least let him know he was still alive. Just standing up from his bed made it beat the way it did fifty years ago when he and Marilyn were still young, when they used to make torrid love on a blanket on the levee Uptown, back before respectable people did that sort of thing without any shame. On hot summer nights in high school, when they explored every square inch of each other in the sweet grass and grime and the cloistered heat.

When his heart slowed, he made his way to the kitchen, prepared himself some dry toast and a small pot of black coffee. About all he could eat at one time anymore. As he drank his coffee he took down Marilyn's cup, just held it, fingered the baked-in trace of lipstick still there, four years after he found her on the kitchen floor that morning, stiff in her pale-blue nightgown. Her half-full coffee cup was still on the counter, her face frozen with the same look of surprise she had worn the day they found out she was pregnant again with Matt, fifteen years after the second of his older brothers had been born.

He checked his messages again, and decided he would leave another one for Matt. He wasn't going to yell this time. He had left, what, thirty messages in the last two weeks? It just wasn't like his son to flake off for two weeks. As he looked at the phone in his hand, considering the words he would use, it rang. He jumped.

It was Logan, from the office. His head of security.

"I got bad news, boss."

"Okay, Logan. What is it?"

"Well, you know I've been working here a long time, boss. Watching people. Studying things . . ."

"I'm sorry, I'm in the middle of something, Logan. What happened?"

"I didn't mean to waste your time, boss. I'll deal with it on my own, if you like."

"Just tell me, Logan. What happened."

"One of the blackjack dealers has been working with a patron. Slipping him chips. You see . . ."

Bianchi couldn't really follow the story; the nausea and the winding, grinding sense in his head distracted him.

"Just deal with it, Logan."

Logan lived for things like this, and could barely contain himself from repeating the details again. "I watched him for seven days on the camera . . . it was always the same . . . he was fast with those chips but not as fast as my eye is . . ." The last time they had discovered something like this, Bianchi had gone down there himself and beat the balls off the guy, and enjoyed every single punch. But today, forget it. He just wasn't in the mood to beat anybody or smash the bones in some guy's hand with a hammer. Which, by the way, was the worst thing he had ever done, or ordered done, in his entire career. He had never ordered a hit, and certainly never killed anyone, in his life, despite the reputation that he had left guys at the bottom of the Mississippi for forty years.

"Any word from Matt?"

Bianchi didn't answer, just breathed into the phone. Eventually, Logan got the point, and muttered a few more words as Bianchi listened before hanging up the phone. He poured another cup of coffee and dialed his son's number, then checked his watch. Nine fifty-five. Better get dressed. They'd be coming soon.

It only rang once. "Hi, son, it's Dad. Listen, Matt, I'm really getting worried about you. Wherever you are, whatever you're doing. Whatever you've done. You know how much I love you. Whatever it is. It can't be half as bad as what I'm going through worrying about you. Matt . . . I . . . I know I could have been a better father. I'm sure of it. But please . . . don't punish me like this . . . I need to tell you something . . . I went to the doctor recently. Just, please."

Bianchi hung up the phone. The adrenaline rush of his breaking heart mixed with the yawning maw of hunger as the edge began to come off his high. He wondered how many days he had left on earth, saw winged numbers flying around his head in a daydream. And what, he asked himself, had he done with the days he had been given already? The answers to both came quickly, in rapid succession. Not enough. Not enough.

He shaved and dressed, then drank a large glass of water and turned on the television in his kitchen to wait. A landslide had killed a thousand in India, buried hundreds of people alive. Russian terrorists had taken over a school somewhere, killed god knows how many children. And people said *gambling* was bad for the world. His phone rang.

"We're at the place."

"You have the directions, right? You're two minutes away."

"We got it. We're on the way." The man spoke in a gravelly voice, made no attempt to be ingratiating, to sell himself or his purpose.

"I'll open the gate in ninety seconds. Drive straight in. Don't look at anyone."

"Got it." Click.

The Suburban pulled in as the gate came fully open.

Bianchi approached the car through the humid, sticky morning; its windows were tinted such that he couldn't see inside, could only watch a distorted reflection of his own face as he got closer to the car. He motioned the driver, or where he assumed the driver to be, to pull well ahead, up alongside the lantana hedge so the Suburban would be completely hidden from the neighbors.

Mainly he just wanted to look at them, to try to draw his own conclusions. He'd heard good reports, though he'd never before had a need for men like them. He stepped into shade as the driver rolled down the window.

"Anybody see you?"

The driver turned to his partner, snorted in a knowing way. He smirked. The only name Bianchi knew was Bobby. He peered inside, looked over both of them before speaking again. They were rough guys, certainly. Bobby had tattoos down both arms and along his neck to his jawbone and smoked two cigarettes at the same time. The passenger appeared clean-cut, but he had a bite in his gaze that bored into a man, even one as tough as Bianchi. His eye was turned in some, and Bianchi sensed that the guy saw him clearly even though he seemed to be looking in the other direction. The driver didn't waste time on formalities; clearly, this was the man to whom he had spoken on the phone.

"This is Dave." Bobby motioned with his head toward his passenger. Bianchi tried to stare him down, but Dave took no notice. Bianchi knew it was a risk to have them here; for all he knew those FBI assholes had cameras in his trees. Not that they'd be looking for anything like this, but still. Yet, if he carried through with what he was thinking, the men would have to be here later anyway. So it was best they knew where to park.

They talked. Bobby emanated the smell of machine oil, which he covered with pungent cologne overlaid with cigarettes. Neither of them was exactly a smooth talker, their language peppered with profanities and irregular grammar. But Bianchi knew there was a need for men like them, and such men were generally not a classy lot. Bobby removed his sunglasses, showed a giant, ragged scar above his left eye.

"So you've been there, Mr. Bianchi?"

"I went to his house, yes. I know my son was there. Matt never went to his hotel that night, and I haven't heard from him since."

Bobby nodded along. He had a sharpness in his one good eye that made Bianchi think he was paying closer attention than it appeared.

"I've seen the house. I've seen him. We've watched him several times. But the kid doesn't live with him. The kid lives with some other guy. Next door to where the kid lived with his mother. She got killed two weeks ago. Turner visits him every night over there."

Bobby continued to nod. Dave said nothing.

"You got something for me?"

Bianchi handed him the envelope. Bobby put it directly in the inside pocket of his coat, felt it for thickness. His mood seemed to improve.

"We'll watch him some more, get back to you. Don't worry about a thing, Mr. Bianchi. We're your guys." He reached into the pocket, took out the envelope, thumbed through the bills, and grinned.

"I can see we'll get along. We'll be in touch in a few days. We're just waiting on your word."

"I haven't decided yet. Just give me your report. I'll let you know what I decide."

Bobby slipped his sunglasses back on, put the car into gear. He turned around in Bianchi's circular driveway, waited for the gate to open, then pulled away. As the gate returned to its place, Bianchi watched them go through the opening. He used to have some sympathy in his heart; but losing Marilyn, and then his health, and now whatever had happened to his son, had taken its toll. Whatever had been left, now was gone like the smoke streaming from the Suburban's tailpipe. When the gate was fully closed, the metal wheels gave a screech, and Bianchi knew he was locked in tight.

CHAPTER 19

Tommy was grateful for his work. He was grateful for the relief his routine brought him, the simple peace of going to do the thing he did five days a week, where he knew exactly what he was supposed to do. Every day after work he went home to shower, then returned to his truck to go visit his son. He and Glenn had agreed he should be gone by seven thirty to give the boy plenty of time to settle himself down and get ready for bed. Each night he dragged himself away, told himself it was for the best, and drove home into the oblivion of himself that would fill the next ten hours. One Saturday he took Jamey to the alligator park, where they ate fried gator dogs and watched the primordial reptiles do tricks, devour chicken carcasses, slither across the top of the water in conjunction with one another, all seeming aware of their exact places in the world of beasts.

Yet, when he was at work, he wanted to be anywhere else. He and Otis spent a week thinning a tract at the south end of the parish, then James sent the two of them back to the site they had burned before to prepare the ground for replanting. Not only did the place remind him of Sheriff Norm's phone call that day, when he shared the sad news about Brenda, but each time he drove the truck past what he knew was under that pile of ash and debris, his vision tunneled. All he could do was look straight ahead and hope Otis didn't notice. Or that his stupid hound didn't go off digging.

Fortunately for Tommy, Otis was as clueless as ever. He

snored loudly with his head against the window as they drove to the site. Tommy had to elbow him awake when they got to his mama's house. He woke up with a grin, ran out of the truck and into her arms. One day she handed him a backpack in addition to his lunch box.

"I cleaned him up real good for you, baby." She waved at Tommy, smiled at him with her gums.

"Thank you, Mama."

"Now I want you to make sure you tell Tommy all about him."

"Yes, ma'am."

"And give him a cookie too."

"I always do."

She kissed Otis on the cheek and swatted him on the fanny as he turned back to the truck. She picked up her broom and began sweeping the yard. "Do it right, Otis. You know I'm gon' check up on you."

Otis got back into the truck as Tommy started it and began to back across the hard-packed red clay of his mama's front yard. Otis rolled down the window.

"Mama?"

She stopped sweeping. "Yes, Otis?"

A devilish grin spread across his face. "Just call me Otis Bob, just one time. Now step on it, Tommy!"

Otis belted himself into place, then opened his Spider-Man lunch box as Tommy pulled the truck back onto the road. He shuffled aside his sandwich to find a small baby bottle among the items, and set it between his legs. Then he zipped open the backpack to reveal a pale-brown plastic baby, all swaddled in a blanket.

"Oh, there you are, little baby Jesus." Otis spoke breathily to the baby, as if the sight itself were awesome. He shoved the little plastic bottle into its mouth.

"Just look at him, Tommy." He held his hand behind the

doll's neck, as one would a real child. "Isn't baby Jesus the most beautiful baby in the world?"

Tommy began to speak but decided just to look at him.

"I mean, Tommy. Do you ever stop to think about it? Sometimes I can't believe Jesus died for my sins." Otis looked at the baby dreamily, as if absolutely amazed at the sight. Tommy was oddly touched by the strange display. Otis picked up the baby and showed it to Tommy.

"I can't believe He died for an ol' country boy like me."

"It is unbelievable."

"Yeah, I'm just an old chunk of coal, baby Jesus."

"That's right."

"But you're gonna shine ol' Otis Bob up real good one day!" Otis picked up the baby then and held it over his shoulder, as if its little hands were scrubbing his back.

"Shine me up, baby Jesus! Shine me up!"

Otis returned the baby to his lap. "You believe in Jesus, don't you, Tommy?"

"You know I do, Otis. I wouldn't be anywhere without Him."

"See there! Even ol' Tommy believes in you!" Otis grinned a dastardly grin at the baby then, grabbed its little chin and began to ooh and ahh. He reached behind the plastic head and twisted it side to side, grinning wildly all the while.

"You don't believe those two old biddies on *The Waltons* were sisters either, do you, baby Jesus?" The plastic head moved side to side.

"No, you don't! No, you don't!"

Jamey was tired that afternoon when Tommy stopped to see him after work. He said he had been working hard in school, and that every night he kept waking up from bad dreams. His hair, normally oily, seemed dry. His eyes drooped. He pepped up when Tommy asked him about going to the gym with Glenn.

Glenn invited Tommy to stay for dinner, made chicken and rice for the three of them. Jamey and Tommy sat at the bar in Glenn's kitchen, Jamey suddenly eager to share weight-lifting stories with his father. He demonstrated the exercises he had been doing with Glenn, and kept asking Glenn to look up from his cooking to make sure he was doing it all right. He went to a closet, found a broom. He returned to the living room where his father waited, lay down on the floor, and proceeded to lift the broom over his chest again and again as both men watched.

"That's called a bench press, Daddy." Tommy glowed. "I use weights on mine the size of little plates. But when Mr. Glenn does it, he uses *huge* weights that look like train wheels." Tommy and Glenn laughed, together, at this description.

"Mr. Glenn says I might be stronger than he is, when I grow up."

Tommy tousled his son's hair. "I bet you will, buddy. Sounds like Mr. Glenn is taking really good care of you." He choked back a sudden rush of tears.

"Do you want to feel my muscle?" Tommy squeezed his son's hardened arm.

"Ooh! Wow! It's so big!!" Jamey showed more gap than tooth when he smiled.

They ate, and Jamey helped Tommy with the dishes while Glenn left the room to make a call. When he returned, he asked Jamey about his homework.

Tommy moved toward the door, not because he wanted to, or because he didn't think he could help with the homework. If he learned one thing in prison, it was that he wasn't in charge. He kissed Jamey on the head, thanked Glenn for the dinner.

"Good night, buddy. I'm gonna go home."

Jamey looked up at him with the sweetest eyes, held his arms out to be picked up.

"Good night, Daddy. I hope you can come back tomorrow."

CHAPTER 20

Back at home, Tommy looked for something to eat. Glenn's healthy meal was delicious, but the way he ate, it was no wonder Glenn still had a flat stomach. Tommy moved some things aside in his refrigerator. His spirit jumped when he discovered a plate of ravioli that one of the ladies from his morning meeting had brought him. He heated it in the microwave and took it to the sofa to watch television and get his mind off things. But everything was boring pap. All he could think about was the next day, when he would see his son again. Everything else was as empty as a shed snake skin.

The phone rang. He didn't want to answer; the number was blocked, and he wasn't in the mood for a surprise. It was probably just some sales call, or someone else from the program who wanted to reach out when he needed some help, yet kept his own number a secret so no one would do the same thing to him. Tommy answered. Rule number one of Tommy's new life: *Deal with things.*

"I know you're lying."

At first he thought it was Uncle Vance. A sudden flash of the man in his short-billed engineer's cap, his Texan face a road map of fine lines and wrinkles, appeared in Tommy's head. But Uncle Vance was dead, and he hadn't seen or spoken to him since Tommy was ten years old. Still, the man on the other end of the line had the same stuffy, screw-you tone Tommy remembered of his uncle.

"Hello?"

"Matt didn't stay in his hotel room that night. You were the last person he saw. We've already established that. I know there's something you're not telling me."

Tommy straightened himself, muted the television. "I told you, Mr. Bianchi. He was here." His forehead burst into a pool of sweat. "That's all I can tell you." *Or you'll kill me.*

Bianchi was silent, simply breathed into the phone. After a minute Tommy asked if he was still there. Bianchi didn't answer, continued breathing loudly, his breath a death rasp. The hair on Tommy's neck stood up. The dread of what he knew was next settled into the heart of him. He was grateful Bianchi wasn't there to see him sweat, couldn't open him up and see the lines of grief and fear cast in webs through his insides.

Bianchi's tone softened. He had long known how to get what he wanted. If Turner wouldn't give anything up out of fear, maybe something could trip him up.

"Can you give me any more details?"

"Sure, Mr. Bianchi. What would you like to know?"

Bianchi measured his words. "Anything. Anything you know. How did he smell, what was he wearing?"

Tommy exhaled loudly. "He had some sort of cologne. I've smelled it before; I don't know the name of it. He was wearing jeans and a dark-blue T-shirt, a nice shirt, not a work-type shirt, you know? Not something I would wear to work. And he had a windbreaker on. Which surprised me, because it was warm that night."

"Did he say anything about where he had been? Where he was going?" Bianchi had asked these same questions before, and only asked again to see if Tommy would give different answers.

"No, sir, I'm sorry, he didn't. He just stayed a few minutes. He wanted to know when I was going to pay off all my debt."

"And that's all you remember."

"Yes, sir. I told him I've been working, saving my money. I told him I could start making payments, on top of the points. To get it paid off. He said he only wanted the points. Until I had enough to pay it all off at once."

Bianchi had a tremble in his voice, a momentary hesitation when he spoke.

"Mr. Turner."

"Sir."

"Does my memory serve me correctly? Didn't you learn to gamble with your father?"

"Yes, I did, Mr. Bianchi. My father used to take me with him for weekends at your house."

"So you were brought up to this world. You understand the meaning of risk."

"Well, sir, if you mean cards, then sure. I guess my father didn't think he had anything better to give me. That's all he had for me."

"So your father forced you into this world."

"Well, no, sir, I chose it for myself. I could have gone a different way. He led me there, sure. But I stepped across the threshold myself."

"And I understand you have a son."

"Yes, sir, I have a son. He's six." Tommy's eyes widened, blinked nervously; his breath wheezed shallow with panic.

"And do you know where he is?"

"Sure I do, Mr. Bianchi. What are you asking me?"

"Only that it must be a great comfort knowing where your child is. Knowing that he's safe, cared for."

"It is, of course it is, Mr. Bianchi. What . . . what . . . I'm sorry I can't help you any more with Matt. He seemed like a nice man, that's all I can say. I didn't want him to come here, but I know he was just doing his job. I'm sorry you can't find him."

"And what is your son like, Tommy? My condolences on the loss of his mother."

Tommy completely stiffened.

"How do you know about my son?"

"I know everything about you, Tommy."

"Mr. Bianchi, look. I can't tell you how much I wish I could help you . . . I wanted you to know . . . I've been going to church. I've been praying you'd find your son."

"And if your son were lost, you'd do anything to find him, wouldn't you, Tommy?"

"Of course I would, Mr. Bianchi." Tommy's voice was an octave higher. "My son isn't lost. He's staying with a friend."

"Because your son is a part of you, isn't he, Tommy? Yet you brought him into this world that you and I both know. You chose this route for him, much as your father chose it for you. Didn't you, Tommy?"

"No, sir. No, sir, Mr. Bianchi. I chose this route for myself. I've made mistakes in my life. Many mistakes. But I keep my son away."

"It doesn't work that way, Tommy. Your son is a part of you. Wherever you go, he goes."

"Mr. Bianchi, all due respect, sir, but I have to work early in the morning. I am going to get your money together very soon. I promise. If you'll excuse me, I need to get some sleep."

"My money?" Bianchi shouted, and began to cough, struggled to catch his breath. He reached for his pocket and pulled out a napkin, expelled a thin stream of blood into it.

"I don't even know how much you owe me, Tommy. Matt's not here to let me know. You're not going to be through paying me until I find my son."

"Mr. Bianchi . . ."

Bianchi intended to shout, but spat blood into his napkin again and felt himself calm.

"There's something you could do for me, Tommy." Bianchi's heart began to race and he thought he would pass out.

"What is it?"

"Make sure you enjoy your son, while you still have him. I wish I'd enjoyed mine more. They grow up so fast."

"I absolutely will, Mr. Bianchi. You don't sound good. Are you okay?"

"I'm fine, Tommy. I feel fine. But make sure you do that."

"I definitely will, Mr. Bianchi."

"Because before you know it, he'll be gone."

CHAPTER 21

Tommy switched off the television, sat back down in his chair, and looked around the room at the bare white walls of his house, as if unsure where he was. The silence around him was like a scream, built to a crescendo. His ears ached from it. *God, where is Brenda?* She would know just what to do. He saw Matt Bianchi's face on the wall, the deadness in those eyes, on the ceiling, reflected in the television; he clawed at his own eyes as if he could pull them from his face.

He drove straight to Glenn's, sat fully erect. Every car on the road looked unfamiliar until they got close and, invariably, the drivers waved. A Suburban approached from behind, way too close for Tommy's comfort; finally he pulled to the side and it whizzed past, its darkened windows revealing nothing of the occupants inside. He looked both in front and behind, making sure no one else was on the road before he turned off the highway down the dirt road leading to his destination.

A little light was left in the sky. Jamey's face lit up as his father approached. Jamey waved at him from the front yard of Mamaw's house, where the boy squatted under a tree patting her dying old dog. Tommy had only been gone an hour, yet he felt as if he had arrived on an altogether different day, the water of yesterday's river long downstream on its unending path to the Gulf. Glenn sat on his front porch holding a football. He took the steps down into his yard, tossed the football up, caught it, tossed it up again.

Tommy didn't look Glenn in the eye when he got out of the truck. Jamey ran through the yard, said "hey, Daddy" as he passed, then shouted to Glenn with his hands up.

"Long pass!" Glenn tossed Jamey the ball and Jamey caught it. Tommy slammed his door. Fireflies had begun to glow and their orange, crepuscular lights shone randomly in the air all around. Crickets rioted in a deafening chirp, so loud Tommy couldn't hear what Glenn said to him at first. He wondered if he should wait to be invited, but reconsidered and turned toward his son, hands out for the ball.

"I know I should be getting him settled, it's too late for this. But the cool air was so nice. It's so pretty tonight." Tommy only nodded, joined the game with no further comment.

Jamey threw his father the ball, then approached and hugged him from behind as Tommy stood looking at Glenn through the muted light. He felt a bath of relief just seeing his son, which grew when he thought he could make out a look of serenity on Glenn's face, or if not serenity, at least something other than annoyance at his return. The evening was cool, and Tommy felt the freshening breeze on his face and arms, a notable distinction from the cloistered feeling in his chest. Glenn finally emitted a sliver of a smile and put his hands up for the football. He wore a glowing white tank top, and in the dimming light his arms were absolutely huge.

"Mr. Glenn was showing me how to play football," Jamey said. He put his hands up again to catch a pass. "Maybe I'll grow up and be as fast as Grandpa Charlie."

Tommy pretended to try to tackle him, didn't resist when the boy began to squirm away. He was grateful for the breeze and the twilight, which dried the tears bursting from his face and disguised his feelings entirely. Jamey got away and rushed toward the oak tree. Rascal forced himself up to bark before collapsing back into his bed between the surface roots.

"Touchdown!" Jamey slammed the ball into the ground, then picked it up and brought it back.

"You'll be even faster than Grandpa Charlie if you keep lifting those weights and exercising." Jamey ran and jumped into his arms, raised both of his own in victory.

"Touchdown!"

Glenn approached, patted the boy on the back. "Just a few more minutes, Jamey." He took the ball again and tossed it straight up. Jamey snatched it from the air, still suspended in his father's arms.

"Hey, Tommy. You just out for a ride? What brings you back?"

Tommy held himself together. He let out a long breath. Glenn's eyes widened when he finally saw the look on Tommy's face.

"Actually, I just wanted to talk to you a minute. I wouldn't have come back if I thought it could wait."

"Okay. Well, let's get Jamey settled, he's already done his homework. Let's get him ready for bed and we can talk a bit. You don't look yourself. Even in this light I can see that."

"It's . . . that's a good idea. I appreciate you inviting me in."

Glenn reached one hand to Tommy's shoulder. At that, everything inside Tommy began to pour out. Glenn noticed, quickly reached, and took Jamey from his father's arms.

"Let's get inside, Tommy. I've got a fresh pitcher of tea if you'd like some."

"I'd be grateful for it. Thank you."

Jamey caught a firefly as they walked, then let it go. It winked its tail in appreciation. They went inside.

"Can we play Sorry?" Jamey eyed his pile of board games on a shelf in the kitchen.

"No, you need to get settled down, honey." Glenn didn't wait for Tommy to answer. "After you get your jammies on, you can have some tea with us and then watch a little TV. Just fifteen minutes or so." Jamey sauntered off to his bedroom.

Glenn took down three glasses from the cabinet, then put them back and took down two others. He tried to figure as he stalled. *Here we go again.* He knew that Tommy Turner had had a rough life, certainly tougher than his own. He had put up no resistance when Glenn asked for the temporary custody order, as if he had suggested the thing himself. He hadn't even balked when Glenn suggested it could be permanent. *Now he wants something. Glenn, stop it.* Glenn saw people like Tommy in his work every single day, living through one little hell or another, jumping from one crisis to the next. Utterly incapable of seeing beyond their next meal, cigarette, drink. All of it seeming to go back to something that happened years before. Genes. Maybe it was in the genes. *Maybe he can't possibly get things right.*

But he had to admit. The guy was trying. More than most.

Tommy was totally silent as Glenn put ice in the glasses, poured tea from a steaming pitcher, and slid Tommy one across the counter.

"There's sugar in that bowl. I don't put any in the tea. And Mamaw brought some cookies over if you'd like one. She knows I don't eat things like that, and I don't want Jamey to eat them all." He handed Tommy the plate.

"Can I have one?" Jamey reentered the room. Tommy stirred sugar into his tea, then put a little in his son's glass and stirred it in too.

"One small one, Jamey. And not too much sugar, right?"

"Yes, sir." Jamey picked out a cookie.

"Jamey's learning that too much sugar is bad for you, right, Jamey?"

"It makes you fat and rots your teeth out so they all fall

out. Then you have to smile like this." Jamey folded his lips over his teeth, contorting his face into a bright-eyed rictus.

"Mr. Glenn has good advice, buddy. Too much of just about anything is bad for you." Tommy reached for a cookie himself. He had always had a wicked sweet tooth.

"Except cookies."

Glenn drank his own tea, without sugar. "Beautiful day today, wasn't it, fellows?" Tommy and Jamey both nodded yes as they ate their cookies. Glenn was floored by the resemblance between the two.

"Jamey, you've finished all your homework, right?"

"Yes, sir. I only had one page tonight. Can we still do my spelling words in the morning?"

"Sure we can. Your dad and I need to talk. You can go watch some TV if you want to."

"But I want to stay and talk to y'all."

"We'll talk before I go, okay, buddy? Mr. Glenn and I need to have a grown-up talk."

"All right." Jamey stood from his chair, slumped his shoulders. He checked the clock. Suddenly he pepped up. "Eight o'clock!" he shouted. "*SpongeBob* is on!" He disappeared into the other room. In a minute the sound of the cartoon carried into the kitchen.

Glenn began to empty his dishwasher, not sure how to proceed. He felt Tommy's hot eyes on the back of his neck.

"So, Tommy. Everything going okay?"

Tommy drank his tea, stared down at the counter. He began to rub a hand on the surface, over and over again, as his face grew redder and redder. Glenn sat too, and lowered himself to look into Tommy's face.

"Tommy? You got something on your mind?" Tommy didn't answer. Then their eyes met, and Tommy just began to talk.

"I've got a giant problem, Glenn." Tommy buried his face in his hands, began sobbing now in earnest. Glenn stepped back, surveyed his guest. He had been about to ask Tommy how much money he needed, and was exceedingly glad he hadn't. Hesitantly he walked to Tommy's side and touched him. Tommy sat perfectly still.

"I've got a giant problem," he said again.

"Maybe there's some way I can help you. You can talk to me, Tommy." Glenn heard his tone soften, felt something he thought had been lost to him a long time ago.

Tommy sat like this for a while, then reached for a paper napkin and dried his face with it. He took a long drink of his tea, then swallowed several breaths to compose himself. But when he started to speak again, he quickly ran out the front door and vomited on the dusty ground.

Glenn drew a glass of water from the tap and followed. He found Tommy on the porch, sitting on the steps and rubbing his shaved head over and over.

The night was dark then, and the cool evening breeze had picked up; only a few fireflies remained at the edge of the darkness. The outdoor air seemed to have calmed him, and Tommy no longer cried. When he spoke again his voice was lower, exhausted, resonant with the dregs of anxiety. Glenn handed him the water. He took it without a word, drank.

"Remember how I wasn't supposed to gamble?"

"I've never heard the exact terms of your parole, no. But that makes sense to me. I've had a lot of clients over the years on parole. Terms like that are often part of the deal."

"Well, overall, I've done okay. I've taken care of things. All in all, I've done what I was supposed to do." At that Tommy started to cry again, pulled himself together quickly. "*Dammit*, I've done a pretty good job."

"It looks that way from where I sit. You go to work every

day, stay out of trouble. You've been great about your time with Jamey. Even before . . . we lost Brenda."

"I have. I've tried so hard."

"Really, Tommy, I'm proud of you."

"You don't have to say that, Glenn." His voice was sludgy, exhausted.

"I mean it, Tommy. Honestly, you've done a lot better than I thought you would."

"I have a big problem, Glenn. I didn't want to bring you into it . . . but I don't have any choice now."

"Tommy?"

"I had some debts when I went in. Since I've been out, I've been paying on them. I don't like it, because I have to keep dealing with these people . . . but it's what I have to do."

"So you still have debts? How much?"

Tommy told him then about the payments, how he had sold his Mustang, most of his guns, which he wasn't supposed to have anyway, and his baseball card collection, to stay on top of things. "The guy that was collecting from me, he knew who I was, and knew he had me. So he pushed me further and further."

"So where are you with it?"

With Glenn's question they came to the moment, and Tommy seemed to consider the six-year-old boy in the other room, then continued.

"I was dealing with a guy named Matt; he had me making my payments into a bank account, but I had never met him. I had only dealt with him on the phone. I just wanted to get them paid off and get on with my life."

"Did you have a loan contract? Were all the terms laid out?"

"The terms were, make your payments or we talk to your parole officer. And maybe, we pull out your fingernails."

"I guess that was a stupid question."

"The night before Brenda died, there was a knock at my door and it was this guy. Matt. He came in, tried to play tough guy, where's my money, et cetera. This was Matt *Bianchi.* The big boss's son."

"What exactly did he want? You said you were doing everything by the book."

"That's just it, Glenn. I don't know why he came by. He was high on something. Talking crazy."

Tommy sobbed once now, then caught himself and spoke again, his voice even more subdued.

"Glenn?"

"I'm listening."

"Are you sure you want to hear this?"

"I'm glad to listen, Tommy. I feel terrible for you. Obviously this weighs heavily on you."

Tommy was silent for half a minute, slowly pounded with a fist on one knee.

"Glenn?"

"Yes?"

"You're grateful for me, right, Glenn?"

"What do you mean? Of course I am."

"I've done some good things in my life, haven't I?"

"Well, you saved my life, Tommy. And then Jamey . . ."

"He pulled a gun on me, Glenn."

"Oh no. Oh, Tommy."

"Glenn, I don't even know how it happened. I just freaked. I went for it, we struggled. He intended to *kill* me, Glenn. He had every intention of killing me. I could see it in his eyes."

"Oh no." Glenn felt things sinking, the earlier scheme he had considered dissolving completely.

"I only hit him once. It wasn't even that hard . . ."

"Oh my god, Tommy. Are you telling me . . ."

"He just wouldn't get up."

"Don't say anything else. Don't say anything else. Let me think."

"He pointed that gun at my face, Glenn." Now, the dam was burst. Again, Tommy cried. As if on some instinct of timing, Jamey opened the door to the porch.

"What's the matter, Daddy?" Tommy quickly wiped his face. Glenn wondered what he should do. *Should I call the cops? Did he just tell me what I think he did? Do I need to get Jamey away from him?*

Tommy pulled his son onto his lap. "Daddy's okay, buddy. I was just telling Mr. Glenn about how much I miss Mommy. That's all."

"I miss her too, Daddy." Jamey snuggled into his father's neck.

"Mr. Glenn and I need to talk some more, okay? I'll come put you to bed before I go, okay?"

"Okay." Jamey went back to the television.

"Look, Tommy. I have some questions for you. Please just answer the questions and don't say anything else. This is the best way for me to help you.

"I don't want to know what happened after you hit him. But my god, Tommy. It must have been awful." Glenn was surprised how much sympathy he felt for the man.

"Why didn't you go to the police?"

"Glenn? Prison? Carlo Bianchi?"

"You have to go to the police, Tommy. You have to."

"They'll never believe me. And you know it."

"You have to. It was an accident."

"These are bad people, Glenn. Matt's family. There's no way I could have gone to the police *before* what I did. Much less now."

Glenn sat down heavily then, blew out all his breath. He'd seen plenty of screwups in his life, people who would never get it together, whose teenage mistakes led to young adult mistakes, then middle-aged mistakes and, finally, elderly ones. He hated that he felt that way about Tommy, the man who had once saved his life. At the same time, he felt a sympathy long lacking in his work. Living with Jamey was part of it. All of that goodness came from somewhere. And not all of it came from Brenda.

"I don't want to know any more about that, Tommy. Please. I *can't*. It's best."

"I agree. That's all I'll say."

"But you've been dealing with this alone."

Tommy only nodded.

"So what now?"

"I wish I could just move on with my life. But there's another problem. Even bigger."

"I'm listening."

"His father. Carlo Bianchi. He's been calling me. He knows Matt came to my house that night."

"Oh my god! You told him that?"

"Carlo came to my house. He asked me. I told him Matt had been there. He already seemed to know it."

"But you didn't tell him more."

"I told him I wished I could help him find his son. That's all."

"And we're talking about the guy on the news. *Reputed* New Orleans mafia boss Carlo Bianchi."

"Him."

"Oh shit." Glenn's next thoughts were random—did he remember to turn off his computer before he left the office, was it time for an oil change in his car, what was Louise doing right then, and what would she think if she could hear this conversation?

"Tell him I'll pay the money." Glenn surprised himself when he said it; he hadn't even been thinking those words, not consciously anyway. But, there it was. He wouldn't back off; he looked straight into Tommy.

Tommy stopped, drank more water, waited. He seemed to want to object, yet at the same time was too exhausted to do so. He watched as a bat swooped down into the yard as the distant barks of nameless dogs echoed in the recesses of the night.

"That's not why I came here, Glenn."

"I know it isn't. It's just an idea I had. I could help you. Maybe it would get him out of your life."

"I would repay you every dime. I'm paying them. Or trying to. I would pay everything back with interest."

"I don't want the money. I don't need the money. I just want you to keep Jamey in my life. That's all. You didn't deserve this, not if everything you say is true. Tommy, you've got a lot on your mind. It's been a struggle to get yourself well enough to be a father."

"Yes, it has."

Both men turned toward a sound that came from the yard, from the darkness beyond the ring of light made by Glenn's porch lamp. A shuffling, scratching sound, uneven footsteps. Into the ring of light stepped Rascal. He moved slowly, pivoted over his stiffened front leg as he went, then fell hard on the other as if pole vaulting on every step.

"Hey, Rascal, what are you doing?" The dog stood panting in shadow, stared at them with bright-red eyes. "I haven't seen you so far from home in a while." Then Rascal barked once, turned, and moved back into the darkness, making the same sounds as he went.

"Glenn, look. I know I'm a screwup, all right? I admit it. I take responsibility for all of this." He gestured with his hands, as if to encompass everything around. "I wish I could change things. I do. All I can do is what I'm doing. I've been working.

I'm sober every day for two years now. This is what I can do. But all this I'm telling you, this is why I haven't been able to take care of Jamey. And I can't tell you how much I appreciate your help with that."

"You're doing great, Tommy. You are."

At that, Tommy stood. Glenn knew he wouldn't talk about it anymore tonight.

"There's something else."

"Okay."

"Bianchi called me earlier and said something really strange. Something that made me nervous. That's why I came back."

"What?"

"He was asking about Jamey. Asking what my son was like. He's not well to start with, I can tell. He's desperate, his son is missing."

"Oh shit."

"All the things people say about him, mostly that's just talk. Reputation. But on the other hand I don't know what he's capable of."

"Look, Tommy, he just wants his money. He can't connect you with anything. Let's get him his money, then maybe he'll leave you alone."

"I'll think about it for a couple days."

"Good idea."

"I just freaked when he was asking about Jamey. That's why I came back."

"I'm glad you did. You're welcome anytime."

"Glenn?"

"Yes?"

"This is between us, right? What I told you?"

"You didn't tell me anything."

Tommy nodded his understanding, looked out into the darkness. "We should get Jamey to bed."

Glenn agreed. They both went inside. Jamey lay on the sofa with the television blaring, slumped to one side diagonally across a large, fat pillow. Glenn turned the TV off and began to step forward to pick the boy up. Quickly he thought better of it, backed off.

"You get him. I'll get his bed ready." Tommy moved in, lifted the little boy with perfectly smooth skin into his hands, pressed the bobbing head into his own chest. Glenn turned off the light in the den as he exited the room after Tommy. He scooted around, clicked on a lamp by Jamey's bed and pulled back the cover, then quickly moved toward the two of them, reaching out his hands.

"His head, Tommy. Hold his head up." Tommy grabbed the boy's lolling head, and laid his son down gently. He and Glenn turned to leave the room. Then the two men pivoted, moved back toward the bed. With silent understanding Tommy went first, and then Glenn, as each in turn bent down to kiss the little sleeping beauty on his cheek.

CHAPTER 22

Glenn went home quickly at lunch and put a low heat on the gumbo he had started after putting Jamey to bed the previous night. Outside, the temperature rose all afternoon as Glenn sat in his office back at work, lulled by the low-grade roar of the paper mill half a mile away as gathering clouds buffeted about the darkening sky. Tommy called at three o'clock to let Glenn know he was leaving work early and wanted to pick Jamey up from school and take him to the zoo in Monroe for the evening, and that he would drop his son at the bus in the morning after Jamey spent the night at Tommy's place. Glenn didn't argue, but simply went along with the plan and thanked Tommy for calling.

"Looks like we'll be alone for the evening." Louise stood in the door of his office as he hung up the phone. She told him she'd been out surveying a space for another sewing center she planned to set up, and couldn't wait to drink some wine and relax with him after work. "You sure you can't skip your work-out today? Just get straight to it?"

Glenn stood as a thundercloud cracked overhead, rattling the windows. "Don't encourage me toward bad habits, honey," he told her, tousling her hair as he passed. "See you about six thirty?"

"I guess I could do a little more work. I'll pick up a few things and see you then."

Glenn was soaked by the time he got to his car, and got

soaked again going into the gym. He hit the weights hard, groaning loudly each time he pushed out an extra rep, blood pumping through him so viciously his head throbbed. He missed having Jamey there with him, but on the other hand felt himself relax at the thought of a night without responsibility.

The evening rain had slowed to a steady sprinkle by the time Louise arrived at his house. Glenn sat on his swing, listening to the patter of thousands of fingers at once on the veranda roof. Though darkness was still two hours away, the heavy clouds had brought on evening early, and her headlights cut through the thickened air as she came around the curve and splashed through puddles in the road. Rascal barked once, from his bed on Mamaw's porch, as she passed. Apparently the weary dog still had the sense to get out of the rain. The rain brought with it a coolness, a tickler of a breeze that boiled the smells of heat and decay from the humid ground.

Glenn watched Louise from the porch as his gumbo simmered on the stove. He figured she didn't see him as she shut off her car, then twisted the rearview mirror in her direction, applied more lipstick, ran fingers across her eyelids, and adjusted the bandanna she had tied on her head. She finally caught sight of him sitting in the shadows when she stood from her car, and to her credit she didn't insult herself for her primping, but simply smiled.

"Hello, Glenn."

The rain had fully stopped then, the suffusing after-drips crackling on dried brown leaves scattered about the hard-packed clay underneath his mammoth live oak tree. Pockets of steam began to rise. She moved through the purplish haze with a paper bag of groceries under one arm, the muted-blue bandanna bringing out the soft color of her eyes as if in a scene from some romantic movie. She was the picture of happiness then, willowy light dampening her otherwise angular features, as she approached his porch with her bag of vegetables. *Mother used to look that happy,* he thought. *She loved her bandannas too.*

"Hey, Louise. You look beautiful."

"Oh, Glenn. Listen to you." She stepped onto the porch, leaned on the railing, set the bag down beside her. A glistening sheen of sweat coated her upper chest, and Glenn noticed for the first time how muscular she was. Inside the bag were cucumbers, a head of broccoli. He admired the way the bag stood open, not like these shiftless plastic pieces of junk all the stores sent you home with anymore. Light streaming from the open door highlighted the warm, creamy color of the bag against the darkened greens of grass and shrubs in his yard. The image was positively lovely in the clean, supercharged air of the evening. For the moment, Glenn thought, things were as they should be.

Inside, he put on a CD and they listened to Chopin nocturnes, piano solos that fit the mood of the graying evening. Outside, the rain began to fall again in earnest. Glenn repeatedly lifted the lid of the pot of gumbo, stirred in more Tabasco or Worcestershire as he bathed his face in the heat rising from the melding concoction. Louise sliced two cucumbers, arranged them on a plate with a pinch of dill, then proceeded to cut up broccoli and set it in the steamer.

"Are you sure that gumbo's spicy enough?" She lifted the lid and smelled. "I like it spicy. And maybe just a touch more rosemary.

"Try this." She sprinkled black pepper on a cucumber slice, held it up to him. Glenn ate it right from her hand, nodded his approval. Then she turned and added a quarter cup of water to the cooking broccoli as a bath of steam rose in a cloud.

"Gary taught me this method. Blast the florets with steam three different times as they cook. They stay firm and all the nutrients stay in."

"I look forward to eating it. There are few things in life better than fresh, crisp vegetables."

"Very few," she answered. "Glenn Rosen. Is that bread I smell?"

Glenn went to the oven then, removed a pan of cornbread muffins. He tested one with a toothpick, placed the pan on a mitt he had set on the countertop.

"Such decadence. We're having rice!"

Glenn pulled a top from one of the muffins, ate half and handed her the rest. "I know, I know. And bread is not good for my diet. But I love these cornbread muffins with my gumbo." He wondered what Tommy and Jamey were up to just then, and forgot it as quickly.

She tasted it, marveled. "I like it. Buttery, not too sweet."

"Everything has sugar in it now. I make these myself."

"This is phenomenal, Glenn. It smells like a bakery in here. And this gumbo! Do you buy the roux at Whole Foods?"

"Ohhh!" he gasped. "Do not make me spank your butt, Louise. What kind of a *knave* buys premade roux?"

"Um, gosh, I can't imagine who would do such a thing. When you could stand there and stir for forty-five minutes without stopping."

"It's worth it, believe me. Well worth it. Hey, I have an idea." He moved toward the front door. "It's cool enough now to leave this open. What do you think?"

"And leave off the air? Great idea. I hate air conditioning."

She joined him at the door. The two stood, looking out. Gumbo continued to meld on the stove, its parts slowly transforming into a whole. Glenn's one streetlight winked on at that moment. The rain came down in sheets. Rascal bayed at the streetlamp as the last few seconds of light in the sky faded to black.

Glenn simply couldn't remember the last time he was so full. The rain had slowed by then, and a cool spring breeze blew in through the heavy screen door with its fleur-de-lis pattern. He loosened his belt, pinched his stomach when his back was to Louise as he walked over and opened the screen to let in even more of the breeze. He told himself he was probably not as fat as he felt at the moment.

"Would you like a little more?" Louise poured herself more of the dry white wine, slipped a dash into his glass when he didn't answer.

"Just a splash. Why not."

"That's the right attitude, Glenn."

He returned to the table, lifted his glass, drank, yet never looked away from her. She demurred, cast her eyes down. Suddenly she was pensive.

"What? What is it?"

"Oh, nothing. You looked at me so . . . seriously." She took another sip from her glass.

"That was intentional. Because I have a question for you. A very, very *serious* question." Glenn was just tipsy enough, he couldn't stop his giddy smile from leaking out.

"Oh my. Should I have a lawyer present?"

"A lawyer can't help you at this point. Oh, no, no, no, no, no! For there are times, darling, we all must face the *ineluctable* truth on our own."

"Now you've got me worried. Using legal words."

"Oh, you should be worried. You should be very worried." He paused here for another sip of wine, then set the empty glass in front of her without a word. "Because if the answer to my question is yes, I would like to take something from you that you may not have intended to share with me." He grinned now, a wry smile.

"Now I'm positively scared."

Glenn took another drink from the glass she had refilled, then slapped his hand on the tabletop with a medium amount of force, to accent his point. "Louise Michelle Andrews. Did you, or did you not, bring two large peaches to my house tonight in the paper bag that previously contained broccoli and cucumbers?"

Louise was visibly relieved. Without breaking stride, she turned the tables, looked at him and squinted conspiratorially.

"Yes, I did, Mr. Rosen. I brought two nice, firm peaches for dessert. Round and *perfectly* ripe. Filled to bursting."

"Mmmm! Because I was thinking. My Mr. Louisiana contest isn't for another month. So I gain a couple pounds!! Water weight!! What's a few extra minutes on the treadmill, huh? Maybe I'll run and get us just a leeeeeetle carton of ice cream."

"Oh, I'm so glad you said that!" Louise made a big show as she stood, then sneaked into the kitchen and returned with just such a container.

"Ohhh! You demoness!" Glenn gasped ostentatiously. "How did you get that in here? You jezebel! You veritable whore of Babylon! Corrupting my hallowed home with wickedness!"

Louise looked at him, cockeyed now. "A girl has her ways, doesn't she? I put it in the freezer when you went in the bathroom."

"Well, what are we waiting for? I'm a forty-something-year-old man, I can't wait forever. Let me get my hands on those peaches."

Fingers of rain tapped again on the veranda roof as the two glided, almost imperceptibly, on Glenn's porch swing. The ice cream and peaches swirled in his mouth in a succulent burst of flavor, the taste so rich he swore he felt hives form on his arms. In the distance a crackle of lightning brightened the night sky in veins, momentarily showed the twisted shapes of trees and cars and everything around. Glenn thought he saw a car without lights passing by on the road, but it must have been his imagination.

"Glenn?"

"Mmm-hhh?" He licked the last bits of ice cream from his spoon, patted his stomach again.

"Thank you for inviting me over. I mean it."

"Of course, Louise. You know I love your company."

"I mean it, Glenn. I don't know another soul here in Branden. It means so much that I can connect with you." She playfully slapped his wrist. "And such a good cook!"

Was she moving closer?

"Well, honey, I've lived here my whole life. And believe me, you've been a real find for me too. I only have a few friends myself. And I'm sad to say I just lost one." He looked toward Brenda's house wistfully.

"Sounds like she was nice. I can tell you miss her."

"I do. I just hope I'm not making a mistake, taking in Jamey. I'm very attached to that boy. It will kill me if Tommy takes him away."

Now, she reached out to rub his arm. "You're a good man, Glenn. I know you're taking a risk. But you have to take it."

"You're right. Tommy's in no condition to be Jamey's only parent." Glenn shuddered then at what he knew, which he couldn't possibly share with her or anyone.

Louise sighed, began to rub Glenn's knee. "Gary never wanted to take any chances."

Glenn prepared to sigh himself, tired as he was of hearing about Gary. But the alcohol had taken off his edge, and he let the comment pass.

"He never wanted kids. I thought that would change, hoped it would." She sighed again. "But it never did. Eventually, he stopped finding me attractive. Which I guess I understand. I'm not the girl I used to be."

"Louise." He took her hand from his knee, squeezed it tight, pressed it to his lips. "You're a beautiful, wonderful woman."

"At least you know how to talk to a girl, Glenn. Ironic, I know. But unlike me, Gary just kept looking better." She turned to him. "He's not as big as you, but he works out a lot. He looks great, better than he did years ago."

Another bolt of lightning hit, charged the air around them. Louise went back into the house, returned with the bottle of wine and her glass. She poured it full and took a sip, offered the glass to Glenn. He suddenly felt fastidious and refused.

"I told him, we all age, Gary. Of course, things aren't like they used to be, are they?" She took another long sip. "For better or for worse, right? I told him, we can age together. It doesn't have to be all bad. Even if we don't have any kids. It's like he *wants* to end up a lonely old man or something. Are you tired of hearing about him?"

"Not tired, exactly. Annoyed, I guess. I just wish he were here so I could spank his ass." He stuck a finger in his ear, blocked out whatever she planned to say next, gave himself a moment to think.

She laughed despite herself, squeezed his knee again. "I'm seeing this picture of Gary bent over your knee. It's an awfully funny picture."

"Well, he deserves it, I tell you."

"In a way, he does. But anyway, thank you, Glenn. For listening."

"You're welcome. I'm glad if I can help you."

"I know he was with others. He wouldn't admit to it, but I know he was. For the last couple years. Something about him was just . . . *different*. Anyway, he's definitely with her now." She gulped the rest of her wine. "Probably got his hands on the bitch right now. That redheaded whore." She reached for the bottle and refilled her glass. "Probably got one of her surgically enhanced titties in his hand right now, squeezing it so hard it could pop!"

"Lou-ise! I'm sorry! I've never heard you talk that way."

"Pfff!" She drank again. "I do now. Anyway, que será, será."

"Sometimes, that's all you can say."

She stood then, went behind the swing, put her hands on his shoulders, and began to massage him.

"Oh, that feels nice. Thank you."

"You just seem so uptight lately."

"Too much exercise. I'm not as young as I used to be."

"Pfff! You and me both." She pushed his head to one side. "There, just relax. I'm good at this." Once again his mind filled with the most random imaginings—did he send in the papers he was supposed to complete that afternoon? Did he ever change that light bulb on the back porch? Will that fat raccoon come back tonight? A blooming of feelings spread across his chest.

She began to knead the areas on either side of his neck, in slow strokes at first, then deeper, more aggressively. He had expected to be annoyed by the massage when she started—few people had any real idea of the depth and complexity of muscle tissue, preferring the easy path of rubbing his skin until it itched—but he was pleasantly surprised.

She pounded on his trapezius muscles with the edges of her hands. "So uptight. Just relax."

"It feels great." He moved his head and neck in consort with her movements. "You're better than I expected you would be."

Now, she dug even deeper, moving out to the bony area on top of his shoulders, and down over the edge, to the rippling deltoids. "Oh, I'm good, all right. I know how to use these hands. The trick is to put your whole body into it." She hiccuped. "I'm a little tipsy too."

"Well, it feels great."

"You know what feels great, Glenn? You feel great. I appreciate you letting me touch you." She kneaded the triceps now, dug her thumbs into his massive biceps. Reflexively, he tightened his arms.

"Wow, Glenn. Are those your arms? They're as big as most men's legs."

He laughed. "You stop it. But don't stop what you're doing."

She pressed her palms across his back, slid them up and around, over the top of the shoulders and down his arms until she had to bend over to reach her hands all the way around him and into his. Then she slid her hands back up along his forearms until she came to rest on his shoulders again. She giggled and turned her face into the back of his neck.

"Look at me. I'm just making a fool of myself."

"No, you're not, Louise."

"It's just so nice to touch somebody. I trust you, Glenn. I know you won't hurt me or push me away."

"Don't stop. Do it again." His voice was suddenly high, reedy, nervous like a thirteen-year-old. He turned and looked over his shoulder at her, tried to speak again, but he couldn't.

"Do you like it?"

"I'm all alone here, now. Mother's gone." He still looked at her.

"Gary always talked about his mother. Often, at the worst possible times."

Suddenly he turned, mysteriously emboldened. He stood and tried to shove the swing to one side. It hit the brick wall and ricocheted back. He tried to move around it, but he couldn't get it out of the way. He reached over the top of the swing for her, his mind finally clear of random thoughts, flailed for one of her arms with his calloused hand.

"Don't say another word, Louise. Your husband is a baby. A coward and a fool." He was breathing hard now. "If he were here right now I would slap his ridiculous face. To let a woman like you get away." The swing was still in his way, and he let her go long enough to grab both chains and yank it from the ceiling, straightening the S-hooks holding it up, then set it gently on the floor, stepped over, and picked her up as if she were no larger than Jamey. She weighed less than the dumbbells he lifted in sets of ten on the flat bench.

Louise threw both her arms around his neck and pressed her face into the side of his. Glenn carried her into his room, his heart ringing in his ears. Then, suddenly, he was filled with a dreadful feeling, as if all the air had been let out of him, as if he were doing the worst kind of wrong. But he simply didn't slow down. "Mother's gone," he whispered, and carried her to his room. She must have wondered what he meant, but after a bottle and a half of wine, she probably couldn't think how to ask.

He sat himself on the edge of his bed, let her down so she stood on the floor between his legs. The two interlocked in an electric kiss that positively sparked when another lightning bolt illuminated his room for an instant. She was absolutely shaking. He reached up to push the wavy hair out of her face, felt the wetness of a tear on his thumb as his hand ran across her cheek.

"Here. Sit down." He tried to guide her onto a spot beside him, but she was resistant, didn't want to move from between his legs. She turned away shyly at first, then looked at him with a hopeful smile. The glow of the streetlight softened her face. Glenn pulled her down into his lap. "Are you okay with this?"

She didn't answer in words, instead began to kiss him deeply, only slowly this time, as if the fire inside her had been dampened to a slow, steady burn. "I want this, Glenn. Just be gentle, okay?"

"There's no hurry, sweetie. No hurry at all."

"Just be gentle. Okay?"

"I'll say the same to you, Louise. I've never been with a woman."

She took his hand, seeming hopeful again now. They kissed some more. Then she pulled his hand to her mouth, ran it down along her breasts, across the outer part of her thigh. He pulled it away from hers, and continued in this fashion on his own until she took his hand, again, and placed it on the top button of her shirt.

He eased her back onto the bed and she lay perfectly still, hands at her sides, as he worked, through his trembling, at the buttons of her blouse, then released the snap and the zipper of her jeans and slid them down over her ankles. She never once opened her eyes. When she was naked, Glenn stood and removed his own clothes, kissed her again, and lay down beside her.

He knew how it was done—he had certainly seen movies—and he told himself just to climb on top of her and start. Suddenly she opened her eyes and touched him there. Her hand was so strong. Then a billion thoughts came into him again, and his mind just raced.

He lay down beside her, unsure how to proceed, what to do. He went into the bathroom to gather his thoughts; when he returned Louise seemed more drunk than she had before and talked incoherently with both eyes closed, called him Gary, and suddenly fell asleep. Glenn stood naked looking down at her, apologized to the woman sleeping on his bed, and finally put his underwear back on, lay down beside her, and fell asleep himself.

Later, in the night, Glenn woke. He reached for her, but she wasn't in his bed. A light was on in the bathroom, and he began, again, to stiffen at the thought of her. He rolled over to see her standing in front of his mother's old vanity, a beautiful piece that he couldn't bear to let go, in front of which Darlene had spent ten thousand hours of her life. Louise was still naked, and stood looking at herself in the beveled mirror. In the finger of light trailing from the bathroom, Glenn could see she was smiling. She heard Glenn moving and turned toward him.

"Glenn. Did we . . . ?"

"No. We couldn't. I'm sorry. You fell asleep."

She sat down on the bed, reached a hand out to grip his shoulder.

"It's okay, Glenn. We really drank some wine, didn't we?"

"I guess we did."

"You're a good friend, Glenn. I really needed a good friend, and that's exactly what you are. You're a good friend."

"Louise."

"Glenn. Just listen. I don't blame you for this. I'm just as responsible for this happening as you are."

"We're just two good friends, being friends to each other, Louise."

"Yes, Glenn. That we are. And I know I have some things to work out."

"I appreciate your trusting me, Louise. To be your friend."

"I do, Glenn. But you're obviously working something out too. Tonight is the first time I thought about that. Have you thought about that, Glenn?"

"I'm not sure what you mean."

"I'm not some teenage girl who will get her heart broken, Glenn. I know you're gay. I didn't come over here expecting this to happen. We're obviously both confused about some things."

"But I like it, Louise. I like it. We can try again. I'm feeling better now."

Louise sighed. She turned her head and smiled at him, a beatific, teenaged smile, a smile so bright it seemed a light shone from behind her.

"If you're confused, Glenn, that's fine. Take me to bed, I'm yours. You're a specimen of a man. And I could use a good time. Seriously. It's been way too long."

Louise bent down then, grabbed his face. "You're a beautiful, remarkable man. Whatever your proclivities. Just don't make a fool of me."

"I won't. I'm sorry. I'm sorry."

Louise stood, began to dress. "I think I'm going to go."

"No, Louise. Stay. Please stay."

"I think I'm going to go. Thanks again for the wonderful dinner." She quickly finished dressing, then kissed him on the cheek on her way out the door. Glenn thought about getting up, but he knew she had made her mind up and couldn't be stopped. He lay back on his pillow and turned away from his window, watched the lights from Louise's car sweep across the wall as she drove away from their unexpected night.

CHAPTER 23

Bianchi got less than two minutes of peace and quiet after the girl was out the door, before he had to run and vomit into the sink. It was the first thing he noticed when she stormed out, before he bolted to the bathroom: how the room went from a chorus of expletives and shouting to total quiet, just like that. In fact, the quiet was better than her company anyway; he only wished he'd figured that out much earlier, so he could have had more than those two minutes of relative happiness before the unpredictable wave of nausea washed over him. He never knew when it was coming, but one thing he did know: it was coming.

He couldn't even remember her name. She'd spent the night a few times, and he'd found a handful of things he could talk about with her. He liked her more than most. She was probably thirty—she had a little maturity to her anyway, not like one of those shallow young girls who looked like they came straight from the hand of God but couldn't put five words together on anything other than hip-hop music, their body, or Facebook. Bianchi was a seventy-year-old man—what would he possibly want to know about Facebook?

Michelle. That was it. For a thousand, she'd spend the night, do whatever he asked, and tell him what he wanted to hear. He'd never really felt right about bringing the girls back here to his house, to their bed. Sure, he enjoyed the company of beautiful women from time to time when he still had his Marilyn. What man didn't? Or didn't want to, anyway. Their house was Marilyn's domain. But after a few years of marriage, when he was thinking about it all the time anyway, women all over the casino rubbing themselves against him like cats in heat, what was the difference between that and just indulging himself from time to time? If anything, it made his marriage better. He didn't want anything from these girls, and if they wanted anything from him, he didn't pay attention to what it was. He just did what he did from time to time, then went home to his wife every night and paid attention to her. And gave her whatever she wanted. Which, more and more, was his attention.

He knew it was back. He knew it the morning he woke up three weeks ago. He just had a feeling. The doctors told him at the time it would probably come back within ten years, and that was thirteen years ago. They'd called him three times now, leaving messages of varying lengths about how important it was that they talk, but he didn't plan to go back. He was done fighting. Some mornings, when his mind was still quiet, lying in the half light with nothing to guard him from all the deeds of his life, he wondered how many days he had left. Then he forgot about it. Only God knew the answer to that question. And He wasn't talking.

Since Marilyn had been gone, an hour or two with a woman just wasn't enough. He could keep himself busy enough at the casino all day, often convincing Matt to let the old man take him out to eat or for a cup of coffee before heading back to work to check on things in the evening. But eventually, he had to go home; they didn't really need him there at all, certainly not in the night when the place went hopping mad with tourists and drunks and all the high rollers chasing an elusive dream. It was those quiet hours after midnight, when it was way too late to get on the phone and talk to whichever of his friends were still around, when he just couldn't sleep, he'd never been able to sleep; it was in those quiet hours he was grateful for company.

Now he missed her. Now that he was awake, feeling better for the moment. Michelle. What did she know? It wasn't her fault he woke up in a bad mood. So she'd reached for Marilyn's cup to use for her coffee. He was the one who had invited her to stay and have some breakfast, who had made the pot of coffee, instead of her just leaving after their morning session as she normally did. She didn't know. On the shelf it looked just like any other coffee cup. She put it back, just like he had asked. Then she got another cup and made too much noise slurping her coffee. What was the big deal? She was just a girl who was taking his money to make him feel less lonely for a little while. So what if Marilyn never would have made a noise like that? Michelle was not his wife. Michelle was not the one who spent days at the hospital with him when he had the surgeries. Michelle was not the one who sat up all night holding his hand, who asked Matt to get a dozen balloons or make that "Get well soon—we love you" sign. She was just a girl who came to be with him so she wouldn't be lonely all night at her own house. And because she needed the money.

He figured he may as well drive in to work and see if anything was going on there. But today he just wasn't in the mood to smile and shake hands. A cattlemen's convention was in town, and he couldn't understand why, but those guys all seemed to know who he was and wanted their picture taken with him. Without those guys, and thousands more like them from all over the country, chasing impossible dreams, he wouldn't be able to live in this gated, secluded mansion, and he knew it. But today, he didn't care.

He checked his phone again for messages, slipped it back into the pocket of his robe, and went upstairs to the attic. It was hot up there already on that early morning, and before long he was sitting in a leather wing chair that Marilyn had been meaning to get re-covered, wearing nothing but his underwear.

He dialed Matt's number. He'd heard that same recording of his son's voice a dozen times a day for two weeks now, yet in all his anger, he didn't tire of it. This time he took a conciliatory tone when he left the message, begged his son to call him back. *No questions; just come home.* He finished and dialed again right away, this time shouting, demanding in a rage that Matt call back or face his father's wrath.

Finally, he set the phone to the side and began to look for what had taken him to the attic in the first place. There it was, in a large plastic box in the corner. He dug it out, opened it, and began to remove the clothes one at a time. He finally understood why Marilyn had made a point to keep a pair of pants and a shirt from every year of Matt's youth. First he took out the baby suit, this tattered sailor's suit Matt had loved so much when he was a baby, though he constantly pulled at the drawstrings in the pants and left them forever frayed. Bianchi took it to his nose, begged for just a drop of the smell of the baby, somewhere still embedded in the material.

He couldn't even remember what the other boys looked like when they were babies, much less point to anything they might have worn. Matt, though. Matt lived on Daddy's knee when he was small. Sure, Bianchi was well established by then, had a lot more flexibility with his time than he had with the other boys when they were small. Hours and hours he spent with Matt in his first year of life, feeding him, singing songs he had learned from his grandmother, straight from the old country. Mark and Daniel—he couldn't remember a day with either of them. No surprise, his three sons never spoke to each other. And now, Mark and Daniel didn't even know their brother was missing.

He went downstairs to his computer, typed the name of the newspaper into the search box, then wrote the number down, went upstairs to dress, and made himself comfortable in his living room before dialing. The receptionist asked who was calling, and he preferred not to say. She put him through after a long pause.

"Daniel Bianchi."

"Daniel?"

"Speaking. Who's calling?"

Another long pause. "It's me."

"Dad?"

"Yes. It's your father."

"Dad?"

"Yes, son. It's me."

Bianchi heard the sound of the phone being dropped, a staticky rattle as his son must have felt for it on the floor. "Dad, it's been, what, five years since we talked?"

"Has it?"

"I must be dreaming."

"Have you heard from your brother? Matt?"

Daniel didn't answer. The buzz Bianchi heard then grew louder and louder until all he could do was go straight to his car and drive.

Later, he couldn't even remember where he had been. He knew he had driven around all day, back and forth through the city, down every street he ever remembered driving, thinking maybe he was here, maybe he was there, just this one more turn, down where he fought those guys, to that little apartment building where the tall blonde one lived, the one Matt said once he hoped to marry. When he saw it was six o'clock, he pulled into the nearest parking spot and took out his phone. That was the time he had decided on, and Bianchi always stuck to his plan.

Bianchi held the phone to his ear, breathed with labor, waiting for the answer. He only had energy left for one emotion, and he didn't choose it. It chose him. "Yours was the last number he dialed. He didn't make another call after that."

"Mr. Bianchi, he never called me. He just showed up that night. Have you heard from him?"

"You know I haven't heard from him, Tommy. You know I haven't."

In his living room, Tommy quickly switched off the television. "Mr. Bianchi, take it easy. I'll pay you. I have all your money. All twenty-five thousand."

Bianchi snorted into the phone. "You'll pay me what and when I tell you to pay me, Tommy. I already know that. Or you don't want to know what will happen."

"I have your money right here, Mr. Bianchi. I have it right here."

"Maybe I'll drive up there and get my money, and I'll still take care of you. How would you like that?"

"I have it. I have every dime."

"And how much is that, Tommy? You could owe us a hundred thousand dollars, for all I know. Matt kept all that information. I have no way of knowing when you'll have us paid off."

Tommy began to sweat.

Bianchi felt that surge again, that wave that started in the middle and worked its way to both ends of his body. He flushed and felt a tightening in his scalp.

"You're not listening to me, Tommy. Do you think I care about that money? Where is my son, Tommy? Where is my son?"

"How can I get the money to you?"

Bianchi suddenly cooled, as if a rain cloud had floated over him, pulled him into it.

"You want to know how to get me the money? Here's how."

He laughed, once. "Get a package. Put all the money in. Then go down to the post office. Send the money to hell. That's where we're both going. Just send it to hell."

"Mr. Bianchi, please. You're scaring me. I mean it. I have your money."

"You know what? I just want to talk to you. Forget about the money. Just come to my house. When can you get to my house? I'd like to see you in person."

"Mr. Bianchi, no. I don't see how that would accomplish anything. Let me just pay you your money."

"Tell you what. I have a jobsite. Off Carrollton Avenue, just north of Saint Charles. Meet me there, eight o'clock tomorrow night. I have some questions for you. Meet me there."

"I have your money, Mr. Bianchi. Can't I bring it by in the daytime? To your office?"

Then Bianchi hung up the phone. For the moment, he felt okay. He drove down Canal Street, past the casino, but didn't park, just pulled his car to the side and looked for a while at the glitter and lights. Then he turned his car toward home. He thought maybe he'd make an early evening of it. A Clint Eastwood marathon was playing on TNT, and he couldn't remember the last time he just stayed home, turned off the lights, and sank into the same chair he'd been sitting in for the last twenty-five years. Bianchi went inside, settled himself into the spot, checked his messages again, and dialed Matt's number one last time.

CHAPTER 24

Miss Mabel and Bonita were whispering to each other when Glenn walked into the office in the morning. He was a half hour later than he normally came in, and they both eyed him as he passed, then turned back toward one another and laughed like little girls. Miss Mabel had a new style, her hair in ringlets and a foot longer than it had been the previous day. She wore a large ring in her nose—Glenn had asked her, more than once, not to wear that thing to work, but he headed straight to his desk with only a cursory "good morning."

The message light on his phone was blinking as he entered his office. *Louise.* His chest filled with an expanding feeling, and he caught his breath and sighed twice to try to get it out. He reached for the phone, drew his hand away, reached again, then moved around the desk, fell into his chair, and just stared at it, confused.

"Glenn?"

He looked up. Miss Mabel stood in his door.

"Yes, hi, good morning, Mabel. Miss Mabel."

"You and Lou-ise had a fight?" Her tone was inquisitive, nothing like the loud and boisterous tone in which she normally spoke.

He opened his mouth to tell her to mind her own business, then wondered if she knew something he didn't. *Maybe Louise told her something.* The expanding worm in his stomach continued to gnaw its way out. Mabel averted her eyes, as if feeling sorry for him, then grinned. Her nose ring reflected the light.

"Why do you ask?" Glenn felt foolish for saying it.

"'Cause I'm the first one here every morning, and today Louise just about bust the door down trying to get out when I'm comin' in. Carryin' a box with most of her stuff in her hands. I know she went to your house last night."

"Um, yes. She came for dinner last night. I don't know what you mean about a fight, though." *Shut up, Glenn. Just . . . shut up.*

"Glenn. Gleeeeennnnnn."

"What is it?"

"A lady get a certain look when she had a fight with her man." She cocked her head to one side. "Not like no other look. Louise don't know nobody else here. She at your house last night. She here early, don't want to see nobody, cain't wait to get out of here. I put two and two together." She smiled again, the lady sleuth. Glenn had to admit, she sometimes showed powers of observation that surprised him.

"You her man, Glenn?"

"Louise and I are just friends, Mabel." He cleared his throat, quickly sat up straight. "Miss Mabel. Just friends. I'm sorry to hear she was upset about something. Maybe she'll talk to me later about it. Whatever it is."

"Well, she must have some other man, then. 'Cause I know that look."

Glenn shrugged. She flashed the nose ring again.

"Glenn. Gleeeeennnnnn. All these years I've known you. You surprise me. I thought you was the other way."

He shrugged again. She looked him up and down.

"You do have a good body, though. A lots of ladies likes those big muscles."

"I got your message." Louise busied herself with her potted

flowers as Glenn sat on one of two wicker chairs on her small concrete patio, the only furniture she had on the tiny deck. He had invited himself in when she answered the door and didn't seem in a hurry to invite him in herself.

"I guess I'm not really surprised to see you here." She stopped digging with her trowel but still didn't look up at him.

"I haven't been able to think straight all day. I just had to see you."

"I knew you'd come by. Gary was always doing that." She laughed, once, then shook her head as if to dislodge the connection. "Always rejecting me, then chasing me around to tell me he wasn't rejecting me."

"Louise."

"It never occurred to me until this morning that maybe I've just been doing the same thing I've always done."

Glenn went to her, bent down, and tried to look into her face, but she turned her face to the ground.

"Louise. Louise. Of course I'm not rejecting you. It's just . . . I've never been with a woman before. You know that."

"You know, you've brought something good into my life, Glenn." Finally she turned toward him, but Glenn somehow knew not to move any closer. "You have, and I appreciate it."

"I appreciate you too, Louise."

"So many things are changing."

"Louise. May I touch you? I'm dying to hug you."

At that, she stood, and Glenn quickly followed. She reached her arms out to hug him, but still she looked away, as if unconvinced.

"Louise. Maybe we could make this work, Louise."

Now, she looked up at him. "What are you talking about, Glenn?"

Glenn met her gaze. "I mean it. We could do it. I'm all alone. I can do whatever I want."

"You've always been alone. You could always do whatever you wanted."

"No. I couldn't. I never could. I've only felt this way for a little while. I've never been . . . free." Suddenly, he smiled wide, pulled her into him tight. "Maybe this is meant to be. Maybe I'm not really gay, Louise. I mean it. Maybe we can do this. Jamey needs two parents."

"He already has two parents. You and Tommy."

"Okay. Fine. Then he needs three parents." He reached down to kiss her, and this time she let him.

"You can't try to love someone, Glenn. I've had a lot of years with a man who didn't know what he wanted. I can't take anything like that anymore."

"Maybe I'm not. Maybe I'm not gay after all."

"I've never heard a man say that before."

"No, but I mean it. Maybe everything has just been leading me right to this place."

Louise looked up at him then, and didn't say anything in return for a very long time. Finally she moved toward the chairs.

"I think I need to sit down."

"Mamaw?" Glenn had always felt funny calling her by that name, and avoided calling her anything at all most of the time, even though they were neighbors. But when he called her that afternoon from his car and she answered the phone—*haaaallllloooooo!!*—Mamaw was the first word that came to his mind. For as long as they had been neighbors, he had never actually met any of her grandchildren, all of them said to be away in Texas and Oklahoma and various places in the East. But everyone in the neighborhood—and everyone he had ever known, including Sheriff Norm, for that matter—always called her Mamaw. It was the only name she ever responded to. Years ago, as a younger man, he tried to

call her Miss Corinne once, as he had overheard her sister say one time. But she had made her feelings on the matter perfectly clear that day twenty years before, as she pulled him into a hug.

"Honey. Honey. Call me Mamaw."

"Hey, honey!" Mamaw lit up when she heard Glenn's voice on the phone. "My goodness, it's so good to hear from you. My goodness! Who is this?"

"Mamaw, it's Glenn. Your neighbor." He ran through a red light at that exact moment, just as he had run another one four blocks back. "I got tied up this afternoon and I'm pretty sure I'm going to be late to meet the bus. Can you go out and bring Jamey inside if I'm not there first?"

"Aw, pfff! Sure I can! I'm not doing anything. All my shows are over and *Gilligan's Island* is on, but I wasn't even watching it. This one's all about Ginger. I never did like that redheaded tramp!"

"Mamaw, I'll be right there. Just please look for the bus and I'll be right there."

"I made some cookies this morning. Chocolate chip."

"I'm sure Jamey would enjoy a cookie, Mamaw."

"But I didn't have quite enough baking soda so they're a little bit flat, but not too bad. Still better than those hard little things they sell down at the Piggly Wiggly. I'll make sure Jamey has some with a big glass of milk."

"Okay, Mamaw. Not too many, okay?"

"I made some extra for you boys to take home too."

"Oh, well, that's okay, Mamaw. I really can't eat sweets."

"Aw, pfff! You need to fatten up a little bit. I'll save you two dozen."

Mamaw was sitting on her old metal chair in the shade of her oak tree when Glenn pulled onto their road. Rascal lay prone between the roots of the tree and didn't get up, only moved his eyes to look at Glenn. Glenn in turn looked at the old woman, puzzled.

"They ain't made it yet. Mighta had a flat or something. Or . . . you never know . . . bus mighta got the vapor lock."

"The bus hasn't made it yet? Okay. Well, thank you for waiting. I wonder what happened. I can take it from here, Mamaw. I'll have Jamey stop over and see you in a little bit."

Mamaw wasted no time getting up and heading back toward her house. "I better get on in, then. *Sanford and Son* is about to start."

"I just realized why the bus isn't here, Mamaw. I'm early."

"Well, that's all right. I'll just watch *Sanford and Son*. It's a good show, not like all this crap they got on TV now. All these girls walking around with their perky little titties sticking out! I'm telling you! *Sanford and Son* is from the good ol' days!"

"Yes, ma'am."

After his confused rush to get home quickly, Glenn tried to catch his breath. He checked his watch again. The bus wouldn't come for another ten minutes, at least, and he began to feel antsy again, wondering what to do while he waited. He walked to his porch and tried to relax, but all the feelings welled inside him, and he got up again and walked back to Mamaw's yard and waited for the bus.

All he wanted to do was get in his car and go back to her. Jamey needed him home; Glenn knew that, certainly after all the boy had been through. But maybe just this once, he thought, he would just take off and let Mamaw take care of him for the afternoon, while Glenn went back to Louise. Jamey would want to spend an hour or more out there anyway playing with Rascal, trying to coax just a few more days out of the ancient dog. Why not let somebody else worry about things for the afternoon? For just a little while.

When he heard the bus approach from the other side of the curve, he wiped his cheeks, put on a good face, and stood up to

wait. The bus stopped in its usual spot on the dirt road in front of Mamaw's house. Children in the bus shouted and screamed, threw wads of paper at one another. The driver looked to the back of the bus in her rearview mirror, then yelled at a group of boys to sit down and pipe down. A little girl stared blankly out the window toward a patch of grass in a finger of sunlight and never even blinked. Jamey's head slowly glided down the aisle until the exit door opened on the other side of the bus with a screech. Jamey's head disappeared in the doorframe, then the door squeaked closed, and the bus pulled ahead and leaned hard after the holly hedge that separated the far side of Mamaw's yard from the red-dirt road.

After the bus passed, Jamey smiled and waved at Glenn, then moved toward the oak tree, where Rascal lay waiting, flapping his tail into the ground, sending up little puffs of dust. Jamey said something to the dog, then Rascal slumped down to one side until he was nearly flat on the ground.

The whine of an engine broke the silence left by the departing bus, then suddenly an SUV, a Suburban with tinted windows, tore onto the road from around the hedge the bus had disappeared behind. It was going way too fast, and Glenn jumped and ran straight toward it, yelling *"Slow down!"* and thinking to himself if only he could catch up to it, he'd drag the genius out from behind the wheel and stomp the living shit out of him for going so fast.

Then, when it blocked his view of the boy, the Suburban slammed to a stop. Two men got out of the car, the passenger running around the front and the driver diving out his door in the direction of Jamey.

Jamey looked up at the men then, his face showing no sign of recognition. Rascal continued to lick his hand. Then the driver had his arms around Jamey and covered his face with a small white rag.

Glenn bolted around the back of the car toward the man

and Jamey. Then a searing flash of pain tore into the base of his skull and he fell. The one who must have hit him went then to the other man as Jamey writhed in his arms. Glenn tried to stand, but his whole body was off, and the tree and Mamaw's house and the car all stood at an angle, and halfway up from the ground he fell back to the dust. Warm liquid coated his neck and he got to one knee, and then the ringing in his ears drove him back to the ground.

The two men struggled with Jamey. The boy kicked and shouted, twisted his face against whatever the man tried to shove into it. Glenn watched the scene as if through water, the whole thing slowed, exaggerated, so clear he could see every detail, the mask of determination on Jamey's face, his blue eyes wide, fine baby hair flying, jaw clenched into a wolf-like grimace despite his missing front teeth. He landed a kick in a soft spot, and the one with the rag yelled out curses. Glenn tried to stand again, but once more fell onto his face.

They got him to the car and still the boy didn't give in. Jamey grabbed the doorframe with both hands and kicked and kicked. Finally Rascal stood and barked at the scene, prancing like a Thoroughbred as the momentum of his vigorous barking carried him forward in inches and he backed himself up after each bark. Rascal quickly abandoned the tactic when it got no response. Glenn watched as if in slow motion as the dog brought himself to a gallop in the few short strides between his tree and the car. Rascal threw the bad leg forward, the stovepipe, the goddamnable leg that just wouldn't bend, and pivoted over it with extreme prejudice in his eyes, one, two, three, four times, leaving the ground with each step. Then he planted the leg one final time like a pole and vaulted over it into the middle of things.

Rascal sank his teeth into one man's upper leg. The man cried out and began punching the dog's head with both hands, tried to back himself up to dislodge Rascal from his leg. Jamey

let one hand go from the doorframe and poked the other man's eye with his thumb.

The other man grabbed his eye with one hand and shoved the boy into the car with his shoulder. The first man continued to scream at the dog, then tried to drop to the ground on top of it. Rascal snarled and pulled against him, refused to go underneath. He screamed louder now, tried to wedge a hand into Rascal's mouth and get it open. He poked at the dog's eyes, but Rascal closed them tight and ignored the pain, refused to give him an instant's mercy. Jamey kicked at the man pushing him, then landed several blows into his face, neck, groin, and stomach. Then Rascal planted all his feet and began to back up, as if to drag his prize away from the scene altogether, shaking his head and sinking his teeth in farther all the while.

The other man wasted no more time. He reached into his waistband, took out a cold Glock and thwacked Jamey across the back of his head with it. The boy crumpled into the seat and offered no more resistance. Then the man slammed the door, stepped away from the vehicle, took two steps toward the man and the dog. Rascal's eyes were open and he watched the other man approach, but he didn't let his captive go. Then, when the other man was close enough, Rascal released his grip and immediately went for the new arrival, who raised his gun and fired.

Rascal's eyes came wide, and he fell to the ground. He pawed at the air as if running as the gunman helped the other man into the car. Then Rascal slowed, his bad leg laid out in front of him, once more no different from the others, as the car with the two men and the boy inside it traveled down the road.

Glenn tried to get up, wanted to get up, struggled to his knees and then to his feet, but then the ringing began and he fell back in a heap. He could feel himself cursing but couldn't tell if he actually made a sound. In his mind he saw himself stand, felt his legs begin to run toward the car with little

Jamey's face peering out the back window, the boy's eyes wide not with fear but with a certain disappointment, as if to say, *I knew something like this would happen.* But instead he could only lie on his stomach and watch the car drive away, could only watch as the child he loved disappeared to an unknown place.

He had no idea how much later it was, but when he finally got to his feet, Glenn felt nothing but pain. Finally, he was able to stand. The sky was a beautiful blue and a crow shouted from the top of Mamaw's tree. With his head buried in his shoulder, Glenn shuffled over to the dog. Rascal's eyes were open and his tongue lolled in the dust. Apart from the hole in his head, and the ants crawling over his tongue, the dog looked purely at peace.

The distant chatter of Mamaw's television spilled out from her open back door. The mayhem had come and gone as if it had never happened. He looked up and down the road, twice in each direction, saw no one. Glenn rubbed several handfuls of dirt on Rascal's head, which was still warm. He tried to brush away the blood, to disguise the injury. To be safe, he dragged the dog well off the road, behind some bushes. Then he returned to the road, threw more dirt onto the pool of blood gathered there. He continued looking around, his breath shallow. He didn't know what to do, but some instinct told him not to involve her.

He went to Mamaw's door. She sat engaged in her program; she had clearly neither heard nor seen a thing. She cackled at something on the television just as he approached.

"Mamaw?" She turned toward him without her teeth, flashed a gum smile.

"Hey, honey. Where's Jamey? He ready for some cookies?"

"Um, Mamaw, I forgot he was going to his dad's today. But I'm afraid I have some bad news for you."

She fumbled for the remote, turned the set all the way down, and looked at him blankly.

"I'm afraid Rascal has died."

"Oh no. Where did you find him?" She moved toward the door.

"I don't think you'll want to see him. I found him in the road. It's pretty bad. I saw a car go through here too fast a few minutes ago. They must have hit him."

"Oh, goodness."

"I'll take care of him for you, Mamaw. I'll give him a good burial."

"Well, thank you, Glenn. Oh no. Jamey will be so disappointed. He didn't get a chance to say goodbye."

CHAPTER 25

They took him.

They took him?

Yes. They took him. Maybe twenty minutes ago. Somebody hit me with something and knocked me out. They killed Rascal when he tried to help Jamey.

Did you call the police?

No. I don't know why I didn't. I called you first. We need to call the police.

Wait. Glenn. Wait. Don't do that. Please. Don't call them.

Tommy. We have to call the police.

Glenn. Wait. He wanted me to meet him in New Orleans. I told him I had the money. I told him I would get it to him. I never thought he'd do this.

Well, he did. Somebody did. We need to call the police.

Wait. Glenn. Wait. I'm screwed if we call the police. They can't get involved. I don't think Bianchi will hurt Jamey. He doesn't want Jamey. He just wants me. But I'm screwed if the police get involved.

It's not about you, Tommy. We need to get Jamey back.

I promise you, Glenn. If we call the police, we won't get Jamey back. I know how he thinks. He doesn't want Jamey. He just wants me.

Tommy. Tommy. These men are dangerous, Tommy. I saw them. I was close to them. They are dangerous, Tommy.

Yes, they are. I know they are. But they're taking orders

from Bianchi. And he won't let them hurt Jamey. He just wants what he wants from me.

So what does he want? What does he want you to do?

He wants me to face him, Glenn. He wants me to see him, on his turf. He knows I saw Matt. He knows nobody else saw him after that. He knows what happened. He can see right through me. I can't hide anything from someone like him. I never could. He only did this to get me to meet him on his field.

Tommy . . .

He's dying, Glenn. I heard it in his voice. I've heard it before. I know what it sounds like. He wants to know what happened to his son.

And. What will happen then?

He has nothing to lose, Glenn. If we call the police, we won't see Jamey again. I should have seen this coming. I should have known he wouldn't settle just for the money.

But. What does he want you to do?

He wants me to come to him. He knows I will come to him if he has my son.

And?

I have to figure out how to get Jamey back. I have to think. I have to let him think he is in control. I have to think. Let me think. I'll be right over. I'm on my way.

Tommy drove. He didn't exceed the speed limit. He didn't run a light. *He's only trying to prove a point. He doesn't want Jamey. He only wants you. He won't hurt your son.*

He couldn't possibly handle any questioning about Matt. Couldn't possibly. If it all came out, he was dead. He was as good as dead already. Tommy pounded the wheel, again and again. But it didn't matter now. He had only one goal. He had to end this. Bianchi had nothing to lose. He had Tommy's boy. *I have to end this. It's my problem now.*

The crush of things in his head became too much, like

overloud music that can't be turned off but can only be turned down, little by little, until a new song began to form from what before was barely music. He began to think about Brenda, and he simply took that seed and let it grow as he drove.

It was before Jamey came. They had spent a month together, nearly every day, nearly every moment she wasn't at work or he wasn't somewhere playing cards, which was in fact his job at the time. They made love in the morning, at noon, in the evening, late at night; she touched him and he touched her and, when they were together, neither was afraid.

In their hours apart, things were different. He doubted every decision he made. He couldn't make decisions. Brenda told him every day that she loved him; no matter what he did or what he had done, she loved him like her soul, and only asked that he love her in return. No requirements, no gamble, no risk. It was there. She was there. It was as if she had opened a hole inside him, had pumped him so full of her love, but the hole wouldn't close, like a tire with a zillion tiny punctures that just wouldn't hold air.

His game suffered. He lost his heart for the risk. No longer could he look hard at the other players and know what they were thinking. He tried to go straight, worked offshore where he couldn't gamble, clawed his way through the moments when he was away from her. He quit that job and tried it again, ran on fumes and bluffed his way through and won hands again, made it for a while, then Jamey came and then drugs and then it all disappeared in a puff of smoke and ash and deception.

Glenn was sitting on his porch, and stood when Tommy pulled up. He would have only one goal now. He wouldn't call Bianchi or contact the man in any way. He wouldn't let anyone know what he was thinking. They wouldn't hurt Jamey, he didn't think they would; Tommy had been away from his son before and could do it again. For a little while. He had walked a hard road, learning to express his feelings to the people he loved. But for a little while, he would have to hide them all again. He couldn't let them know. But he knew. Soon, Glenn would know. And Glenn would help. Glenn would certainly help. Glenn loved Jamey. Tommy loved Jamey. And that's all that mattered. Nothing else mattered.

CHAPTER 26

Bobby knew how to use a needle, and had Jamey dosed with the right amount of ketamine that allowed him to wake up but not to speak. Bianchi had told them to take care of the boy, not let him get hurt, find a place to hide, and do most of their driving after dark. Bobby had learned a bit about sedation in his work and had come to prefer this method. The objects would sit there, staring out a window, breathing normally, and he could tell quickly if anything was wrong. It sure as hell beat wondering if the poor bitch or bastard was going to wake up or not, and not having to worry that he or she would wake up screaming and thrashing and grabbing the door handle at sixty miles an hour was a big bonus too.

He was especially glad about it this time, because even though he played nurse on these jobs, today he had to drive. Dave sat in the passenger seat moaning, grinding his teeth against the pain in his leg. He groaned every time Bobby hit a pothole.

"Ayy! These roads suck, Bobby."

"Just let me find a place to pull back into the woods where nobody sees us. I'll give the kid another dose and I'll help you out with that."

Dave's lip beaded with sweat. "Just. Hurry."

"Okay, buddy. Take some deep breaths."

"God! That dog looked like he couldn't bite a sausage."

"Yeah." Bobby tried to lighten the conversation, looked in the rearview mirror he had trained on the back seat as Jamey began to stir but didn't sit up. "Looked like he was going for your sausage. Good thing you only got a Vienna."

"Just drive the car, Bobby."

South of Winnfield, Bobby braked quickly and darted down a road through the woods, traveled a good quarter mile, then turned around in the road and got out. He left the engine running and left his door open too. The Suburban was dirty; he'd made sure of that before they left New Orleans, and he checked again to make sure the license plate couldn't possibly be read. Then he opened the back door, slapped Jamey lightly three times to make sure he stirred, and inserted the needle into the boy's arm, plunged in the premeasured dose from the syringe, and taped the needle onto Jamey's arm and removed the syringe. He retrieved his large first aid kit from the wayback, cut a section out of Dave's pant leg, poured peroxide onto the wound, then gave him a shot of fentanyl for the pain. Dave grimaced but didn't scream.

"You think I got rabies?"

"Wouldn't matter if you did, kid." Bobby rolled gauze around his partner's leg, then covered the gauze with tape. "A wild man like you. You're more likely to give out rabies than you are to get it."

Dave grabbed his leg. "Come on, let's go."

"Son, I take it back. You don't have a Vienna sausage at all. Move that thing to the other side so I can tape this bandage on."

They waited behind the Baptist church at the outskirts of Dry Prong until dark. Bobby dosed Jamey two more times over the three-hour period, and the opiates began to work for Dave and he leaned back in his seat, smoking cigarettes and talking to himself. Finally they pulled onto the lonesome state road, rolled through Alexandria without event, watched the terrain flatten, and got to Baton Rouge about ten o'clock.

Bobby half expected to see an Amber Alert flashing on the electronic signs above the road, and was surprised when he didn't. Bianchi had told them it would never happen, not to worry about it. That Turner didn't want the police involved in this affair. Maybe the old man was right. Periodically Jamey stirred in the back seat, and Dave continued to groan and grab his leg, but all in all the ride was quiet.

At the edge of New Orleans, Bobby cut south on I-310. Dave opened the window for some air as they crossed the giant river again and continued south into darkness, the three-quarter moon dancing off water nearly everywhere they looked. Eventually they drove down the country road Bobby had scoped out two days before and continued to the end. Bobby got out and opened the gate, then pulled the car around to the back side of the house, just as Bianchi had instructed.

The day had been an especially tough one for Carlo Bianchi. He just couldn't eat. Since the morning he had felt it, this slow, inexorable ache inside himself that he was going to have to admit was getting worse every day. The doctor's office had called again that morning; this time it was the doctor himself, the gorgeous young man with beautiful hair who no doubt believed he would be that way forever, that there couldn't possibly be a problem in the world that he, with his youth, his confidence, and his smarts, couldn't fix. When Bobby carried the boy into his house at midnight, Bianchi felt good for the first time all day.

He was in his pajamas and robe when they came into the house. He smiled and directed them to the room he had set up especially for this, at the end of the hall. Bianchi felt his mind clear out as soon as they entered, felt his worries subside along with the pain in his body. He had done a lot of bad things in his life, true, and had begun to consider those things more and more in the last several days. He had made a good living watching other men ruin themselves, had built a fortune on the backs of these poor ignorant bastards who paid him dearly for the chance to ruin themselves, and he had to admit, he had enjoyed all his victories.

It wasn't the thing itself that excited him. Taking the child, he had no particular feelings about. Any average man would doubt himself, wonder, regret. Feel sorry for the kid or for the kid's father, the so-called victim. But Bianchi knew. He was dying, he knew that. He had lost just about everything that was important to him too. But he wasn't confused. He was happy to know it. Everything else was gone, but he wasn't confused. He would do what he had to do, for his own flesh and blood. What man wouldn't?

Everything had a price, and more and more, he watched men gamble their lives away, all because they flat out didn't have the guts to pay the price to get what they wanted. Always putting faith in some irreconcilable dream to get what they thought they wanted. Everything had a price. If the kid had to go, so be it. It wasn't up to him. Turner had left him no choice. The situation would take care of itself now. Bianchi couldn't wait to see Tommy Turner here. To ask him, again, what happened to *his* son. And then, to see the bastard beg. To see that look on his face when he thought that he, or his worthless little seed, would have a chance to walk away. Why? Bianchi didn't ask why. Why was for the weak.

"You okay, Mr. Bianchi?"

Bianchi pulled the rag away from his mouth, went to the sink for a drink of water as the men returned from the back room. "You lock that door?"

"Yes. But he's not getting out, Mr. Bianchi. He won't wake up. You sure you're okay?"

Bianchi looked at the bright red spots on his handkerchief, then refolded it and coughed into it once more. He took another drink of water, and this time rinsed the handkerchief out in the sink.

"It's nothing. I'm fine."

"Doesn't look fine to me, Mr. Bianchi."

Bianchi reached out and squeezed Bobby's shoulder. "I'm fine. Don't worry about me. Just take care of the kid."

"All right. If you say you're okay. You hear from Turner?"

"Not yet. We will."

"I'm going to try to get some rest. He'll be down for the next few hours. He shouldn't wake up."

"Go ahead. I'll be up awhile. Good job getting him here. I can't sleep anyway."

CHAPTER 27

A whole bunch of birds were singing when Jamey woke up in the morning. When he first heard them singing, he was so relieved. He hadn't opened his eyes yet, and hadn't quite figured out where he was, but he knew his bad dream was over, the dream that had his whole body tingling. In the dream he was standing at the edge of a giant hole, kind of like a picture of the Grand Canyon he saw in a book, but not as big as the Grand Canyon. Down in the hole a giant tree was growing; it was so big that even way down in that hole it looked as big as a tree growing right next to him.

The weird part was the car. Way, way up in the top of the tree, which was as high as the edge of the canyon, there was a car. An old car, a powder-blue car like Mamaw used to drive. Somehow it had got stuck in the top of that tree, and the really weird part was that it wasn't even beat up; it was just parked up in that tree like it would be parked in a driveway. Jamey really wondered why. In the dream he made his way down into the hole, walking down the hill in zigzags. When he got to the base, a giant ladder was growing into the tree, so he began to climb the ladder, all the way up until he got to the top. He couldn't believe it. It *was* Mamaw's car, except it was all blue and shiny like it was brand new. He was so happy to see it, he forgot it was in the top of a giant tree. Where was Mamaw? He got inside. It smelled just like Mamaw smelled. Then, all of a sudden, it was rolling. It rolled out of the tree, fell through space, then hit the ground. Jamey woke up just as it hit, his whole body tingling. He was happy to hear the birds. But he still wondered why Mamaw's car was in that tree.

He didn't know where he was. The last thing he remembered was Mr. Glenn watching him get off the bus. And then there was a car that drove up real fast and a man got out and that's it. He was in a grown-up's bedroom, or maybe it wasn't a bedroom at all. There was no bed in it; in fact there was no furniture in the room at all, only a bunch of boxes marked "clothes" piled nearly to the ceiling. He lay on a little mattress on the floor with a blanket and a pillow, but besides those things, it didn't look like a bedroom at all.

The door to the room was partway open, so he got up and opened it and walked out into a hall. There was no light on in the hallway, but he could see pretty well; there was a light coming from down at the end of the hall, and the carpet was white, which made it easier to see. A television was playing on the other end. Jamey thought maybe he'd go down there and see if somebody was there. Where was Glenn? He was scared. His heart began to beat so fast. Then he heard a man laugh; it sounded like a nice person's laugh, not a scary laugh like the scary man on the cartoon he saw the other day, who laughed as he shouted, "I will rule the world!" The day was sunny outside and there was a nice man in the house, so there probably wasn't anything to be scared of. He walked down toward that light, remembering as he did what he had learned in Sunday school, and thinking it to himself as he walked.

And yea, though I walk through the valley of the shadow of death, I shall fear no evil. For Thou art with me, Thy rod and Thy staff, they comfort me.

The man was laughing harder as Jamey approached the end of the hallway, then Jamey heard another laugh. The other man sounded friendly too, though he kind of sounded like a

snorting hog. He walked into the room. The sound of the television stopped.

"Hi, Jamey," the big one said. He stood up from his chair. He tried to smile. He was trying to be nice, but he had a big scar on his face and one of his eyes looked purple. His muscles were huge, even bigger than Mr. Glenn's, and both of his arms were covered in tattoos. Jamey looked at him but didn't say anything. He was smiling in a funny way, like he didn't really mean it. His whole face was sweaty.

"Hi."

"Did you sleep okay?"

"Where am I?"

"You had a little accident. Don't you remember?"

"No, sir."

"We're just taking care of you here, for a little while. We're friends of your daddy's."

That sure made him feel better. "Where is my daddy?"

"He's not here right now. He should be here later. Here."

Bobby led him into the kitchen. Dave stayed in his chair and didn't look at Jamey. "Let's get you a drink of water."

"Why do you talk funny?"

Bobby laughed then. "You're funny, Jamey. We're not from Louisiana. We're from another state where people talk different."

"Where's Mr. Glenn?"

"You'll see him again too." Bobby led him back into the living room. "Come on. I need to give you your medicine. The doctor said make sure you take your medicine."

Bobby had babysat like this before, just once, and he had to admit it was a welcome change from his normal routine of strong-arming and intimidation. Jamey was a decent kid—he wasn't a brat or a crybaby or any of the things that made Bobby glad he didn't have any kids of his own. All Bianchi had told him was that Jamey's dad owed him some money, and that he had a gripe to settle with him. Whatever the amount of money was, Bobby figured it was the gripe that had motivated him to pay Bobby and Dave to take the boy like that, and to keep him here all day. And it must have been something awful to make Bianchi so certain the guy wouldn't call the police. Bianchi said the guy would probably show up at the casino looking for him sometime today, and he and Dave were to wait there at the house for their instructions on what to do with the kid. No doubt Bianchi wouldn't like it if he knew Bobby had let the kid wake up and left the door unlocked, but he didn't like to keep them knocked out all day. And he damn sure didn't want the kid waking up and freaking out like he had been . . . kidnapped. It was all for the best, this way. Bianchi had gone for the day, and left things in Bobby's capable hands.

They just needed to stay sober enough to deal with whatever it was they would have to deal with. So far, he was doing okay. Though he wasn't so sure about Dave.

Jamey didn't say anything when Bobby plugged the syringe into the needle taped to his arm and injected the liquid into his vein. Bobby marveled at how quickly the boy passed out. That stuff was just a miracle. Worked so fast, and when they woke up, they didn't remember a thing.

Bianchi hadn't heard a word from Turner, and Turner hadn't shown up at the casino either. Finally, late in the afternoon, Bianchi gave up pretending he could make himself useful there, and began to drive back to Des Allemands. Normally he would listen to WWL, just about the only thing about New Orleans that hadn't changed; he could always count on a familiar voice there. But today he had too much on his mind. He turned it all the way down so he could only hear a buzzing sound. He would have turned it off altogether, but just having something on in the background kept his mind focused. Sometimes pure silence was just too much, left him with a sensation that he would just float up off the road and into the clouds.

He wondered as he drove if Turner had any idea what he had gotten himself into. Sure, Bianchi was an old man now, but didn't his name still send men into shivers? He was frankly surprised Turner hadn't shown up yet. He'd told Logan, the security man, the night before that someone would be showing up to look for him. Then he got himself into work early, pretended to be busy, stayed in his office all day. Nothing. Before leaving he had instructed Logan to let him know the minute Turner showed up. He hadn't decided yet how he wanted to handle it. Probably he'd have Logan give the guy his address, or maybe just tell him again to meet and do an exchange in that lot he liked to use, over off Carrollton. It was dark there and completely invisible from the street. He figured he would decide when he had to decide. His instinct had never failed him.

Back at the house, both of the goons were watching cartoons. They had obviously been smoking weed inside, which lit his fuse as he had told them not to smoke at all in the house. But it was better they didn't go outside, and they both assured him they hadn't. His place was fairly private, but with all the technology these days, you just never knew who was looking.

"What's up, doc?" Bobby looked at him with heavy eyes. The other one didn't even look up, continued staring at the screen as if trying to keep his eyes open. Periodically he laughed out loud, whether the action on the screen called for it or not.

"You monitoring his dose?"

"He woke up once, Mr. Bianchi."

"What!"

Bobby stood. "Relax. I've done this before. It's better this way. I want to make sure he doesn't get hurt."

"You let him wake up?"

"Mr. Bianchi. What are we going to do if the kid stops breathing? Call a doctor? Besides. He won't remember a thing. I know what I'm doing."

"Fine. Fine. Just keep him down now. Make sure he stays down all night. I don't want him waking up."

"No problem, Mr. Bianchi. Where is this guy? I thought you said he'd be here by now."

"He's coming. Don't worry about it. He wants his kid back."

Dave sat up straight then. "How much longer we gotta wait on this, Mr. Bianchi? We did what you asked of us. We're ready to get back to Jersey."

"He's coming. I just need you two to babysit a little longer. Then you'll get your money. And lay off the shit. I need you two sober."

Bobby chimed in. "Mr. Bianchi. All due respect, sir. We did what you asked of us. We'd like our money."

"Give me until this time tomorrow. I'll make sure you're paid."

"Twenty-four hours, Mr. Bianchi. We leave at sundown tomorrow."

"I've got it, fellows. Don't worry. He's just thinking. He'll be here."

"Twenty-four hours."

"No problem."

Bianchi went into his room, checked his phone again for messages, and tried to settle into his bed and relax with whatever he could find on television. But he was too restless. He made himself some spaghetti and offered the others a plate. They all sat at his table and ate.

"Delicious, Mr. Bianchi," Bobby said. "Thank you for the dinner."

"You're welcome."

"Mr. Bianchi. How's that cough?"

"Comes and goes. Not a problem today. Say. You guys remember Charlie Turner?"

"Never heard of him. I know him?"

"Football player? LSU? The Miracle Run? November 1968?"

Bobby shook his head. "We weren't born then. In Jersey, we don't pay much attention to Louisiana, besides."

Bianchi thought about responding, but instead took his plate to the sink, washed it off along with the silverware, and stacked it all in the drainer. He felt an overwhelming disappointment, and knew as much as he ever knew anything that it had nothing to do with the little boy in the other room whose life was about to be changed for the worse. No. The feeling was about his own life. Here he was, nearing the end, fraternizing with low-life idiots who didn't even know who Charlie Turner was. Now there was a guy who knew how to make something out of nothing.

"Make sure he doesn't wake up."

By the time Bianchi reached his bedroom, the disappointment had washed away, and only the anger remained. When he opened his room to what remained of Marilyn's smell, what little was left on the clothes still in her closet, he felt at peace with it all. He couldn't change anything now. He'd always dealt with things this way. No doubt, in whatever time he had left, he always would.

CHAPTER 28

Tommy checked Jamey's bedroom three times after he and Glenn went inside the house. Glenn stayed in his chair at his kitchen table, softly rubbing the bump that had formed on the back of his head. Tommy looked under the bed, inside the closet, even pulled out drawers from the antique bureau where Glenn stored Jamey's clothes. Each time he returned to the kitchen, looked at Glenn once, and went back to the bedroom. Glenn never looked up at Tommy, only sat rubbing his head and breathing.

"It was a Pennsylvania plate?"

"Yes. First three letters were *GQR*. Or *OOR*."

"Black Suburban?"

"Black. Definitely."

"And the one guy. You said he had a scar on his face?"

"That's the one who shot Rascal. He was the driver. Neither one of them said anything. Tommy . . . I'm . . ."

"It's not your fault, Glenn." Tommy sat, took Glenn by both shoulders, bent himself down to look in the other man's face. "I don't like it either. But they won't hurt him, Glenn. Not if I handle this right."

"How do you know?" Glenn stood, wrung his hands.

"I know how he thinks, Glenn. The guys that came, they're following orders. Bianchi has played his hand here. I know what he wants. He only wants to draw me in."

"And?"

Tommy stopped then, rubbed his head. "He'll let Jamey go if I come to him."

"Let him go? What's he going to do with you?"

Tommy stood then, went to his truck, and returned with a pack of cigarettes. He lit one at the table without asking if he could. He smoked it all the way down, then stubbed it out in a glass, lit another one, and smoked it all the way down too. Glenn took a cigarette himself and lit it. The two men sat, smoking.

"What will he do with you, Tommy?"

Tommy stood. "He's expecting me to call him. He used to have a place out in the country outside New Orleans. I went there with my father a few times."

"They could be anywhere."

"I'm going to New Orleans."

"Tommy. No."

"I have to think about how to do this. But I'm going to New Orleans."

"It's too dangerous."

"I told him I had the money. He doesn't care about the money."

"What if I talk to Norm? I know he will help. He'll know what to do."

Tommy went to Jamey's room again, and this time just sat on the bed awhile before returning. Back in the kitchen, he sat at the table, blew out an exhausted breath.

"I'll go back in just for the parole violation, Glenn. Two more years just for associating with gambling interests. If I knew that would get Jamey back, I'd take it. I'd take that deal."

"You don't know. Maybe . . . there are extenuating circumstances."

Tommy reached across the table, took both of Glenn's hands in his. Glenn swallowed hard.

"I can't face the sheriff, Glenn. I can keep this quiet. I can eat my feelings for as long as I have to. For as long as I'm living. But I can't face the police. I couldn't even face Bianchi. He knows."

"He can't know, Tommy. He just suspects."

"I only told you because I didn't know what to do, Glenn. I felt like he was threatening. And he obviously was. I should have known this would happen." Tommy slammed his fist on the table. "I should have protected him."

"It's not your fault, Tommy."

"Look. Glenn. I know you hate me."

"I don't hate you, Tommy. I owe my life to you."

"I deserve it. I wasn't worth a shit to Jamey until lately. He needed me. Just like Brenda needed me. And I wasn't there."

"I was there for you, Tommy. I was there. I owe you. I'm going to pay this money for you, and we'll be even."

Glenn went to the back of the house and returned with a small satchel. He set it on the table and removed several stacks of hundred-dollar bills.

"My mother left this. She spent so much of her life poor. Then when she finally had money after Fred died, she hoarded it in her house. I found nearly a hundred thousand just in shoeboxes in her closet.

"I'll count out the money you owe him and put it in a bag, and I'll go with you."

"No, Glenn. No way."

"You say he'll trade you for Jamey. I'll bring Jamey home. Just in case. I'll go with you."

Tommy started to object, but instead looked at his friend and didn't. His mouth drew into a hyphen. He stood and returned to his truck. This time he didn't bring back cigarettes. Instead, he lay a Glock .19 and a short-barreled .38 on the table.

"Just in case. You won't have to use it. The state took away all my other guns. They didn't know about these."

Glenn reached for the Glock, checked to make sure it was empty, then held it and looked it over.

"How are you going to find him?"

"I haven't made it that far yet. I'll think it through. It's in God's hands now."

"Then ask God to bring him back."

"Doesn't work like that, Glenn. God won't bring him back. I have to do it."

He sat on Jamey's bed, held his son's shirt to his face, and breathed in the boy's smell. He touched Jamey's pillows, stuffed animals, his Lego airplane and robots. Then he stood and went into the backyard, picked up a football, tossed it into the air, caught it, and threw it up again. He looked up to the north, to the same guiding star he and his father once had studied. He held the ball tight, as if he would run with it, and run and run and run.

"Where are you, little boy?" Tommy asked the heavens.

But the stars didn't answer. In a little while he carried the ball to the porch, left it on Jamey's chair, and went back inside.

"Why don't you stay, Tommy? We can figure out how to find him in the morning."

Tommy didn't say anything, only nodded. He walked slowly down the hall into his little boy's room, while Glenn went to brush his teeth. A few minutes later Glenn knocked lightly on the door, asked if Tommy needed anything. When his guest didn't answer, Glenn opened the door. Inside he found Tommy asleep, curled up like a newborn in the child's bed with all his clothes on, holding Jamey's stuffed cow, Billy Joe, tight.

CHAPTER 29

Sheriff Norm walked into the station at six o'clock sharp, as he did Monday through Friday every week. An overzealous morning sun was just coming up across the courthouse lawn, sharp fingers of light refracting in a million directions when it hit the grime-smeared glass of his office window. Dewy trails of steam rose from the watered grass. Norm rubbed the inside of the window with a rag; it didn't make the slightest improvement, so he typed an email to Katie to let her know it was time to have the windows cleaned again. *Best to send it now,* he thought. He would definitely forget by the time Katie wandered in to work.

Deputy Peterson typed a report out in the common area. Norm had asked him a hundred times to fill those out by hand; Peterson couldn't type three words without making a mistake, and Norm had no doubt the paper would just look terrible when he was done. Not to mention that the amount of Wite-Out on the page made the paper so heavy he practically needed both hands to hold it up. Peterson shifted in his chair and the leather of his holster creaked. Peterson had been on the phone when the sheriff walked in, and they hadn't yet spoken.

"Deputy?" Norm hollered out from his office. Peterson's chair creaked again. *He's probably trying to sit up straight,* Norm figured, and he smiled at the thought. Peterson was the nervous type.

"Sheriff? Good morning to you, sir. Nothing unusual to report, just the same old same old."

"Sounds like a winner to me. You got any coffee out there?"

Suddenly, a flurry of commotion. Peterson tried to stand quickly, somehow knocked over his bottle of Wite-Out, then when he tried to grab it he upended the whole table, knocking the typewriter with his report still in it onto the floor. He didn't say anything. Norm just listened. Finally, Norm got up and went to the door for a better look.

"You okay?"

"Yes, sir. Just a little accident, sir." Peterson was a great deputy, *a steady hand,* as Norm's father used to say. A little lean in the common sense department, though.

Peterson stood over the fallen table, looking confused. Norm helped him stand it up, then lifted and repositioned the typewriter. He knew better than to laugh or kid Peterson in any way. To do so would surely send the young man into a storm of apologies and self-flagellation.

Peterson followed him into the kitchen, where Norm spied a full pot of translucent coffee. His heart sank. Another thing Peterson couldn't do was make coffee.

"I just made it, Sheriff. Twenty minutes ago, so it'd be ready when you got here. You know I wouldn't let you down." Norm had been hoping to find an empty pot so he could make some fresh himself. Yet, he was the sheriff. The leader of the bunch. He poured himself a small cup, figured he could make it another twenty minutes until Peterson was off and he could dump the whole business down the drain and start over.

Maybe Andy would bring in some muffins today. Ever since Cynthia died, Andy's wife had been sending Andy in with food for Norm at least once a week. Sometimes twice if she made a big batch of something. She obviously fed Andy well, judging by the way his uniform fit. Norm could sure have used a couple of those banana muffins right about then. He'd already had a big breakfast—six slices of bacon, four eggs, two thick pieces of toast with butter and jam, half a pint of orange juice. Same thing he ate every morning. Cynthia was always trying to get him on diets, to cut down on the fat, grease, cholesterol. Now that she was gone, he tried not to think about those things as he stuffed himself for the first thirty minutes of every day. He must have gained forty pounds as a widower. Yet, it didn't matter how much he ate. Less than an hour later, when he began to settle into his office for the day, he was hungry again.

Norm took his cup of watery coffee into his office. Now that sunlight had flooded the room, he turned the light off before sitting back down. It wasn't much, but it kept him a little cooler than he always felt under those burning fluorescent lights. Norm figured out long ago that this was the trick to staying cool. Stay ahead of it. He sharpened two pencils in his electric sharpener, then sat and blew on the coffee before taking a sip. Peterson walked into Norm's office and dropped a stack of reports on his desk. Thankfully he didn't stay and ask about the coffee.

The news wasn't too bad. Just like the old saying: no news is good news. Not a month ago he had been called out on a Saturday night—the night before Easter—to a dogfighting ring a few miles north of Quitman. He had spent all night up there doing interviews, making arrests. They had nabbed thirty-seven people in a ring that had been carrying on across north Louisiana for two years or more. All night he stood there, then watched a rarefied sun rise on Easter morning, giving shape to trees and automobiles and a steaming pond in the distance, to trash and empty beer bottles and the carcasses of two dogs on top of a tarp, to just and unjust alike. He had driven in after eight that morning to spend another half a day in his office, thinking about Jesus's resurrection and at the same time about how little he was paid to do a job so important. Break this thing down by the hour, he figured that morning, and he could make more money hauling pulpwood. But. Law enforcement was in his blood. He loved his job. He just didn't like staying up all night dealing with rings of lowlifes anymore.

He shuffled through the papers on his desk and perused a report filed by Branden's resident crazy old lady, Mrs. Lolley, reporting a stolen chicken. Norm laughed out loud when he read it and had to grab his trash can to spit Peterson's watery coffee into it. She must have been in shortly after he left yesterday; no way she would have left her house after dark. Sometimes he had to entertain the old people, even when they did start to get a little dotty. Thirty years ago her husband, Joe Lolley, practically ran the town as head of the paperworkers' union, and Mrs. Lolley was a respectable lady in her own right. But then he died, and she started collecting chickens, right there in the city limits, not two blocks from the courthouse, those stupid feathered birds constantly getting out of the pen and wandering down Main Street. She must have had forty at one time, but she couldn't have six left, and now she thought people were stealing them. Norm laughed again. As if anybody younger than fifty would know how to kill a chicken and pluck it. Why would they? When you can buy the whole thing in a neat little package for four bucks at Walmart?

Norm heard a noise outside and glanced up at his window again. It looked halfway clean now that the sun wasn't piercing through it like a knife anymore. He read the next report. Looked like James Madison got picked up again. Another drunk and disorderly. Norm went to school with James. Unlike the other three, James's fourth wife had apparently refused to leave him, and every time the deputies brought him in, James said he couldn't stand to stay home anymore when he went on his benders. Looked like there was another shooting. *Those dumbasses down in Ward 10 are at it again.* Norm shook his head. He considered what his daddy used to say, after he had given up a twenty-year career as a laborer at the paper mill to be sheriff himself: "Son. If you wanna do this job one day, better learn to swim. A law enforcement officer ain't nothing but a lifeguard at the shallow end of the gene pool."

The ringing telephone startled Norm from his daydream. As was his habit, he answered quickly. The sound of a ringing phone had sent him nearly into a panic since he was a young man. He always made it stop as soon as he could.

"Norm Allen."

"Norm?"

"Speaking. Glenn?"

"Hey, Norm. I'm glad you answered."

Norm felt himself relax. After all these years, after all the phone conversations he'd had in his life, they'd carried bad news—what, twice? About his daddy, then his brother. And the call about his brother was, what, forty years after the call that night about the drunk who tried to kill Daddy with a deer rifle? Still. It was just in his head. Phone rings, bad news.

Norm sank into his chair. "Mr. Rosen. Good morning. I don't normally hear from you this early."

"Well, I was just up early. I couldn't go back to sleep so I figured I'd try to get some things done. I had a couple things I wanted to ask you about, figured I'd catch you when I knew you'd be at your desk."

"Yes, well, here I am. Slow and steady Norm. Same time every day. Say, did Donnie Parker come around and see you the other day?"

"What? Parker? I think so. I know he's been in at some point. Probably talked to one of the girls."

"I sent him over to talk to y'all. I was just hoping you could point him somewhere. Hell, anything, Glenn. Sacking groceries would be an improvement for that fellow. Hopefully he can get himself doing something so we don't have to keep picking him up once a week."

"I'll follow up with Louise about it. I'm not totally clear on it right now."

"Oh no, Glenn, hell, don't worry about it. I just wanted to ask you before I forgot. Speaking of which, how is Louise?"

"Well. Maybe not the best subject right now. I appreciated your thoughts the other day, though."

Norm sat up straight. He knew enough to know this was the time to be professional. "I apologize, Glenn. I didn't mean to be too personal."

Now, Glenn stammered. "Oh, no, Norm. Hell. I enjoyed talking to you about her. Things just went a little sour the other day, that's all. We'll get it straightened out."

"I'm sure you will, Glenn. So listen. What's got you calling me so early? Must be important, calling so early and on my back line at that."

"I didn't want to go through reception. Truth is, it's kind of private."

Norm craned his head to see into the main office, though of course he knew what he would see. "Well, Katie's not in yet, anyway."

"Oh. Okay."

Norm lowered his voice, spoke slowly to stall for time on some instinct. He hadn't kept this job for nearly forty years without developing a sense of things. "Glenn?"

"Yes?"

"Something going on?"

"Um. Norm. Are you alone?"

Norm didn't ask to be excused. He stood and closed his door. "Sure I am. Deputy Peterson's working on a report in the other room. That's all. What's up?"

"I need a favor."

Norm felt a rush of relief. Finally, something he was good at. People were always asking him for favors, for money or to speak to a group or to put in a good word with the judge about one prisoner or another. But rarely did someone he liked ask for one. Especially someone he felt indebted to.

"Well, you called the right place, buddy. I'm full of favors, and I owe you plenty of them. What can I do for you?"

"I need an address."

Norm considered several funny things he wanted to say, but let them all pass. He was having trouble reading what kind of a mood Glenn was in, and he had chastised himself for being too personal once already. He couldn't totally resist, though; the tension in Glenn's voice was obvious, and the reason for his call was clearly more than simple convenience. He settled for a jocund line, not a joke per se, just something to slow things down and give him a little more time to figure out what was going on.

"Now, Glenn. You're not planning to go out hunting and open up a can of whoop-ass on somebody, are you? Somebody messing with you? You can tell ol' Norm."

Glenn came right back, laughed for just the right amount of time. "No, Norm. Nothing like that. It's . . . well. I'll tell you the whole story if you want to hear it. I'm afraid there's not much to it, though."

"No, Glenn. I'm just playing with you. Anyway, I guess it's somebody hard to find, or you could get it yourself, right? Am I right?"

"Yes, well . . . Norm, I wouldn't call you if it weren't important. It's a really long story. I owe somebody a favor . . ." Norm heard Glenn shuffling paper; he seemed to be reading from some notes. "And she thinks he might be the father of her child . . . She wants to get him a message . . . I promise, Norm . . . nothing will come of it for you. You know you can count on me."

"Well, shit, Glenn. I'm not worried about that. But you've got me curious now. Who are you looking for?"

"It's an address down south of New Orleans somewhere.

Or maybe not. I could really use addresses for all residential properties this guy owns."

"I need a name, buddy." Norm laughed.

"Carlo Bianchi."

Norm's arms began to shiver. He certainly knew *that* name. Bianchi's influence didn't extend into Branden Parish, but Norm had heard talk of it in Lincoln Parish, right next door. Bianchi, to hear it told, had an old-fashioned racket going, the kind of stuff the Feds and state and local officials had broken up in most other states. But Louisiana had always had a soft spot for corruption, and the present day was no different. Of course there was that deal with the insurance commissioner and the lengthy trial for rate fixing; that was down in Baton Rouge, but Ray was just a small-town boy from Branden, just like Norm himself was.

"Did I hear you right?"

"Norm, I know you weren't expecting this. It's what, six fifteen in the morning, and ol' Glenn has already got you worried, right?"

"Glenn. Don't bullshit me. Are you in trouble?"

"No, Norm. Nothing like that. To be honest, it's kind of embarrassing. Like I said, I'll tell you anything you want to know. It's a really long story . . . goes back to my mother."

"Are you sure you're all right? Is there some way you could get me a message? Is someone coercing you somehow?"

"I'm fine, Norm. Really. I'm glad to know you're worried about me. Glad to know I have some friends out there."

"I'd do anything for you, Glenn. Does this have something to do with Tommy?"

"It's one of my clients, Norm. You know her. I'm just trying to help her out a little."

"Okay, all right. Fine. I'm just making sure."

"I understand if you can't do it, Norm. I do."

"Aw, hell, Glenn. You wouldn't hurt me. I trust you."

To Norm, Glenn sounded like he was about to cry. "No. No I wouldn't. If you can find it, I'd appreciate it if you'd keep this between us."

"Of course I will. I have to be honest, though. It scares me to hear you mention that name."

"I understand. I do, and I appreciate it. Like I say, it's nothing to worry about. It'll be anonymous, just a letter. She wants to send him a letter at every address she can find for him. She's afraid if it goes to his office, he might never see it. That's why I'm looking for residential addresses. She says they went to a place somewhere down south of New Orleans, down near the water, way out in the swamp."

"Well. You know I owe you, Glenn. I've told you many times before . . . for making my job so much easier. For keeping half the idiots that come into your office out of my jail. You're a great citizen, Glenn. You really are."

Silence came over the line. Finally Glenn continued.

"I've been telling Jamey I could show him your office. He thinks it's pretty cool that I know the sheriff. He thinks I'm a big shot, I guess."

"Of course you can, Glenn. Anytime. Let me know. We've even got some honorary deputy badges we give the kids now. I'd be honored to pin one on your boy's shirt."

"That was a great idea. Was that yours?"

"Noooo. Katie's. Even law enforcement can use a woman's touch from time to time."

"I'll tell her so myself, then. Say, Norm. Can you call me back when you find the addresses? She was hoping to send the letters out today."

"Actually, I'm at my desk right now. Just hang on. Keep talking to me. I can look it up as we speak."

Norm began typing, humming and muttering to himself as he did. Glenn didn't say anything.

"Glenn?"

"Sir?"

"So. I've got an address here, but that's on Saint Charles in New Orleans."

"I have that one."

"Okay. And then there's an apartment, it looks like on Chartres Street . . . that's the French Quarter."

"Anything else?"

"Oh. Look here. *Bayou Bend Road.* That sounds like a rural address to me. This one's in Des Allemands. Looks like"—*click, click, click*—"he's had this address since 1978. That's a good hour south of the city."

"My pen's ready."

"Okay. Here it is."

Norm heard the commotion as he hung up the phone. Andy walked into his office with a large cup of coffee for Norm in his hand. Norm felt his spirits rise. For in Andy's other hand, there for Norm to see, was a rustling paper bag, held out at such an angle that Norm knew it was meant for him, and him alone.

CHAPTER 30

"He knows more about gambling than I do. There's no doubt . . . in my mind . . ." Tommy hesitated, raised an arm to wipe his face on the sleeve of his shirt, to brush away the intermingled sweat and tears on his face. The two had been silent until Tommy spoke. The first hour of their trip, Tommy had whispered his thoughts too quietly to hear, from the driver's seat of Glenn's car, and allowed his tears to flow freely down his face. Glenn had merely stared at the towering pine trees whizzing by as they passed through Winnfield and Colfax and numerous collections of falling-down houses before the sky began to open and the earth began to flatten as the two neared Alexandria.

After studying aerial pictures of the address online, Glenn and Tommy had decided to leave home at noon, rather than trying to kill an afternoon somewhere between Branden and Bianchi's address south of New Orleans; every place they would stop, every time they'd be seen, would be just another opportunity to blow their cover. Tommy had no doubt Bianchi had eyes everywhere, and they would be looking. The house where Tommy figured Bianchi had his son was down a wooded road, just as Tommy remembered, with no neighbors for half a mile. How he and Glenn would sneak in there and confront the men who had Jamey, they intended to work out on the drive. Glenn had called Jamey's school to say he was sick, and Tommy had called Otis to tell him they couldn't work today. Otis was happy for the news and offered that he and Red would go right back to sleep.

"I figure he was thinking, either I know something about Matt or I don't. He's sick, and he's tired of waiting. So he figured he'd up the pressure."

"I'd say it worked."

"Yes. It definitely worked."

"Is he going to hurt Jamey, Tommy?"

"I don't think they've hurt him yet. He'll be drugged, for sure. They won't let him be awake. He would be a nuisance. They'll just want to keep him quiet."

"But then . . ."

"He didn't expect me to wait this long. He expected to hear from me by now. He figured, if I knew something about Matt, I wouldn't go to the police. And he probably knows I haven't been to the police, because he would have heard about it. I have no doubt he has people everywhere . . . If I had gone to the police, he would have heard about it by now. So he knows I haven't."

"And so."

"So he figures I know something. And he's waiting."

"So why haven't you contacted him?"

Tommy breathed out. Without a word he pulled Glenn's car to the side of the road, got out, walked around the back of the car, and stood by Glenn's door on the passenger side. Glenn took the clue and got out himself, stretched, and moved around to the driver's seat, belted himself in, and pulled back onto the road. Tommy adjusted his seat and looked over his shoulder to the contents of the floor behind him. He reached back and lifted the paper sack, which held fifty thousand dollars in hundreds, and spied the two small pistols shining on the floor underneath, before placing the bag back on top of them.

"He's a professional, Glenn. He's been watching people's faces for a long time. He was sure I knew something about his son, or he wouldn't have taken Jamey. So I didn't see the point of calling him and lying to him again. He already knows better. I figured the best thing was just to bluff him. To wait him out. To see what I can make happen."

"I'm nervous about this, Tommy." Glenn watched the road as he spoke, yet still Tommy could feel Glenn's judging eyes boring into his skin.

"Listen. Just listen. Bianchi—he's very sick to do this. He wants to be comfortable. He'll be there. He wants to be in his own house, where he's comfortable. Probably the other guys will still be there too—we'll see. They don't want Jamey—they want me. Maybe they'll trade him for me. I don't know."

"Trade him? Tommy!"

"I don't know, Glenn." Tommy slammed the dash with both hands. "I don't know! These guys—no doubt, they know what they're doing. The best bet we have is to outsmart them. Bianchi doesn't figure I'll be able to find him—and maybe I won't—he's counting on me to call him. He expected to hear from me already."

"And what if they're not there?"

"I don't know, Glenn. I don't know. I just know we're best off looking for ourselves. Not calling the police and asking them to look. Bianchi would hear about that and be gone immediately. Not calling him to see. Then he'd be ready for us. If this doesn't work, we'll try something else."

"I don't know what else we can do."

"They planned this, Glenn. They knew nobody but you would know about it. Or Mamaw, maybe. If she had seen it go down—they had a plan to deal with her, believe me."

"Thank God that didn't happen."

"Yeah, well . . . the truth is, you're complicit now. You're in on it. If you want out, now's the time to get out. Turn around and take me back to get my truck. Give me a good head start and call the cops. If that's what you want to do. I don't recommend it, but . . . you don't have any other choice now. Other than to go with me and try to get Jamey ourselves."

"Family Serv'ces."

Glenn felt a rush of relief at the familiarity in Mabel's voice, and had an incalculable urge to turn around and go back to Branden. Instead he held his phone to his ear as he continued driving.

"Miss Mabel?"

"Glenn? Is that you? Where you been? We been worried about you all day."

"I know, I'm sorry. Jamey was so sick today and couldn't go to school, I completely forgot to call and let you know I wouldn't be in today. Have I missed anything?"

"Aw, naw, same old." A squeak erupted loud enough for him to hear on the phone, and Glenn pictured her lowering her ample frame into her chair. "You been home all day, Glenn?" She tsked. "You forgot to call your own people. You supposed to be the boss, Glenn. Set a good example."

"I apologize, Miss Mabel. I just kind of forgot about it today. I've been so worried about Jamey."

"He got a fever?"

"Oh, yes, it's . . . nothing. He'll be fine. I'm just not used to being a parent, I guess."

"Make sure he drinks lotsa water, Glenn."

"Thank you, Miss Mabel. I will. Have you heard from Louise?"

She began to smack her gum loud, and Glenn imagined the large, toothy grin erupting on her face. "Naw, Glenn. Louise gone. She told us she won't be back."

"I know. I just wondered if maybe she forgot something. I didn't get to say a proper goodbye."

"Oh, okay. I hear what you sayin'. I miss her too, Glenn. Nice to have somebody new aroun' here."

"Miss Mabel?"

"Yeah, Glenn?"

"You might've noticed Louise and I have been very close."

"*Pfff!* Uh, yeah. Anybody can see that. Something happen 'tween you two, Glenn? You scare her off?"

"We just enjoyed one another's company, that's all. Anyway, listen. There's something I've been meaning to say to you."

He could tell she was filing her nails; normally this would annoy him, but today he let it pass.

"I'm listenin'."

"I've enjoyed working with you all these years, Mabel. You're a real asset to our team. I just wanted to say that to you."

"Aw, Glenn. That's nice. You never say anything nice to me and Bonita."

"What? Sure I do."

"Okay, Glenn. If you say so. But thank you for the compliment. It's much appreciated."

"You're welcome. I mean it."

"So where you now, Glenn? It sounds like you're in your car."

"Oh. Just out for a drive at the moment. I'll be back Monday. I'll see you then, okay?"

"Oh, that sounds nice. It sure is a nice day for a drive."

"He'll definitely be drugged. Wherever he is." Tommy drove now, leaned forward to adjust the back of the driver's seat. "Bianchi will want to be somewhere comfortable to him, at one of his houses. He'll want to be comfortable. But they will have him sedated. No way they want him up making noise or trying to run away. Even if they're out of the city, like we've been guessing."

"They better not have hurt him."

"They haven't hurt him. Not yet, anyway. Bianchi's waiting to hear from me, and he's surprised he hasn't yet. After he does—who knows what will happen."

"Don't even say it."

"A few days ago I talked to one guy I know who still works at his casino. I was thinking about going down, trying to take him the money. This guy told me that Mr. Bianchi never comes in at night anymore. He may leave Jamey with these guys in the daytime, but he'll be home at night."

"It's hard to try to guess at all this."

"I'm just trying to think like him. Like someone desperate to find his son and with nothing to lose."

"You've been there before."

"Not like he is. Not until now. But desperate, yes, with nothing to lose. I've been there. It's not a good place to be."

An hour from New Orleans, he exited the highway and drove into the parking lot of a small store. Tommy parked at the edge of the lot, where no one would pay particular attention to them, and turned to face Glenn. He took a small cooler of food and bottles of water from the back seat, and the men each ate a sandwich of cold cuts, chewing slowly as if to ponder things in the silence that fell between them. Glenn had suggested before leaving Branden that they should bring food with them—no point showing their faces anywhere they might be remembered—and had filled the car with gas, alone, before returning home to pick up Tommy.

"The guys who took Jamey," Tommy said. "They're getting impatient. Guys like that don't like to babysit. They're from out of town, no doubt."

"I couldn't fully read the license plate. But Pennsylvania, like I said."

"They had it covered somehow, I'm sure. But they're not crazy about waiting around like this. Especially when they have no idea what is going on."

"So they're ready to leave. Distracted. Not expecting us to just show up."

"Exactly. But they'll have him drugged, like I say. If he's there, and we find him, we'll have to carry him out. Bianchi won't be alone with him yet. They'll still be there. Just not for much longer. But my plan is to catch them not paying attention, get in, threaten them, and get out with him. You don't have to come in, not right away. I can signal you somehow. I may have to hold them off while you come in and take Jamey out."

"And you don't think he'll just send somebody again? Assuming this actually works?"

"If I can get him out of there—I've been thinking about this. We'll get him back to Branden and I'll tell Norm everything. I can't run from it. I'll do what I have to do. I'll take my punishment."

"I don't know, Tommy. You have no idea . . . Parole violation . . . the body."

Tommy nodded but didn't speak for a while. He got back on the road and drove on, opened the window a crack. The setting sun shone from behind, reflected off the rearview mirrors.

"I'll tell him everything. I just want Jamey out of Bianchi's hands. They'll look at all the circumstances. They'll arrest Bianchi. As for Matt—why did I want to kill the guy? I've never done anything like that. It was an accident, Glenn. I mean . . . they'll dig the body up and they'll find a wad of money on him. I knew it was there. He flashed it at me, showed off. Thousands of dollars. I just . . . I don't know. I'll take my chances. If I can just get him back. So they put me away again for a little while. They'll put Bianchi away too, if he doesn't die first. But I'll do it, Glenn. I'll do it. He's my son. He's my flesh. I'll do anything."

"I recognize this place," Tommy said as he sat back down in the driver's seat, and reflexively looked up into the rearview mirror. He had left the engine running when he pulled the car off onto a dirt path on the high side of the narrow parish road. He turned the headlights off before turning the car around and facing it out toward the road. Dusky bits of light reflected in flashes off the bayou on the downhill side of the road.

"What were you doing just now?"

"Sorry, Glenn. It's dark, but there are a few houses along here. And this is the only way in or out. I had to punch out the light bulbs that showed the license plate."

"No problem, fine. That was a good idea."

"You can bet there's not a lot of traffic down here. We'll just ease on through with the windows up. Look straight ahead if you see anybody by the road."

"So you've been here before."

"This is definitely the place. Daddy used to play a game down here. This was back before all these casinos took over. These games weren't legal then. But Mr. Bianchi had games in the house we're looking for. I used to spend weekends down here with Daddy. I was seven, maybe eight."

"He brought you to illegal weekend poker games?"

"Yeah. Till somebody tried to knock the game over one weekend and ended up shot on the floor. We weren't there then, thank God. But we never went back. Daddy said they covered it up somehow, but we never went back."

"Your father would drive you all the way down here to watch men play poker?"

Tommy breathed out. "I guess that sums it up."

"How did he get into this?"

"I guess it was just the thrill of it. The chance of winning something big. Daddy came from flat-out nothing, and he took a gamble and made something of himself playing football. Twenty-one years old and had eighty thousand fans cheering for him. And when that all quit, I guess he just . . . had to find something to replace it with. High-stakes poker was the closest thing he could find. He said . . . nobody ever knew what he had in his hand. Nobody ever knew which way Charlie Turner was going."

"And this was your childhood."

"Hey. Don't knock it. It was better than staying home all weekend with my drunk mother."

"I don't remember her."

"Yeah, well . . . I've forgiven her for all she did and didn't do for me. Including some things you can't imagine."

"I can imagine." Glenn sat and stared out the window. "Tommy?"

"Sir?"

"Are you sure we shouldn't call the police now?"

"I don't trust them at all, Glenn. Not the locals, parish, state. None of them. We're here. We're just going to walk right in and take him."

"You're sure about this?"

"I'm sure of it, Glenn. We're all good. It's just ahead, if I remember right."

"Okay. I'm ready."

Tommy pulled back onto the road and the men continued steadily toward the end.

"What was that number?"

"It's 16681," Glenn said. "We must be close."

Tommy stopped the car, squinted. "It's about a hundred yards ahead. I remember that huge oak tree leaning across the road. I see it's still there." He turned the car around in the road to face away from the house. "I'm going to back up a ways. Get us closer. Then I'm going to get out and take a look. Can you see those lights?"

"Sure."

"Somebody's here. That's for sure. Can't get too close." He switched the lights off, craned around, and began to back the car slowly, periodically lifting the parking brake lever in order not to engage the brake lights. “Funny thing about hedges. No doubt all that was planted so nobody could see in. But right now it’s protecting us from being seen. In the city, the neighbors would have called 911 by now.”

“So what are you going to do?”

Tommy stopped. He cut the engine and rolled down the windows to hear the roar of crickets and night birds and the settling of the car as its engine ticked in the heat. The smell of brackish water clung to the air.

“You really think he’s here, Tommy?”

“I hope so. I’m going to take a look. I want you to wait here.”

“You’re not going in without me.”

“I’m not going in now. I’m going to try to see what cars are here.”

“Come right back.”

Tommy walked away and returned after ten minutes.

“So?”

“Here’s what we got. The Suburban is here. Pennsylvania plate. A Cadillac is here too. I’m guessing we’ve got all of them. Two guys came out and smoked cigarettes. Gotta be two dozen beer cans on the lawn. They’re not expecting us, so no way they’re locking that door. My guess is Bianchi wouldn’t let them drink when he was up, but he’s probably back in his room now and not paying attention. No doubt these guys can handle themselves when they’re drinking, but it just slows them down a bit. Enough so I can sneak up on them.”

“You? By yourself?”

“Glenn. It’s not too late. You can drive to the police station now. Get out of here. I can get him. I’ll take one of their cars and get back home. I’ll kill them if I have to.”

“Tommy.”

“I mean it, Glenn. You don’t have to go in there.”

“I do, Tommy. He’s a piece of me . . .”

The two men just looked at one another.

"So here's what we're going to do," Tommy started.

Glenn grabbed Tommy's arm. Tommy stopped.

"He's the best thing in my life, Tommy. I mean it."

"I know. He's the best thing in mine too."

"What else do I have, Tommy? I'm all alone. I should've been dead that day thirty years ago. He means more to me than anything else in my life."

"Then let's go."

Tommy stuffed his pistol into the back of his pants. He handed Glenn the other.

"Don't take it out unless you have to."

"I know."

"We'll try to keep them quiet. We'll wait outside until they come out to smoke again."

They took one step toward the house. Tommy stopped Glenn with a hand on his elbow, looked into his friend's face.

"And yea, though I walk through the valley of the shadow of death, I shall fear no evil." He stopped then, looked down at the ground, then raised his face again. "For thou art with me."

"Thy rod and thy staff," Glenn joined in. "They comfort me."

After fifteen minutes waiting by the door, Tommy moved closer. He watched the men through the gauzy curtain. Both of them were still awake. One pointed the remote at the television and switched channels. A commercial for dog food was on; the one with the remote muted the sound.

"See if you can find a movie, Bobby." The other man rose, tilted back a can of beer, and drank it down to the dregs. "Two hundred channels and nothing on worth a shit." He disappeared down the hallway.

Glenn focused on managing his breaths. He swallowed against the wave of nausea crawling up from his stomach.

When the one called Bobby turned the volume back on, Tommy slowly slid the door open. Glenn by now had lost all hope of keeping his breathing quiet; once they were inside, he exhaled quickly. A commercial with a talking cat came onto the screen; Bobby snorted at the picture.

Tommy walked straight toward the man in the chair, then turned to look at Glenn and pointed at the hall. He reached into the waist of his pants and pulled his gun out, sticking it to the back of Bobby's head, before leaning down to Bobby's ear.

"Don't move, sir." The man in the chair remained quiet. "I don't want anyone hurt. I'm just here for my son." Only then, when Tommy felt the contact between the barrel of his gun and the flesh of this stranger's head, did Tommy feel a hardening inside himself.

"Where's my son?" Tommy whispered, and shoved Bobby's head forward with the end of his gun. "Answer quietly, or I will kill you."

"You must be Tommy." Slowly, Bobby raised his hands. To Tommy's surprise, he remained totally calm. When he spoke, he sounded almost jovial. "You've got me, pal. I'm dead to rights. Just take it easy with that piece, my friend. Everything's just dandy here, amigo."

Tommy slapped the back of Bobby's head with his free hand. This didn't seem to surprise Bobby, who kept talking.

"Shut up. Where is he?"

"He's here, Tommy. He's here. Don't worry. Please. Everything's fine. Come on around here, let me introduce myself."

"Put your hands down! Now I'm going to ask you one more time." Tommy shoved Bobby's head again with the end of the pistol. "Where is my son? I have Bianchi's money. I'm going to leave it here and take my son home."

Slowly, Bobby lowered his hands and began to turn his face toward Tommy. Tommy slapped the man's head repeatedly as he moved. Still Bobby turned until one eye was in Tommy's view.

"Tommy. Please. I want to get a look at you. Please. This is undignified. I know you're afraid for your son. I understand. I have a son myself," Bobby said, fidgeting, as he continued to inch himself around. "I'm sorry we had to take him like we did, but I can assure you, everything is fine. We've just been playing some games, and he watched some television with us. Cartoons only, I promise." He began to raise his right hand as if to promise, but lowered it again when Tommy shoved him harder with the pistol.

"Nothing inappropriate for children. I promise."

Quickly Bobby turned his head the last few degrees until their eyes met. Tommy read something there, below the scar that had totally disfigured Bobby's eye, a bite in Bobby's gaze and a blackness, a blankness, that startled him. Bobby must have seen the flicker of fear in Tommy's eyes, the hesitation, like an animal crossing a busy road, and reached for his middle. A glint of reflected light bounced off the metallic object he drew from his waist. Tommy squeezed his trigger, felt the pulse of heat in his hand and the warm, sticky blood that splattered his face when Bobby's head exploded.

Dave tripped coming out of the bathroom and fell against one wall. Glenn, from the dark around the corner when he heard the shot, quickly turned to see what Tommy had done. Dave charged him from behind. Glenn partially turned, elbowed the man in the face as he approached, knocking him back against the same wall.

Glenn turned again and pointed his gun. But Dave ducked and went for his waist, this time planting Glenn against the opposite wall. The two men went to the floor. Glenn, much the stronger man, got himself on top and planted a forearm under Dave's chin.

"Okay, okay, you got me." Dave turned enough to see

his friend lying motionless on the floor and forced a breath through his body. Slowly he brought both hands up toward his chin.

"You've got me. Put the cuffs on me. Tie me up if you want to. Just don't kill me."

Tommy cut his way in, pulled off his belt and wrapped it several times around Dave's wrists. Glenn lifted Dave by an arm as Tommy tied his hands.

"Where is the boy?" Tommy asked. Dave got to his feet.

"Third door on the left. He's fine, man. He's not hurt. We just gave him something to help him sleep. He's fine."

Tommy leaned in, breathing heavily, his face inches from Dave's. He stuck a finger in Dave's face.

"He better be fine. Or you'll be down there with your friend."

"It's cool, man. He's fine."

"Who else is here?"

"Just the old man. This was supposed to be an in-and-out thing, man. All this wasn't supposed to happen."

Tommy took two steps down the hall and stopped, turned back. He returned to the sofa and picked up a blanket, opened it, and spread it on what remained of Bobby on the floor.

"Can I sit down?" Dave asked.

Tommy looked at Glenn, head pointed toward the sofa. Glenn shoved his pistol into Dave's back and pushed him toward the sofa.

"You guys are good, man. We weren't expecting you here at all." Dave half turned and looked over his shoulder. "I'm sorry about that knock I gave you yesterday too, man. I didn't want to shoot you, you know?" He laughed, once, then quickly made his move.

Dave wheeled on his feet and planted a foot convincingly between Glenn's legs. He had somehow worked the belt loose, and shucked it off and knocked Glenn's gun away. Then he dived for Glenn with both his hands out, reaching for his eyes.

Tommy began to move toward them, then froze where he stood. He saw the movement in his periphery from the other end of the house, and knew right away what it was. He fired a shot into the cabinet, shattering glass.

"That was a warning, Mr. Bianchi. Come on out."

Bianchi moved into the kitchen and laid his gun on the counter between them. Tommy faced him now, his back to Glenn and Dave as the two men struggled on the floor. Bianchi smiled. He was still high from the pipeful of weed he had smoked before falling asleep in front of his television an hour before. He surveyed the scene, Bobby's body covered with his blanket, Dave and another guy wrestling for control on the floor. He smiled at the devastation. It wasn't exactly what he had hoped for, but it would do. For the first time in ages, he felt at once so certain of things, his heart pounding in a way it so rarely did anymore. Finally Tommy moved closer, pointing his .38 squarely at the old man's face.

"I'm here for my son, Mr. Bianchi. Your money is in that bag. I'm going to leave it—there's fifty thousand dollars in there. I'm going to take my son and leave, and we are going to forget about all this. We are going to be even. Do you understand me?"

"Looks like you've left me a mess, Mr. Turner."

"You brought this on yourself, Mr. Bianchi. I'm sorry you lost Matt, wherever he is. But taking my son won't bring him back to you."

"Tommy Turner." Bianchi coughed once, then appeared contemplative, his face whitening in the dim overhead light.

"I'm going to take my son, Mr. Bianchi."

"I remember you that night on your father's shoulders. What were you, three years old then? Four?" Bianchi shook his head. "Time certainly has a way of changing things." He put both his hands flat on the countertop between them and continued. "I suppose I owe you. Your father put quite a bit of money in my pocket at one time." Bianchi reached for a pack of cigarettes on the counter, shook one out of the box, lit it, then offered the box to Tommy, raising his eyebrows as if asking a question.

Quickly Tommy glanced at Glenn and Dave on the floor. Glenn was on top now, and punched the other man repeatedly in the face.

"Come around the counter slowly, Mr. Bianchi." Tommy kept the .38 trained on Bianchi. "As you can see, I'm not scared to use this gun. We're going to walk down the hallway and get my son."

"Where is my son, Tommy?" Bianchi asked coolly, and took a deep drag on his cigarette. He watched the men fighting on the floor as if amused. Tommy glanced back quickly as well. Bianchi began to reach for the gun on the counter, but Tommy yelled out to stop him. Bianchi drew back, this time looked up toward the hallway.

"Oh, look who woke up now." Bianchi smiled in the direction of the hallway, over Tommy's shoulder.

Tommy turned quickly then, and when he did, Bianchi grabbed the gun on the counter and shot him once, in the middle of his chest. Tommy stood still, his eyes widening, looked down at a circle of red growing in a pattern in the middle of him.

Glenn shifted then, positioned Dave's head between his bicep and forearm and squeezed. Dave slapped the floor with both hands, his head wedged tight under Glenn's massive arm. Glenn looked up at Bianchi then, who stood gloating in his bathrobe looking at Tommy. Bianchi slowly began to turn toward him. In one motion Glenn turned Dave's head until he heard the crack of skull separating from neck; then, as if he had practiced the movement, he reached out with his other hand, grabbed his gun from the floor, and began firing in Bianchi's direction.

Bianchi, like Tommy, stood heart-shot. He fired off several rounds into his ceiling, blasted the chandelier over the dining room table that Marilyn always loved so much into a shower of glass. Then he slowly shuffled backward until he leaned against the countertop behind him.

Bianchi and Tommy stood looking at one another, Tommy's face a blanket of surprise and Bianchi's almost amused at the absurdity of it all. Glenn watched them both, his pistol outstretched.

"This didn't have to happen, Mr. Bianchi," Tommy said. "None of this had to happen."

"Few things do, Tommy," Bianchi said. "We both made this happen." A bloody foam began to creep out of the corner of his mouth. Then Carlo Bianchi slumped to the floor and closed his eyes.

Glenn approached Bianchi then, started to pick up his gun, and decided not to. He kicked it across the floor and went to check on his friend. Tommy had fallen into a chair. His breaths came out short, bloody bits forming at the corners of his mouth.

"Tommy. Look at me." Tommy turned slowly to look at his hand, the bright crimson almost pretty in the garish fluorescent light from the kitchen. Glenn pulled Tommy's face up by the chin.

"Stay with me, Tommy. Say something."

"Find Jamey."

Glenn bolted then, stepped over the stiffening body at the edge of the hallway. He switched on every light in the hall, opened doors, and switched on more lights there. He entered the third room he came to. Half a minute later he walked back into the hallway. He carried Jamey like a baby in one arm, the boy's spindly legs hanging down like little white sticks.

Tommy looked up at the two, his mouth agape, everything around him swirling in a mad mix of colors like the marbles he had shot as a boy with his father. He told himself to stand, but couldn't get up off the chair.

"Just give me a minute. I think it went through. See if it went through." Tommy leaned forward, tried to reach around behind himself. He felt warm liquid on the back of his shirt.

"It went through, Tommy. You have to stay with me. Let's just go." Glenn grabbed his friend with his empty hand, tried to lift Tommy off the chair. "Just get to the car. Then we'll figure out what's next."

Tommy stood shakily and tried to speak again, but just the standing had taken all his energy. He reached out lazily and patted his son on the back. Jamey didn't wake up but stirred, then settled back to sleep on Glenn's shoulder and moaned contentedly.

Then, as quickly as he had stood, Tommy slumped back into the chair.

"You can't take me to the hospital, Glenn. You can't. I'll take Bianchi's car. Get Jamey out of here. Get him back to Branden."

"Come on, Tommy. I'm not leaving you here."

"Get him out of here. You can't be here. The police will come. I never wanted him here. I never wanted him around this life."

"Tommy."

"Just get him out of here, Glenn. Get him back to Branden. Where he belongs. I have money. I can take Bianchi's car. I can take care of myself."

Glenn looked in his friend's face then, and slowly turned and began to walk toward the door.

"Glenn?" Glenn stopped.

"Tommy?"

"I haven't been all bad."

"Of course you haven't, Tommy. I owe you my life."

Tommy nodded, struggled to breathe. "Pay me back. Take him home. Be a family."

At that, Glenn nodded once at his friend, and this time, carrying Jamey, he walked outside. The door stayed open, and Tommy watched Glenn duck through the cut-open fence by the street and disappear. He held his breath and listened until he heard Glenn's car start and begin to drive away.

Tommy forced himself up and into the kitchen. Bianchi's keys lay on the counter, and he grabbed them and shuffled outside to the car parked under a giant live oak tree. Each breath came harder than the last. Thoughts jumped randomly through his head. He fell to one knee, but kept himself upright and stood again to take a few more steps. Before he got to the car, Tommy fell again. This time he sat in the grass and watched the movie reel that began to play in his head.

He threw a football with his father, then Daddy just stood looking into his face. Charlie Turner was handsome and strong and he looked like he could knock down a brick wall with that football, could outrun a freight train, could jump over a tree as tall as the one Tommy lay next to now. Tommy stood again and took another step toward the car, the sound of crickets sawing in concert all around him.

Then Tommy fell again, back to the earth, and lay down quietly in the grass. Daddy stood next to him and smiled, a look so loving on his face, and Tommy couldn't remember the last time he had felt so good. Charlie Turner came down on both knees and put his arms around his son until Tommy's breathing became even and a warm, tender feeling washed over him and he lay there happy, basking in the glow of his father's love. Charlie stood and opened his shirt to show his son the hole in his own side, the scars he had earned from his life, and the way they had all healed so nicely. Then both men looked up as a star shot across the sky. Charlie stood and reached down, and Tommy Turner reached up and took his father's outstretched hand. The two jumped from the ground and climbed up on that star, rode across the sky in the light and the heat and the warmth surrounding them, Charlie Turner holding his son tight. Finally the two looked down and watched as the world grew smaller and smaller as they went, all the filth and abstraction and brokenness melting away until they gained enough distance and everything down on earth became perfectly clear.

CHAPTER 31

"I took him to the hospital about three a.m.," Glenn said. He held his head in his hands, his elbows planted on the desk as he sat across from Sheriff Norm, while Norm read the newspaper.

"He was hallucinating . . . he kept saying, 'It's loud. It's loud.' He was burning up, so I took him in and they admitted him. He wasn't feeling well yesterday, so I kept him home from school . . . but it wasn't anything like this."

Norm put down the paper. "What a tragedy."

"I can't believe it, Norm. What will happen to Jamey now? He can stay with me . . . I'd like it if he stays with me."

"Turner took a secret to his grave. You can bet on that."

"What's going to happen to Jamey?"

Norm stood. Glenn stayed in his chair. "I'm going to help you with that. Staying with you would be the best thing. I'm going to make that my personal mission. I'm going to stop anyone who tries to take him anywhere else."

Glenn rose and looked at his friend. Neither spoke. After a minute, Norm nodded at him and the two moved toward the door.

"We should go together and talk to Jamey. It's best if we go together," Norm said.

"Yes. I agree. Let's wait just a little while, okay?"

"Sure. No problem. Bad news can wait just a little longer."

Norm moved toward the exit. Glenn followed. Outside,

Norm walked away from the building's entrance. He reached in his pocket for a cigarette, took one out, and lit it.

"That boy has lost a lot. He's lucky to have you." Norm turned and blew the smoke away from Glenn.

"I don't know how he's going to deal with this."

Norm put a firm hand on Glenn's shoulder, gripped it tight. "He's going to deal with it. He's going to make it. He'll be very sad. But he's going to make it."

Glenn looked up into the massive oak shading the courthouse lawn, a thousand grackles shouting their morning cries.

Norm smoked his cigarette all the way down as the two men listened to the birds. He stamped it out and began to speak before he looked back up.

"I want to tell you something, Glenn. I got a call yesterday. From an old friend."

"Yes?"

"Now this is a good man, Glenn. I thank the good Lord regularly that I've had a chance to know him."

"It's always nice to hear from people we care about."

Norm took out another cigarette and held it in his hand, but didn't light it. "My old friend, he wanted a favor. Now, I rarely get to help people in this job. Mostly it's just bad news and more bad news. But my friend, he asked for a favor. And it was something I could actually do for him."

"I'm sure he appreciated it, Norm."

Norm lit his cigarette and blew the smoke out once. "This is someone I would trust with my own *life*, Glenn. Someone I have complete confidence in. Do you understand what I'm saying?"

"I understand, Norm. Sometimes our life is in the hands of others."

"This is one of the finest men I have ever known. He could be my own son, and I would be proud if he were my son."

"He's a lucky man. To have a friend like you."

Norm was silent for a minute, smoked down his cigarette, tapped the air several times as he spoke indecipherably to himself. He began to shake his head.

"The Saint Charles Parish sheriff called me about five this morning. A few things don't make sense down there . . . they can't figure out how Tommy got there, if they took him there, what. Bianchi's car was there, and one with Pennsylvania plates. I told him it sounded like he must have gone there with one or the other of them. But it looks like Tommy popped three of them, and somebody got him. Three of them won't be missed anyway. Tommy at least tried to make something of himself."

"They had Jamey, Norm."

Norm quickly put his hand up. Glenn stood silent.

"Glenn . . ."

"It was terrible, Norm."

"Glenn . . . Son . . ." Glenn began to sob then. Norm walked around Glenn, put his arms around his friend.

"I don't know what happened down in Des Allemands. I don't need to know. You want to come over sometime, I'll take my badge off . . . friend to friend. We can talk. They found some money there . . . must have been an argument over money. No doubt, there's a lot we'll never know."

"It's a horrible tragedy. It really is. Tommy was doing such a good job getting himself together."

"I know. I admit I was surprised by it, but I was proud of the progress he was making. But Glenn. Let's talk about him another time, okay?"

Glenn nodded, looked down, crying.

"I guess we need to go talk to Jamey."

"Like I said. I'll help you any way I can, Glenn. You're the best hope that boy has now." Norm paused. "So. How's Louise?"

"Uhhh. I think she's moved on, Norm. Moving on. The truth is, that was just a dream. She's a great woman, but that's just not who I am."

"You've figured out who you are? You have any advice for me?"

"No, Norm. I wish. Still figuring it out. I guess I may not ever completely figure it out."

The men looked up at the birds shouting in the trees.

"They're happy about something."

"They're alive, I guess. That's something."

"Yes, Glenn. I guess it is."

"So how's Rachel?"

Norm blushed. "She's doing well, fellow. Doing well. She texted me at six o'clock this morning. Said she was getting up to get a gumbo started. She likes to let it cook all day until everything just melts together." He stopped, rubbed his stomach. "Mmmm mmmm. I'm gonna think about that all day."

"I don't blame you."

Norm grinned. "Fifty years out of high school, and I still can't believe she loves an ol' working boy like me. Sometimes I can't believe how things have turned out."

"Lotta things we never could expect."

"This is true. Well. I guess we better get over there and talk to him."

"Yes. I guess we should."

Norm took out another cigarette, held it, looked at it, then put it back into the pack.

"I told Rachel I'd keep it down to three a day. I guess I'll save that last one till tonight, after my gumbo."

"You're a disciplined man, Norm. I admire you."

"I admire you too, son. Come on. We can take the cruiser."

They drove toward the hospital through a cool, azure-sky

morning. Norm rolled the windows down and the spring breeze cooled both their faces.

"Better enjoy it, Glenn. Another month and it will be hot even in the morning."

"Enjoy it while it's nice."

Norm pulled into the lot at the hospital, parked in the deep shade of a blooming magnolia. The men stood up from the car.

"Glenn?"

"Yes?"

"It's up to you, Glenn. Whatever you want to tell him."

"Tommy saved him, Norm. His daddy died so he could be free."

"Is that what you want to tell him?"

"They wanted to hurt him. That's what I want him to know."

"Whatever you think is best, Glenn."

"Some bad people wanted to hurt him. Because of something they thought his daddy did. But Tommy wouldn't let that happen. He wouldn't let anything happen to Jamey."

"So Tommy saved him."

"Yes."

"Okay, Glenn. I'll wait in the room while you talk to him."

"It's my job now. I can tell him."

"I'll be there with you."

Glenn and Norm walked across the parking lot together. When they reached the door, Glenn turned and looked back at the outside world, one last time.

Then they went inside to see a little boy.

ACKNOWLEDGMENTS

I once knew a middle-aged gay man who, in his fifties, found himself curiously in love with a woman. His description of the feelings he experienced provided the basis for this book. I also wanted to write about the other subjects that perpetually fascinate me: addiction and recovery, human craving for something greater, bravery shown by deeply flawed people who humbly approach God despite horrific obstacles to peace—often obstacles of their own doing. Of course, I wanted to mix many elements of Louisiana life in there, with a dash of LSU football thrown in. Ultimately, as stories do when a writer dumps many ingredients into a pot, the book turned out differently from what I had planned.

I'd like to acknowledge Leslie Miller and everyone at Girl Friday Books, who sent me back to work many times. My son, Benjamin Holers Gross, was just a pup when I wrote parts of this book, and I'd like to thank him for inviting me to watch *SpongeBob* and all the other shows we used to laugh at together. Ben's little sayings and my memories of him as a boy with his stuffies provided much of the inspiration for Jamey and will always be golden in my heart, even if I live for a thousand more years.

ABOUT THE AUTHOR

Brian Holers was born in the Midwest and raised in the Louisiana Bible Belt, where he played baseball, fished, and made up stories for entertainment. He has one grown son in college in California and has lived in and around Seattle since 1989. Learn more at www.brianholers.com.

ALSO BY BRIAN HOLERS

MUSTARD SEED

A redemption story of family, faith, and forgiveness in small-town Louisiana.

After a lifetime of abuse and loss, sixty-one-year-old Vernon Davidson is ready to get back at God, his coworkers, and everyone else in his northern Louisiana hometown. To numb his pain, he drinks too much, and he shuns his friends and embarrasses himself in the community. The once-cautious Vernon has spiraled into a reckless mess.

When his brother becomes terminally ill, Vernon must track down his estranged nephew, Jody, in an effort to bring the younger man home to his dying father. Jody himself is struggling after a self-imposed exile—having fled his family for a new life thousands of miles away. As Vernon and Jody set off on their journey home, they find themselves on a path that takes them from loss to healing and will ultimately change their lives.

Mustard Seed is a stirring portrait of small-town Louisiana men—grandfathers, fathers, sons, and brothers—that exposes their flaws while showcasing their inner strengths. It forms a doxology, a song of praise, for the male family bond and the emotional ties men hide from the world and each other. Ultimately, it examines an impossibly difficult question: After a man has faced countless tragedies and endless disappointments, how does he go about forgiving a God he has grown to despise—and find his way back to the bonds that sustain him?

Paperback 978-1-954854-88-8, Ebook 978-1-954854-89-5